Dynasty of Summer: Part Two

Ticana Zhu

For more information, visit space-tigers.com

ISBN: 978-1-949195-17-0 (paperback)
Library of Congress Control Number: 2020931248
First Edition

WARNING:
This novel contains depictions of violence and suicidal thoughts.
Reader discretion advised

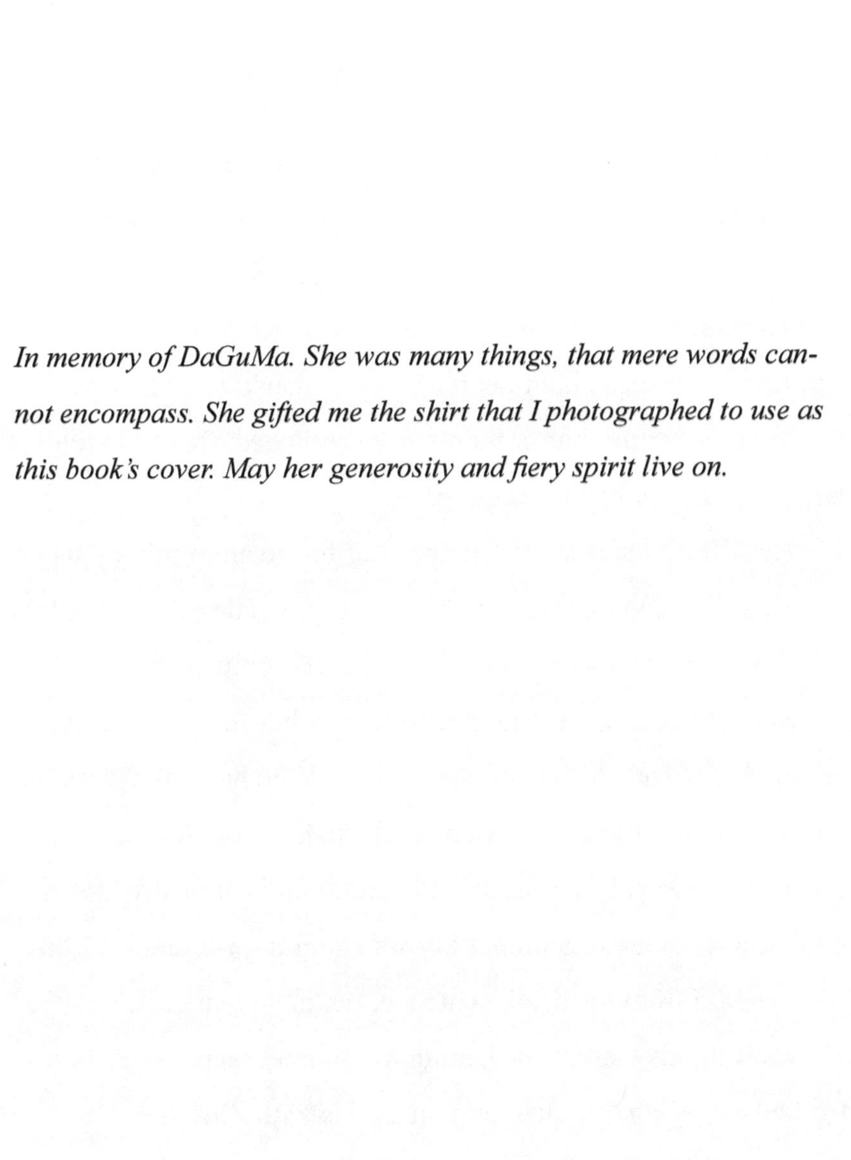

*In memory of DaGuMa. She was many things, that mere words can-
not encompass. She gifted me the shirt that I photographed to use as
this book's cover. May her generosity and fiery spirit live on.*

Dynasty of Summer: Part One
Summary
(contains spoilers)

Princess Summer is raised in the imperial capital, Zhenxun, during the Xia Dynasty. Her father is the Yu Emperor; her mother a descendent of the Tai—rulers of a lost Empire by the ocean.

Those things don't usually cross her mind. Neither do her brothers' warnings about people in her father's court that wish the imperial family harm. Summer's privileged, free to indulge in her penchant for beautiful things.

Her life changes shortly before her fourteenth birthday when she stumbles upon her half-brother's corpse. The events that follow toss her into a world for which she's ill-prepared.

Summer receives the help of Winter—her full-blooded brother, and his friends. But even they cannot keep her safe. Winter has a target on his back and leaves the palace. His friend, Yunkang passes away. His other friend, Hanming is pinned with her half-brother's death. Summer knows Hanming is innocent. She rescues him from his death sentence, but at a great cost.

As if things weren't bad enough, Summer learns she's betrothed to a Kingdom that holds tensions with Zhenxun. Her marriage is meant to garner peace. Holding her head high, Summer accepts her duty.

On the journey to her new home, Summer's entourage is attacked. She's the lone survivor and finds herself at the mercy of bandits, one of them named Elk. She's uncertain if she can trust them. Hanming is among them too, but his behavior towards her has turned cold. Full of fear and alone in the forest, she has no choice but to trust them.

Her trust is well rewarded as the bandits journey to their camp by the river. There, she's reunited with Winter, and makes friends with Silk Deer. Her brother advises to keep their identity as imperials hidden, instead claiming to be nobles.

Winter and Hanming agree it's not safe to return to Zhenxun. They decide to wait out the winter with the bandits. During that time, the siblings make a trek to their mother's fallen empire. Standing amongst the ruins, it's a sobering experience and warning for what may happen to Zhenxun if discord continues.

It is also during their winter journey that Silk Deer discovers Hanming and Summer's feelings for each other. She shares this with the other bandits upon their return to their camp. A mock wedding is held to give them reason to celebrate. Much to the embarrassment of the "bride" and "groom."

Come spring, Hanming is separated from Summer and Winter as they attempt to reenter the palace's inner sanctum. It takes her three years. During that time, the princess sees the underbelly of society she'd been shielded from most of her life. It's left her changed, and fearful of revealing her identity.

Ultimately, she's discovered by the Empress, who places her before her father.

Chapter Twenty:
Catching a Traitor

When we saw the ocean upon our visit to the ruins of the Tai Empire, it was too cold for swimming. Elk said he'd gone in before, as a child. One time, he saw a man dragged away by an undercurrent. The man had paddled furiously, trying to return to shallow waters. He didn't succeed, and his movements grew sluggish.

A calm woman went in after him. When she reached him, instead of fighting the waves, they drifted. People watched apprehensively from shore. Eventually, the waves brought them back.

There's a saying my mother taught me, "Do not fight the abyss. It will ensnare you. You must go through." I wonder if it's an old Tai saying since they had lived by the ocean. Certainly, the man carried away felt as if he were caught in an abyss, doomed to drown.

Upon my return to the palace, amongst my father's enemies, I could not feel more swept away. There were many challeng-

es—all as slippery and capricious as the sea. If I didn't wish to drown, all I could do was keep adrift, and wait to be brought upon an opportunity.

~*~

The war meeting the Empress and I interrupted was called to an end. I was whisked to my father's study. A handful of trusted Lords joined, adamantly prying, "Where have you been all this time?"

I did not respond, insisting on seeing my mother first.

My father forbade it, stating it was too dangerous to leave his side. He promised I could visit her once things quieted. For the time, he ordered, "Child, recount to me your life outside of the palace."

Setting aside my desire for a reunion, I informed them of the attack on my entourage to my betrothed's nation. Then broke into tears to avoid saying more. I hated lying, but I couldn't afford to expose my bandit brethren to the Lords. My heart wanted to tell my father about Winter, but felt sure if word got out, assassins would find him. I didn't trust any of the Lords listening with narrowed eyes and firm mouths.

My father remained patient. He told the Lords I felt tired and sent them away. In their place a physician looked me over. When he was done, beauticians arrived to soften my skin and remove marks of physical labor. In order to keep me safe, the maids were not informed of my identity. Unlike earlier days in the palace, I now kept my ears open. I felt alarmed by how much people gossiped and how quickly word spread.

"Did you hear?" one asked her friend, making small talk, "The lost princess returned! I wonder where she's been all this time!"

The other chimed, "I don't blame her for not going to the Nan Kingdom. I heard they were going to kill her anyway!"

I gulped, keeping my chin lifted.

"You don't know that! Stop listening to your boyfriend's horror stories!"

"But he's right in some degree, you know. She definitely can't go there now. The Nan Kingdom'll send her head back on a platter as a message!"

I shuddered.

"I heard she was kidnapped by Nan mercenaries. At least that's the story they're telling the soldiers to fuel them for war." My hands were placed to soak in lotus water. The friendlier beautician added, "They believe the princess escaped and survived in the wild."

I wished to voice the truth, but recognized it'd be useless.

"My uncle serves in a General's house," the feisty maid spoke. "He says the war is nearing its end. The Nan Kingdom's doomed to fall. The princess' return merely drove our soldiers to quicken victory."

I couldn't listen any more and tuned them out. I feared to think how much blood was being shed.

I trailed my gaze out the windows. Night birds sang sweetly, oblivious to the concerns of war. I wished I had their wings so

I could fly and search for Winter and Hanming. Yet, my father locked me in his private quarters with a dozen imperial guards patrolling. Their presence gave credibility to the maid's words. I needed to remain alive as an icon for war.

~*~

Several days passed and I was still not allowed to leave my father's quarters. Repeated requests to see my mother were denied. I wrote to her instead. Her responses were sweet and composed, like her. She told me to listen to my father and agreed now wasn't the best time to visit. She promised we'd be together soon. I longed to hear her voice. Missing her made my heart weep.

~*~

By spring, we'd won the war. My father informed me personally. "I would like you to accompany me as I announce our victory." I knew it was a command. I bowed and he left me to dress.

I grew accustomed to long gowns again. I didn't trip as I took my first step out of my room in moons. Two dozen guards appeared immediately by my side. They led me to the top balcony of terraced steps where I waited across from the Empress. I kept my head lowered as curious stares tossed my way. Whispered conversations conducted behind sleeves.

"The Emperor has arrived!" a hawker announced.

All present dropped to the ground. My father took his place before the throne and thanked his people for their sacrifice and dedication. "The King of the south has been slain and now the land belongs to us." The crowd let out a roar at this announcement. Birds rose form the trees, circling above. My father held out his hands in acceptance, "We should no longer view the Nan citizens as our enemy, but brethren."

He went on and bestowed honor to each General and presented imperial badges carved from white jade, edged in gold.

Finally, he declared, "New arrangements are needed to govern the land in the south."

I saw Gui Fengbi shift with anticipation. I recounted the whispers, about how he had continuously pushed his Generals to the front of battles.

"After much thought," my father continued, "I've decided to give this responsibility to a man I've trusted for ages." In the dramatic pause, the air crackled with invisible energy. Gui Fengbi wore a smug smile. My father's voice boomed, "I announce Lord Zhan Ji to take over the duties of the new territory. I will assign him additional troops."

My father continued to list names but I didn't hear. I watched Gui Fengbi out of amusement. I thought he might explode. He went from pale as snow to as bright as a persimmon. I kept my face calm, but made note to be wary of him.

Something nudged the back of my mind about the day I was attacked on my journey south. It came back in a flash and I let out a groan. The Empress glanced my way in warning before darting her eyes forward again. I clenched my lips as I recalled a man's torn shirt. I'd spied something suspicious. I closed my eyes and replayed the memory for clarity.

Yes. On the man's chest was tattooed Gui Fengbi's crest.

As my father's declaration ended, I eyeballed Gui Fengbi, silently fuming. My jaw tightened as imperial guards surrounded me to escort me away. I wanted to immediately confront him and confirm he associated with the attackers.

No. I needed to be clever and draw a confession. At least I'd learned Gui Fengbi's weaknesses. I needed to leverage his rage and pride.

Before my disappearance, I was only another princess. Now the title of "The Princess who Survived" followed behind covered mouths as I passed. It came with a level of curiosity. At each banquet, the Lords questioned my journey home in fascination.

I'd confess sheepishly, "I disguised myself as a boy."

This earned gasps and furrowed brows of disapproval. It wasn't proper for a girl to dress as a boy and to be in my presence should be humiliating. But I was a novelty, and I found it allowed me some exception.

"I worked as a kitchen slave, eventually befriending a young girl. She helped me into the palace where the Empress found me."

Some of the older Lords laughed, shaking gray beards. "Oh, you're quite the resourceful girl! Truly your father's child!"

Some asked, "Why did you not come forward sooner?"

I said simply that I'd feared for my life, "Someone powerful near my father wished to harm me." They'd look suspiciously around the room, asking if I felt safe now. I'd chuckle coyly, avoiding a response.

As I entertained implorations, I kept my eye out for my mother. She appeared absent from court gatherings and I grew concerned.

At the latest banquet, my father appeared in great spirits and talked about plans for the recently conquered territory. A village was to be set up, two days travel south. Soldiers would patrol it. "We wouldn't want more people getting kidnapped." He stroked his chin intently. "There will be rebels from the former King-dom."

"I know, Father," I offered in a perky tone. I wouldn't find a better moment than this. "What if you have soldiers disguised as villagers? The rebels will need supplies so they will try to attack the villagers only to be surprised by soldiers."

I glanced around the table. "However, you'd need a way of separating the soldiers from disguised rebels." I asked a question in general, "What would you propose?" My eyes rested on Gui Fengbi. All turned to him.

His mouth pushed into a frown. "You can give them badg-es—"

"Badges can be dropped," I interrupted. His face darkened. I was a young woman behaving rudely. However, as a "The Prin-cess Who Survived," I leveraged my pardon for breaking a few conventions.

Gui Fengbi bore the slight, but having lost the promotion he aimed for, it wasn't easy. It showed in his every move.

"It would need to be something else," I continued. "Something like a tattoo." Approving murmurs rose. Gui Fengbi's eyes narrowed.

"Now, now," the man named Jin Su spoke calmly, waving his hands. I remembered seeing him with Gui Fengbi years ago. He didn't say much usually, choosing his words carefully. "We all respect the princess, but an idea from a girl isn't well thought out. What if these hidden agents were seen bathing and the tattoos gave them away?" He glanced to Gui Fengbi. Jin Su was trying to discredit me.

"Well, is there another idea? Are there hidden paths for rebels to travel alongside the main road?" I asked Jin Su in a childlike voice, eyes wide, waiting.

My father nodded, "Lord Gui, hadn't you mentioned years ago of secret paths you'd learned?"

"Yes, your majesty," Gui Fengbi stewed, shooing away a plate offered to him by a servant at his elbow.

I weighed my odds before taking the gamble. This could be a moment when tides changed, and I can surface from the abyss. I kept my voice even, "Yes, the secret paths he sent his men to attack me. The men who have his crest tattooed on their chests."

Gasps broke out along the banquet table. Many Lords shook their heads that a princess would speak so out of line. Others testified they knew of Gui Fengbi's secret guards with tattoos. Still more challenged my testimony outright.

Gui Fengbi's face deepened to crimson. He stood angrily. I sensed my father warning me with his eyes. However, his silence indicated he wished to hear more.

"I beg your pardon," Jin Su spoke soothingly, "but I believe the princess is speaking without proof."

"Perhaps Lord Gui isn't clever enough to plan such things." I turned my eyes to Jin Su. "Perhaps he had help." I left the insinuation open and it was enough for Jin Su to hesitate as he considered how much I knew. In that moment, he gave himself up to me.

Gui Fengbi erupted. "You spoiled brat! You don't know the cost of victory! People like me go out of our way in the interest of this Empire, only to have the reward go elsewhere!" He turned to my father. "Emperor, how could you?" he pleaded, "I handed the Nan Kingdom to you and you give it to Lord Zhan?"

My father let him rant.

Gui Fengbi clutched his throat, "For years I commanded spies in the Nan Kingdom! I worked with members of their High Court, pushing them to declare war when they believed false reports of our army to be a fraction of what it is. I've done so many things to have the territory handed to you!"

Gui Fengbi had gone too far. My father stood. His stature towered; a dangerous expression across his face. All Lords kept their heads bowed except Gui Fengbi. He breathed hard, like an animal caught in a trap, staring at my father in desperation.

My trap.

"You acted with dishonesty to start this war?" he demanded.

Gui Fengbi sputtered, "Just little nudges… here and there…"

The Emperor demanded, "My daughter was a part of your plot?"

Choosing the wrong moment to be honest, Gui Fengbi confessed, "She's merely one girl, of your many beautiful daughters. Not even named for your house. With her gone, it was inevitable war would lead to us taking the south. Surely that's more valuable to you?"

My father growled. "You see my children, including three of my sons, as expendable?"

Too late, Gui Fengbi and the men around us realized his position. "I would never dare harm your sons!" he cried in terror.

"My brother, Ting told me he was afraid of someone in the High Court!" I shouted passionately, aiming to stir the room. "Days before his disappearance, he warned me to keep away from you!" I demanded, "Tell me, why did you kill him?"

"Lies!" Gui Fengbi shouted, face draining of color.

My father waved to the guards, "Take him away!"

As they grabbed him, Gui Fengbi pleaded, "Your majesty, please!" His eyes locked on me and he grew enraged. "I should've killed you with my bare hands!" He feet kicked wildly as they dragged him from our presence. The large doors slammed and all fell quiet.

The scene should've shaken me, but I felt no remorse. Sensation of the cleaver in my hand slicing a guard's throat reverberated at my fingertips. Defacing Gui Fengbi felt less personal. I deliberated if I'd become a monster; condemning a man so easily. I only told one lie. Ting never warned me of anyone in particular.

No. Gui Fengbi launched our Kingdom into war. I'm ridding a disease.

I reviewed my emotions and when I found no satisfaction, my mind relaxed. I hadn't committed my act from pleasure.

I glanced around the hushed room and saw all but one stared in the direction Gui Fengbi was taken. Jin Su gave a cool, level gaze as if saying, *I underestimated you.*

I returned the look. He appeared more formidable than Gui Fengbi. I would need to be careful.

Chapter Twenty-One:
Ying Guardians

After the banquet, my father pulled me aside to speak in private. It was the first we were alone since my return. He asked, "Daughter, have you lost your mind, creating a scene before the Lords?" I apologized and assured him I didn't act without evidence. He asked, "What would you have done if you were wrong?"

I answered that I'd had little to lose. "A *foolish* girl, Father, was needed to stir things."

My father shook his head, and though I could discern he was pleased to be rid of Gui Fengbi, he still held concerns. "Little Summer, he's not the only traitor. He has allies who would sooner cut of their arm than risk exposure. You're extremely lucky. The backlash could've fallen on you."

"I know father. Men like Jin Su also have motives."

My father sighed. "Yes, Summer. I know about Jin Su, and there are others. Their reach extends deep, into all levels of the courts. Be careful with whom you speak." He brushed my brow.

"Father," I peered into his eyes, clutching his hands. I'd been waiting for us to speak alone. "Winter's alive. He arranged for my rescue from Gui Fengbi's men and took care of me these last years."

My father's face twisted as if it pained him to hope. In his silence, I read years of torment. "Truly, child?"

"Yes," I breathed. "We entered the palace together."

Urgently, he asked, "Where's he now?"

I shook my head in frustration, "We were separated. Last I know, he went to the fields. I haven't heard from him since."

He nodded solemnly. "I'll send out trusted people, in secret."

"Please father, I wish to search for him too."

He shook his head, "Too dangerous." I tried to argue, but he wouldn't budge. As a peace offering, he allowed me to visit my mother.

~*~

"Her chambers are kept dark," my mother's maid explained, "because light hurts her eyes."

I stepped into shadowy quarters. When my mother saw me, her ashen face lit with joy. She reached a thin hand and tried to sit up. "I'm ecstatic!" she wheezed, collapsing. "When one of my maids brought me a gold coin…" she ended her sentence with fitful wheezing "…I'd given you, my spirit lifted." I rushed to her side. "I've waited so long for this day, Daughter."

I felt for her pulse, a technique Hanming taught me. I waited a few seconds to confirm the diagnosis. "Mother," I moaned severely, "you've been poisoned." The words were difficult to say.

"I know child, but it's too late to save me. I'm sorry I couldn't see you sooner." She nodded. "Only recently has my health recouped some. Regardless, my prayers have been answered." She patted my cheek, her hand frail like a skeleton's. "I hoped to hold you before I passed."

I wrapped my arms about her as tightly as I dared, afraid to snap a bone. I crawled into her bed as I'd done in my youth and drew the silken sheets to our shoulders. We talked until she dozed. I kept close watch, fearful she might breathe her last in slumber. Tears dripped ceaselessly from my eyes.

Hours later she awoke and I drew a sleeve swiftly over my face. Some strength had returned to her voice. "Now it's your turn to tell stories," she beamed. "My daughter, where have you been?"

I grinned, "I have been with my brother."

Her eyes sparkled as a welp escaped her lips. "Is he—?"

"We entered the palace together. He sends his love."

She gulped and asked me to continue.

I recounted my adventures and she clutched my hands tightly, weeping at what I'd endured. I even told her about Hanming. "That sounds like a man you can trust," she said.

I nodded but kept from her his mother was the Empress. "Enough about me. Tell me the name of your enemy."

"I was poisoned because someone wishes to harm the Emperor. He's sick as well, through me I'm sad to say, but he hides it well. His deterioration is in the early stages." She squeezed my hand. "You must help your father whenever you can. This Empire needs him. Be vigilant to those who act suspiciously."

A chill spread through my body. My father had always stood as an infallible figure, untouched by slander, swords or disaster. To learn someone had succeeded at weakening him made me dizzy. I promised, "I'll look after him." She pulled my cheek to her shoulder and together, we hummed our favorite tunes.

I tried seeing her regularly, but some days she couldn't wake from sleep. I sat quietly, absorbing what moments I could.

A week later, she passed. Never again would her sweet smile lift my spirits. No matter how strongly I opposed her departure, my mother would never return. A part of me went up in flames alongside her on the pyre. In its place, sultriness entered my soul.

Word of my mother's passing spread through the courts and I kept my eyes open for Winter. I searched every face at the funerary procession, but none were my brother. Unease tugged at me. Only two reasons could stop Winter. Severe Illness or death.

After the pyre burned low, I retreated to my father's quarters to commence mourning. As tradition dictated, I wore sackcloth and white flowers in my hair. My body lost feeling as I sat before the window gazing at a gingko tree. The leaves waved gleefully, their cheer appearing foreign to me.

My father entered late in the day with the two men. He introduced one, "This is Quan Bao, a former top general."

"Before your father put me on special assignments," Quan Bao clarified with a nod.

The other was simply called Spider. He didn't speak.

The two dressed as Middle Court officials, but my father explained, "These are disguises as they searched for your brother."

"We've found him," Quan Bao informed.

I sat up sharply.

My father added, "Winter was in prison—for fighting over food. His health's poor and he's being treated as we speak. They assure me he'll be fine, but keep this a secret. He's still vulnerable."

My breathing turned heavy and my wrists ached. I looked down to realize I'd grasped the edge of a chair. I sucked in air and forced myself to relax. I thanked my father and studied his complexion. Ashen dots peaked beneath thinning hair. On closer inspection, faint traces of gauntness appeared around his eyes. The same symptoms as my mother's.

"Father, how are you?" I asked, heart skipping a beat.

"Child, our fates are written in the stars. I am where I need to be." The unexpected words left me dumbfounded. He continued, "I've assigned Spider to train you. I'll feel better knowing you can defend yourself."

"Father, may I speak with you alone?"

He shook his head, "You may speak in front of them. I trust these men with my life every day."

I studied the two before vocalizing, "Mother told me you

were poisoned through her. If they failed to protect you both, how am I to put faith in them?"

"She told you that?" he asked sadly.

"Princess," Quan Bao bowed, "I'm sorry for your loss, but to do what we do, we need to remain secret. This limits our reach at times." His nostrils flared softly. "Rest assured, we've found the culprit who poisoned your mother and dealt with him." His chin dipped to his chest. "We're sorry it was not in time."

"Clearly the person you dealt with is a scapegoat. What have you done to the mastermind? Does he walk free?" I knew I was being impolite, but grief spoke for me.

My father shook his head, "The person cannot be punished without exposing the secrecy of these two men. It was my consort, Feili."

Fire bristled beneath my skin as I leaped to my feet. I spun around the room, unable to control anger. "That snake! I thought she was my friend!"

"Calm yourself," my father warned. "I figured her out shortly after you were sent away. I stopped seeing her, but never guessed her toxicity was great enough to use the most beloved of my wives." A cloud passed over his face in recounting.

I sat down heavily. "At least my brother's been found," I grumbled. "Thank you both," I bowed to the men, remembering manners.

"Summer," My father redirected the conversation. "I've asked these men here because I have a task for you."

Fury temporarily gave way to curiosity.

"You'll start tomorrow," the Emperor commanded.

Spider and Quan Bao were a part of the Ying Guardians, founded by the first Yu Emperor. Despite mourning rites, I was to become one of them. Their martial arts abilities were unrivaled, and they protected the Empire from the shadows. Traditionally, only three people outside of their clan knew of their existence. The Emperor, Empress, and the heir.

~*~

I awoke at dawn and seated before a royal breakfast. I thanked my maids and moved to pour tea myself. One rushed to take the pot from my hands. I hesitated before remembering myself a princess.

As I chewed, I thought longingly of my mother and the countless breakfasts we'd shared. No more laughter would ring in her courtyard as we played music and read poems. I took those precious memories and tucked them safely in my heart.

Spider knocked on my door, dressed as an imperial guard. I set down my chopsticks and automatically started to clear dishes. This time, all my maids rushed forward and snatched them from my hands. Remembering myself, I stood straight and stepped to where Spider waited.

Without a word he turned and walked, expecting I'd follow. His gait was even and powerful, as if nothing in the world resided outside his control. I held questions on my tongue, but didn't know if it was the appropriate time to ask.

We circled the suites of my father's latest consorts. Passing, I heard laughter and music; the joy within accompanied by sweet fragrances. That used to be my life too. I couldn't say I missed it much.

We arrived at the library and Spider surveyed the area before motioning me to pick up my pace. We trotted behind the building to the servants' entrance. I slowed my steps, but Spider continued past to a rubbish pile. Broken pottery and jagged beams laid piled against a wall.

"Climb onto my back," Spider demanded. I wrapped my arms over his shoulders and griped tight.

Spider took a leap and landed on an old beam. I braced myself thinking it would dislodge and we'd crash atop broken pottery. To my shock, the beam didn't budge. Spider grew airborne and landed atop another. He jumped one last time and I heard a grunt. His large hand closed around a wooden bar at the edge of the roof. He swung his legs over and I found myself on top of the library. Again. Memories of Hutu giving me away to the Empress flashed.

Spider let me slide from his back. I braved a peak over the side. The distance to the ground was nine times taller than my height. "This way," he spoke as I recoiled.

We approached an overhang where the library attached to a larger building. Wooden slits looked as if they were a part of the structure's support. Spider dug his fingers behind a groove and a crack appeared. He slipped both hands inside and gave a pull.

A piece of wall swung open!

I judged an entrance wide enough for us to enter. Spider disappeared inside. I gulped before following.

Only a trickle of light fell through the cracks when Spider closed the wall behind us. I vaguely made out a narrow corridor leading left. I never noticed before, but the hall was built between the inner and outer walls of the library. Only wide enough to squeeze sideways.

I followed Spider and turned to face an equally narrow staircase. The fading light behind me was swallowed after the first few steps. I relied on my ears to listen for Spider's footfalls. It wasn't long until I fell behind. I wanted to call out and ask him to slow, but my pride kept me silent.

Creeping more and more cautiously, I used my feet to search out the steps as my hands trailed against the wall.

Soon, we no longer moved sideways. My hands barely reached both walls as we continued to descend. The air grew cool, smelling of earth. Eventually, a faint glow appeared. I saw Spider waiting for me a few dozen steps down. I picked up my pace.

At the bottom of the steps, we came around a bend and thousands of candles greeted my eyes. They stuck against a wall, the wax melted into a mosaic. I used the opportunity to study my surroundings. The ground was packed solid with rock dust, perhaps scattered to absorb moisture. Wooden beams supported arched walls and air flowed around me, stirring the flames. I inhaled, thinking it tasted oddly fresh.

Past the candles a heavy metal door stood, closed. Spider pushed his shoulder into it and dug his heels. It took much effort before it opened to reveal a well-lit arena. I gaped seeing countless weapons neatly lined along the walls. Ropes hung from a high ceiling and wooden practice dummies scattered throughout. Men and women sparred on the open floor. They repeated motions, never weakening.

A shadow swooped and I ducked, wondering if a hawk somehow found its way underground. Instead, I saw a man swinging from a rope with weights tied to his legs and arms. I caught my breath as he released his grip. For a moment he soared and I feared he'd fall. His arm reached out, catching another rope. I exhaled in relief.

"This way," Spider ordered. I tore my gaze away and trailed him once again. He pointed to a sliding door, "Enter there and change into the robes you'll find."

Inside the room, several benches lined the walls. Some were empty while others held a sash of small weights. Material sat folded on the one nearest to the door. I picked up the robe and turned it around. Men's clothing. I furrowed my brow. "Is this correct?" I mumbled.

After a moment I scoffed, "You're no stranger to men's clothing!"

It took time to undress from the many layers of silk I'd been draped in by my maids. Afterwards, I hung my gown neatly on hooks. I stepped back and jeered. My dress looked amusing against the gray stone.

The men's robes I threw on in little time.

Spider presided as a Captain of the Ying Guardians. His latest assignment was to train me directly.

Though I'd grown strong from physical labor and agile climbing with the bandits, it didn't prepare me for Spider's drills. For hours, I was to hold out buckets with outstretched arms. Once it grew easy, it was required I jump one hundred times without spilling a drop. If a single hint of wetness hit the stones, Spider made me start over.

To hone dexterity, he made me catch birds and insects by pinching their wings without damaging them. This was by far the most challenging thing I'd ever had to perform.

Moons passed before I progressed to hand-to-hand defense with other Ying Guardians. Though I'm sure they were easy on me, by the end of the day my body still screamed. Some days I wondered if my bones would snap.

Spider taught me a meditation for faster recuperation. "You must place your body in a healing aura to lessen aches and pains." As time went on, I did feel a stronger qi invigorating my body.

Winter grew well enough for me to visit. Spider only allowed me free time to catch up with him if I could complete all my exercises by noon. The incentive expedited my progress.

~*~

When I first locked eyes with Winter, there were no words. Giddiness from relief overtook and we laughed uncontrollably.

Despite our joy I felt distraught seeing him weakened. He'd lost enough weight to appear a bag of bones. The thought didn't leave my mouth even as he gave me a mocking look, "Why, you're built like a horse, little sister!

"I'll always need you to watch over me, big brother." I chuckled, assuring him he'd be strong again soon.

In exchanging our stories, I ground my teeth to hear of Winter's suffering in the fields. "Guards whipped the workers as they pleased and we slept under a leaking roof. There was never enough food." He claimed the need to find me kept him going.

"If I were treated the same, I don't think I could've survived." I told him of my time in the kitchens. And with eyes downcast I managed to relate how I'd murdered a man. I shuddered recalling the cleaver.

We made a promise. If we ever came into a position of power, we'd scrutinize the treatment of servants.

I then told Winter of Yang Hengyan and how the Empress discovered me by accident. I left out Hanming's letter to the Empress, fearing it would raise questions I didn't have answers to.

Instead I asked, "Have you heard from Hanming?" Winter shook his head.

I turned the conversation to our mother. We grew somber and Winter let out a breath, saddened by not seeing her before she'd passed. I told him she knew he was alive and it lit up his eyes.

"She was as beautiful as ever," I sighed. "She said to let you know she loved you no less than the day you were born." I cupped his hand. "She gracefully accepted the end of her life." The tightness in his jaw didn't lessen.

I didn't speak of the Ying Guardians. My father warned me not to mention them to another living soul who didn't already know. It wasn't that Winter couldn't be trusted, but by law I could not.

My father had decreed me an honorary member of the Ying Guardians to avoid breaking that law. He'd specified my primary duty was to protect the princess, *myself*. A clever one, my father, much like Winter. I loved them for it.

Chapter Twenty-Two:
Reunion

The blame for Winter's disappearance years ago fell on Gui Fengbi. The palace grew to a fervor and soon, the ruddy man found the death sentence over his head. Despite recent events in our favor, Winter and I knew dangers weren't over. Yet, we couldn't begin to guess how great the threats were until we lost another half-brother.

I heard Ying Guardian recounts after the event.

The Emperor's heir, Yu Longjing strolled through a garden with fellow scholars when a bevy of consorts wandered through. Feili often kept company with princes' wives, being in proximity to their age. Two Ying Guardians tracked her, of course, but couldn't confront her in the open.

Boldly, Feili approached Yu Longjing but imperial guards barred her path. Being a kind soul, Yu Longjing waved them away to receive her greeting. She stepped to him and curtsied sweetly.

"I saw the blade, but couldn't get close in time," a Ying guardian confessed. "As the heir bowed, a sharp object appeared from Feili's sleeve. She thrust it into his heart. Before she could be arrested, Feili took her own life."

Two Ying Guardians had failed. By their code, they took their lives in a private ceremony.

My father said to Spider, "It's not a sign the Ying Guardians have grown weak. Rather our enemies have grown strong."

With a broken heart, he retreated to mourn in private.

I discussed Yu Longjing's assassination with Winter. We both had so many questions. He entered the imperial records hall to seek answers. It was there he discovered Feili and Second Mother had been distant cousins. When I relayed this information to the Ying Guardians, they confessed being already aware. They believed Second Mother and Feili were not cognizant of their relation. The two never interacted and had arrived at the palace a decade apart.

"But Second Mother's son is now in line for the throne," I cried, "Am I the only one to suspect Feili planned this?" No one would corroborate.

Even Winter warned me not to act.

A rumor surfaced about Feili and Yu Longjing being lovers. That she felt spited when he took a wife from another Kingdom. I cringed, thinking of Feili's clever smile. It always seemed distant, as if a cunning mind turned behind it. I always thought it made her a good performer, but knew my honest half-brother held no interest in people like her.

On the day of Yu Longjing's funeral I stood quietly beside Winter, head bowed in reverence. High Court officials lined the courtyard below with heads to the ground. Clouds shrouded the sun and I felt rebellious toward the heavens.

Yu Longjing had loved the sun.

As his corpse carried past me to the pyre, memories of him teaching me to skip rocks and catch crickets surfaced. I loved him as much as Ting and I'd lost both. I reached a hand to hold the corner of Winter's sleeve. "Please be careful," I said under my breath.

Winter peered at me, pupils large. His eyes spoke, *I can make no such promise.*

My spirits lowered even more.

Second Mother stood on the highest terrace singing woefully. When her voice stopped, I peeked with my head still down. Imperial guards approached and announced the Empress. Second Mother dropped to her knees and the rest of us followed suit. My forehead rested on the cool stone of the terrace.

As she passed, I stole a glance at the Empress's feet. Instead of billowing silks in bright colors, coarse linen of bereavement dragged behind. Feeling brave, I glanced higher to observe humble sackcloth over her head.

She approached the highest terrace and Second Mother backed away. The Empress called out, "All rise."

We stood, keeping our eyes to the ground.

Her voice came breathily as if her lungs couldn't find air. Her tone dripped in sorrow. "My fellow countrymen, I come to you today as a mother and your Empress. Such barbarism is indecorous. What has become of our great Empire where the heir is murdered?" She paused. "The Emperor mourns in private and has asked me to be his proxy until the next heir can be determined."

I heard Winter sigh deeply. From distrust.

I myself twitched. Could the Empress truly keep up with duties in her poor health?

Turning her head, the Empress suppressed a cough. "The Emperor's closest cousins cannot leave their posts, ruling suzerainties. Consort Tu is the second wife and her sons are close in age. They are to compete in exams assessing their abilities." I glanced to my half-brothers. "The one who scores higher shall be the new heir. This is the wish of the Emperor."

Second Mother bowed obediently behind the Empress. Her elder son's face drooped as the younger's perked. She'd always fancied herself the Empress. Once a son of hers becomes heir, her status would finally elevate above the current Empress. It made me suspect her collusion with Feili even further.

As the Empress retreated, I studied her movements. The minutia of her simple gestures reminded of Hanming. I gulped, wondering of his fate. Winter and my return had been announced publicly, making it difficult for us to search for him discretely.

I muttered under my breath to comfort myself, "Hanming

is not a son of the Emperor. No one has reason to harm him." I repeated this until my nerves eased.

The pyre lit, and all thoughts washed from my mind. I uttered a prayer to my mother, asking her to look after Yu Longjing.

The Empress left the terrace. I saw red in her eyes and watched her chest heave. A sleeve covered her face and my heart went out.

Besides making occasional appearances around the palace, I spent most of my time with the Ying Guardians. I wasn't privy to their secret information, but tidbits were shared with me now and again.

I learned the Emperor was gravely ill. Poison from my mother finally reached his internal organs. A sour sensation entered my gut. "What can be done?" I asked.

Spider looked to Quan Bao. He nodded. "High members of the Ying Guardians disguise themselves as imperial guards. They stand by the Emperor's bed at all hours, making certain no impatient assassin makes an attempt on his life."

"I meant an antidote!"

Quan Bao bowed, "I'm sorry, Princess. But nothing can be done about the rare poison."

I grew restless and begged to see him. They refused, but I didn't relent. Eventually, Spider spoke with my father and an exception was made. "We'll have a new recruit escort you," Spider sighed. "The Empress personally recommended the young man."

As the recruit entered, I couldn't believe my eyes. Forgetting any pretense of poise, I ran to embrace Hanming. His arms trembled as they closed around me, a deep breath releasing. Eventually he pulled away and I saw his eyes ablaze with cerulean.

"Attention!" Spider called. I remembered myself and stepped away to salute, as did Hanming. Spider rebuked, "There shall be no such display. Recruit seventy-eight, you are to escort this princess to the Emperor and do so with no attention to yourselves. When you return, you shall both perform six hundred squats as punishment." The penance was light.

Hanming saluted, "Yes, sir!" He left to change into an imperial guard uniform.

Spider frowned to me. "Princess, you must not forget yourself. I do not care to know how you know recruit seventy-eight, but you are under my command and you must act with discipline!"

"Yes sir!" I bowed in apology, my insides still somersaulting.

~*~

A rule amongst the Ying Guardians dictated we were not to speak within tunnels. Most were used for eavesdropping, which meant sound could be heard from both sides. When we passed a storage room that I knew was empty, I couldn't help but break the rule. I whispered under my breath, "Hanming, how did you fare?"

He responded in a similar hushed tone, informing me he'd worked as an assistant to many physicians until running into a familiar servant of the Empress. The man arranged an audience with her. She'd wept with happiness and kept in constant contact until Yu Longjing was assassinated. She then quickly ushered Hanming into the Ying Guardians.

"What about you and Winter?" I informed him. He shook his head. "I'm sorry you both suffered. Not a day went by when I didn't think of you two."

I smiled realizing what Hanming meant. He missed my brother one way, and he missed me in another. I wished to ask more, but seeing my father took priority.

We entered the Emperor's room from a back entrance. Dim lanterns cast flaxen light on the bed. I tiptoed to him, aghast to see how he reminded me of my mother; his face pale and lips blue. I knelt by his side and held his hand.

He smiled, "Summer, you stubborn girl. You were always a favorite of mine." He asked if I still missed my mother.

"Of course."

"I do too. I'll be seeing her soon." The words sent a lump to my throat. He must've noticed. "Know I've done all I could for peace. Do not cry for me, Summer. I am where I should be." He took a labored breath. "I'm glad you're here. There's something I need to ask you."

I gulped, but the lump remained. I nodded to indicate I listened.

"Assist the Empress. She's a wise woman and can sense deceit." His breathing grew loud and his eyes rolled back.

"I love you, father," I gave him a kiss on his cold cheek.

"Daughter, I need to rest now. I'm not long for this world."
A weak hand clutched mine for a moment before gentle snores
arose.

On the return trip, Hanming and I remained quiet. The Emperor's poor health meant danger lurked around every corner. I
peered to my friend and felt a spot of warmth. At least I knew he
remained by my side.

Thoughts of our mock wedding drifted to mind. All that jovi-
ality seemed thousands of lifetimes ago. I wondered if we could
ever feel such joy again.

Chapter Twenty-Three:
Past and Future

On a morning I couldn't sleep, I slipped from my chamber's window, away from drowsing guards. Standing against a chilly wind, I gazed east. I didn't mind the cold. It matched the tenderness in my chest. Three stories up, the roof gave pleasant vantage. Watching the sun kiss the land brought a smile to my face. I couldn't see the ocean, but knew the sun's rays saw it for me.

Following the landscape's pools of golden light, I traced my way across territory controlled by my father. Towering walls with carved dragons stood fierce, surrounding the innermost palace. Rings extended outward, stretching farther than my eyes could witness. Someone somewhere once said an Emperor's greatness was measured by the number of walls around the central palace; much like a tree measured its growth by rings.

I looked to my father's room, not far from where I stood. He denied visitors now, even his sons from Second Mother. I saw him again two days ago through the Ying Guardians and asked,

"Father why do you refuse your potential heirs?"

He replied solemnly, "Summer, those two are my sons and I love them dearly. However, both are selfish and are not prepared to rule. I'm giving them tests to ready them. It makes me sad to say this, but I don't trust either." He clutched his blanket in disappointment. "If they see me as weak as I am, they may devise a plan to end me sooner."

I felt disgust hearing him confide this. The thought a son would kill his father was too much to bear.

Yet, before I could speak, the Empress entered. My father smiled. "Ah, my dear old friend. Now it's you who cares for me."

The Empress nodded to me as my father patted my hand in farewell. I bowed to both and took my leave.

It was the last I saw of my father.

During breaks training with the Ying Guardians, I often sought out Hanming. At first we received cautious stares. Once they learned we'd fought side by side outside the palace, they respected our bond.

Winter spent most days in the library, studying political decisions passed during his absence. He tried to sort through what Gui Fengbi reported from what actually occurred between our Empire and the Nan Kingdom. He hardly noticed I wasn't around.

Being forbidden to mention the Ying Guardians, I couldn't tell Winter much about Hanming. I did mention that he now served as a palace guard. Hanming played along when we held a brief reunion. My brother wished to restore Hanming to his former post as a scholar, but Hanming objected. "Leave it be, old friend. The past is the past, and I prefer this role outside of politics."

Winter didn't force the issue, changing the subject with a joke, "How do you think Hutu is doing with Silk Deer?"

"I imagine he's becoming quite the hunting dog," I smiled.

"I believe you're truthfully wondering how Silk Deer is faring," Hanming gave a rare, sly grin.

We reminisced about our time with the bandits. After sunset, we ended our meeting but promised to see each other soon.

My half-brothers, Yu Lei and Yu Dian competed viciously for the title of heir. They refused to speak to one another. I found it amusing they were equally matched. They scored similar marks in all areas of academics and politics. They solved mock crises to the same level of efficiency and when sparring, one couldn't defeat the other.

The Empress reminded that one needed to prove better. The brothers grit their teeth and repeated variations of their tests to see who would finally demonstrate superiority.

I noticed the Empress' complexion had paled further since her son's funeral. I sought her out and asked if she wished to rest for a day. I could tend to my father in her place.

She shook her head. "It's my duty, but thank you child."

One evening after training all day with the Ying Guardians, I returned to find a note from Winter. He requested my immediate presence in the library. I found him slouched in a chair, brow wrinkled. Since his return as a prince, his gut had grown rounded and skin milky.

When he laid eyes on me, his sharp features relaxed. "Any word on our father?"

I reported nothing new. Winter nodded gravely and gestured for me to sit. "Look here," he pointed to a yellowed scroll, ink faded to orange. "Yu ancestors tell of their home in the west, how it grew bitter with drought. They had two options. First, move down river and set up a new village. Second, offer their understanding of the river as services to King Shun and live in Zhenxun."

I shifted to read the scroll, written by an ancient Yu.

Zhenxun is one of three allied Kingdoms. It lies between the Lan Kingdom and their subsidiary, the Nan Kingdom. The ruler in Nan is Yao. Shun is in Zhenxun. Ku is in Lan. Zhenxun cannot grow because they suffer annual floods. They need—

The writing disappeared to rotten paper.

I frowned. "Does this mean we risk war with the Lan Kingdom since we conquered the south?"

Winter nodded, "Since our father's ancestors assumed the throne, broken communication between the North and the South Kingdoms led them to operate independently. Some believe the Lan and Nan only accepted the passing of the throne to the Yu bloodline to avoid bloodshed of their family residing here." He tapped the map under his elbow. "We're like a delta, dividing rivers,"

"I understand Father wished to avoid conflict by marrying me to the Nan Kingdom."

"Even so, the armies south were small." Winter lifted his eyes and I read concern. "Yet the troops of the Lan Kingdom could rival ours. Perhaps they've not attacked because the river running between us is a hindrance."

"Winter, are there Shun people still living here?"

My brother shook his head, "Not for certain, but it's likely some stayed, hoping the mandate to rule will return to them."

"But we've grown Zhenxun into an Empire with outlying territories far greater than either Kingdom. Does this not prove heaven smiles upon the Yu?"

"With the Lan and Nan so near, we must maintain good relationships."

Something dawned on me. I clutched Winter's arm. "There's a man amongst the High Court named Ku."

His eyes clouded, "Are you certain?"

"Remember? I asked you about him when we were in the lower courts, but I could only remember 'Cui' in his name at the time."

"What's his full name?" Winter demanded.

I closed my eyes and recalled his face. I shook my head, "It was too long ago."

"You need to try harder!"

"Can't you find a registry of the Lords?"

Winter rolled his eyes and pushed a second piece of parchment to me, "What do you think I was doing? His name isn't here."

I blinked, "But I swear I met a man by the name of Ku."

"A lot of scholars use pen names or informal titles. It's possible he's one of them." Winter sighed in agitation. "I'll research all of them."

I spoke softly, "Winter."

"Hmm?" He was reading.

"How much of this history do you think father knows? How much do you think Yu Lei and Yu Dian know?"

"I'm not sure how much our father researched personally. He has many Lords who keep him informed. Though they pass information at their discretion." Winter thought for a moment. "But I doubt this ancient history has come up. Our brothers I'm afraid, neither will think to study this."

"What if they their fates end like Yu Longjing?"

Before Winter could answer, shouts reached us from outside. We rushed to a window to witness excitement. Guards darted towards the main courtyard where my father often addressed the High Court. Our ears detected the clash of metal. Amidst the clamor, raging voices of Yu Lei and Yu Dian disturbed the air.

Winter and I dashed outdoors. We shoved through the crowd and climbed steps to a tall terrace. From there, we looked down and saw Yu Lei and Yu Dian with weapons. Soldiers who moved to restrain them were cut down.

The crowd pleaded for them to set down arms. By their stormy expressions, neither would stop until the other lay dead.

I turned to head down to them but Winter grabbed my arm, "No, Summer. I'll go."

"You?" I said incredulously, patting his gut. "You haven't done a day of *gongfu* since you woke up in father's palace. It's a death wish!" By the expression on his face, he knew I was right, but didn't release my arm. Helplessly, we watched from above.

People shouted to summon the Emperor or Empress. Only their authority could stop the brothers.

More guards rushed forward, and I spotted Hanming. My gut lurched, breath growing shallow. My half-brothers Yu Lei and Yu Dian were strong fighters. With Hanming's time in the Ying Guardians short, I felt concerned.

Guards swarmed each and restrained them separately. Yu Dian kicked three away and grabbed his sword. He swung it at Yu Lei. I covered my mouth with weakened knees as Yu Lei's arm came off.

Yu Lei sunk to the ground clutching his shoulder. Guards rushed to stop his bleeding. In the midst of the huddle, I heard an angry roar and witnessed a spear sail. It struck Yu Dian in the chest.

He fell forward, limp. The weapon jutting from his chest kept him upright.

I buried my face in Winter's shoulder, trying to erase the images.

The guards rushed Yu Lei to the physician. In his exertion throwing the spear, Yu Lei had pushed volumes of blood from his body. Word came later that he passed.

~*~

The Empress had slept through the fight. When awoken, it was said she could barely sit. Long nights caring for my father had taken a toll on her already low health. Regardless, it was her duty to announce the death of my father's potential heirs.

Her eyes welled as she spoke on the terrace. When done, she retreated quickly from court members who sought to question her.

Second Mother descended into hysterics. Her mind became ill and it was decided she be carried to a distant suite where nurses looked after her day and night. The maids whispered about servants needing to tie her down because numerous times she'd tried to end her life.

Winter and I fell speechless for days. The sight of our half-brothers slaying each other unsettled us into a stony sensation no words could encapsulate. My emotions walled me in, as tight as a cell with no door or window.

An urgent question remained for all. Who was to succeed the throne?

I reasoned it should be Winter. Our remaining half-brothers were far too young.

However, Winter had often stated he couldn't. "I'm not named for the Yu house. The Lords would object vehemently." I often wondered if it was because he did not wish for the burden. Nevertheless, no further announcement was made concerning an heir.

The future remained precarious.

Chapter Twenty-Four:
Xin

Weeks passed since the deaths of Second Mother's sons. The Empress had yet to make an announcement concerning the Emperor's heir. As the palace waited, I wondered how my life could have turned out differently. What if I had married a prince in the south?

I gulped to think I could be dead.

But one never knows for certain.

As a child, I often heard my sisters chatter about their future husbands. They anticipated details of their appearances and ranks. I remember wishing for someone who could tell good stories, like my mother. I held no interest in rank nor appearance. I wanted a playmate to share my joys and sorrows.

Hanming and I shared much. When near him, strong emotions refused to be tamed, kicking like a wild river. Yet, I was no longer a child wishing to be told a story. This became apparent in many ways after my return to the palace. Most noticeably, my father spoke to me in a mature manner. Because of it, I grew wary of my bloodline and the responsibility it bore.

Hanming was a bastard child, despite noble blood from the Empress. We could never be together.

But could I really love another?

I refused to give the question credence.

There were times I lost confidence Hanming felt the same for me. Sometimes when focused inward, he forgets people around him. Hanming's mind worked to analyze, shutting out distractions not immediately relevant to his question. I'd feel relief, believing it would be easier to forget him if his heart no longer belonged to me.

Then I would catch his eyes and their warmth. It was a look I'd never seen him give another.

One day, we found ourselves in a rare moment alone. I mustered courage to ask if he still felt the same towards me. Years had passed since our moment beneath the waterfall.

In response, he pulled me close—a brazen act. He hadn't touched me since our reunion amongst the Ying Guardians. The warmth of his body glowed blue.

"Please don't look so sad, it injures me. I've kept my distance because you're not meant for me." Forcing himself to pull away, he added, "I will make you this promise. No matter whom you must marry, or where our lives lead, I'll be there if you call. Even if I must travel endless leagues to reach you. And," he gulped, cheeks flushing, "you'll always be the only one to have my heart."

My soul floated to the sky. I leaned my face to his. Closing my eyes, I brushed my smile across his lips in a forbidden kiss. I felt him shudder and the blue disappeared.

"I'm sorry Summer," he ducked away. "I shouldn't have embraced you. We mustn't forget who we are. You're a princess and in this world of propriety, we cannot cross such lines."

I knew well the reasons why we must follow etiquette, but truthfully they felt foreign. The rules didn't cover the scope of my existence. They didn't account for the time I'd spent with the bandits, nor did they consider in the Ying Guardians. Somewhere along the way, my mind rejected rules with disdain. They didn't keep the people I loved from dying, and they couldn't protect me.

In a moment of passion I declared, "If I cannot be with you, I shall remain a maiden and die by your side."

Hanming looked to me in alarm. His hand lifted to stroke my cheek, but he thought better of it. "Silly Princess. It's not our choice." I could hear tears in his voice.

I sighed. Despite how my heart rejected the rules, my mind guided me to abide by them. I moved to stand beside Hanming. His shoulder pressed to mine; the limit of appropriate contact. We stood in melancholy as the sun lowered and tranquil darkness engulfed us.

~*~

By command of the Ying Guardians, I was to have a guard at all hours of the night. Hanming took as many rounds as possible.

I waited up for him those nights. We chatted through a window, often discussing circulating rumors, but mostly refusing to address our emotions.

He told me, "Some fear the Emperor is secretly calculating who's to blame for his sons' deaths. They believe heads would soon roll."

I muttered my agreement.

One night, Hanming asked, "Princess, what do you plan… if your father were to pass?"

I answered there wouldn't be much left for me in the palace. I considered leaving to become a tree bandit. "If I ran away again, you would need to find me like you did before."

He chuckled and promised. Though our words were playful, I knew he meant it with sincerity. "Have you heard from your father?"

"No."

"It seems the palace is holding its breath, waiting for him to emerge," he spoke in his tender way.

I sighed, "Me too." Warm silence settled. "Are you concerned about the plans your mother has for you?"

Through the paper window screen, I saw his silhouette bob. "Always. Ever since I was little, I've lain awake wondering. In recent years I hoped to be a prince of a faraway Kingdom. If that were the case, I'd have a chance to be with you."

I reached through the crack and patted Hanming's shoulder. I knew this confession was difficult. He'd been adamant about appropriate conduct. "For now, we should thank our lucky stars we've survived this long."

He brushed his chin gently against my palm. "I do, Summer."

"Do you remember when I visited you in the dungeon?" I asked withdrawing my hand. A finger accidentally traced his ear. He didn't flinch and I caressed his cheek.

He let out a laugh. "Yes! How surprised I was. If you hadn't brought the pancakes, I might've starved."

The words made my heart quicken. "Remember I met Peng Xu?" Hanming's silhouette nodded. "I was repaying a debt to her, and the Zhan family on behalf of my mother. They were the ones who brought her into the palace."

In a serious tone Hanming asked, "If by freeing me you repaid a debt, then does the food you gave mean I'm indebted to you? It did save my life."

My face flushed. "You can repay that debt by staying with me forever."

His voice grew soft, yet heavy with enough sincerity to out-weigh a mountain. "You only need ask, and I'll swear to do all in my power."

Every ounce of me wished for him to stay. I needed nothing else. Yet, those words caught in my throat. Something inside warned that wishing too hard could lead to sabotage. A soft ache settled inside me. "I cannot. You must serve the Empress first."

He remained silent.

~*~

A moon later, Hanming received a special assignment. He was to escort Lords inspecting territory in the south. The Empress thought this was an opportunity for him to spend time with his adopted father, Zhan Ji. I would've asked to go, but my own father remained ill. I wished to be near should his condition worsen.

Knowing we were to be separated inspired difficult emotions. We met in secret one night to say farewell. Standing above my father's chambers where I resided, Hanming pointed at a cluster of stars. "When I was little, Peng Xu called me Xin because I'm born yin metal, according to the zodiac. Yang Hengyan then showed me this constellation, which writes a different character Xin, or heart. See the dominant two stars? That left connects with the constellation of yin metal. Can you guess the one on the right?"

I beamed, "Yang Water." My element.

"Our stories from this lifetime will live in the same heart for eternity."

I smiled. "Hanming, yin metal is compatible with yang water…"

He chuckled, "Of course, or the stars wouldn't have written us together."

Chapter Twenty-Five:
My Father

The Emperor's health continued to decline. I wrote him letters and each time his response returned slower. He didn't speak on the matter of Yu Lei and Yu Dian. I assumed he felt broken. I continued to send my love and promised to be by his side the instant he summoned. To distract myself, I trained aggressively with the Ying Guardians. At night, I gazed at the Xin constellation in loneliness.

At a meal we shared, my brother casually asked over his bowl, "Are you missing Hanming, sister?" I replied simply that I did. He nodded and said, "Yes, I miss him as well."

I didn't correct Winter that I missed Hanming in a different way. I feared he'd disapprove.

He then went on a tirade. Learning the history of our Empire made Winter agitated. He complained our palace didn't have crucial information. I knew what he wished before he spoke. "Go Winter, do you what you need to."

"Please look after Father." His eyes filled with guilt to be leaving me alone.

I gulped. "I will." I couldn't tell him how ill the Emperor truly was.

Once again, Winter snuck out of the palace we worked so hard to reenter. I was now without my pillars. I knew I must find ways of standing on my own.

~*~

One season after the death of Yu Lei and Yu Dian, the Empress felt strong enough to address the Kingdom. She'd consulted with the Emperor to solve the issue of the new heir. The imperials and Lords gathered around the usual terrace. As I stood listening, her words struck me as bizarre. Many things did not add up.

"As the High Court remembers, I was with child a second time," the Empress spoke complacently. "It was believed to be a daughter, lost to complications. Truth is, I bore a second son. We kept him secret for his safety. He is touring the Nan Kingdom and will return to assume the throne."

When she finished, gasps rattled from those assembled. Questions rang out, loud and demanding, "A second heir?"

"If there was a second, why challenge the other two?"

"Why is this second heir in hiding?"

I too, grew suspicious. A rock settled in my gut and I questioned my loyalty to the Empress. Another child besides Yu Longjing and Hanming?

I needed to speak with my father.

Or did he know about Hanming all along?

~*~

Secret passages I wasn't privy to connected with the Ying Guardian's underground lair. Many led to important parts of the palace. Among these was my father's bedchamber. I didn't know where the entrance to this secret passage laid, but planned to discover it.

I approached Spider and confidently showed him a letter I'd forged. I had signed it as my father and asked the Ying Guardians to bring me to him. I'd carved my father's seal with my own hands from a solid block of wood.

The Ying Guardian leaders looked the paper many times over.

I didn't waver. As a child, I'd often sat on his lap and went through my father's sleeve pockets. He always carried a small seal. I felt as certain of the seal as I was the lines on my face.

Finally, Spider took me aside. "Princess, we know this is a forgery." My skin prickled. Spider remained calm, "Come with me."

My hands turned to ice. Surrounded by Ying Guardians with no place to hide, I obliged.

Spider led me out of the torch-lit arena and behind a bronze standing wall with a large crest of the Empire. It hid a space I was forbidden to enter. Setting foot inside for the first time, hairs stood on the back of my neck. Heavy, locked doors arranged in a semicircle. I gulped, wondering where they led. I looked to Spider. The Ying Guardian could kill me with his bare hands. Yet, something about his demeanour kept me grounded. If he knew I forged the letter and didn't arrest me, something worse must've occurred. I needed my wits to contend with whatever awaited.

Unlocking a heavy door, Spider led me up a dark slope. I marched silently behind him, nerves on edge. Soon, five more doors greeted us. On all sides sliding bars locked in place, carved with characters too dim for me to read. Spider approached the second door from the left and slid its bars in a sequence. I heard a click. The door swung open and Spider grabbed a torch.

I followed him into the dark. He turned and locked the door behind us, checking to make sure it held. My hands grew sweaty.

We continued until we reached a thin metal plate—another door. He took out a flat, circular stone. The character "head" rose on its surface. He fitted this into a notch and gave it a twist. A low groan reverberated as the door swung open. Spider stuck his head through and peered around before waving me to follow.

I stepped forward and found myself in my father's bedchamber, the bed immediately to our right. I approached carefully and my mouth went dry.

Empty?

The only light was cast from the torch. The shutters closed tight and the air stood still. Even so, I listened for the sound of breathing.

All I heard was crackling of the torch's flame. As I stood at the side of the bed, I felt dumbfounded.

In exasperation, I reached forward and patted the sheets to make sure my eyes weren't playing tricks. I demanded, "Where's my father? Why would the physicians take him from his bedchamber?"

"Princess," Spider replied in a tired voice. "Your father has been dead for weeks. With the Ying Guardian Captains as witness, he left all governing power to the Empress."

"The Empress?" I repeated in an injured tone. "The Empress didn't inform the Empire their autocrat is dead!"

"We agreed with the decision," he replied humbly. "We wouldn't have shown you this if we didn't believe you would've caused trouble in demanding to see your father."

I nearly collapsed, "Have I not the right to know?"

"Not when the security of the Empire is concerned."

I fell to my knees beside my father's vacant bed, clutching silk sheets. I had no mother, no father. The fate of the Empire left to an adulterer.

How could the Empress keep this from us?

"Oh my!" I gasped as realization struck.

"What?" Spider asked and peered around, alert. His hand went to a knife at his belt.

"N—nothing. May I be left alone where my father last laid?" I sunk to the floor and lowered my head to my knees.

There was silence for a few moments before footsteps moved to the corner of the room. By the shuffling, it seemed he turned his back. That was the most privacy I'd receive.

My thoughts tumbled like a river. How could I not have suspected my father's passing? All this time I believed he was resting. What was the Empress plotting? What if the second son she spoke of was Hanming? What if Hanming was to be the next Emperor?

This was more complicated than I thought.

Who truly fathered Hanming? Is the unknown father blackmailing the Empress? What new dangers lurked in our Empire?

Spider moved to the bed and smoothed the sheets where I'd clutched them. "Princess, someone's coming. We must leave."

Obediently, almost blindly, I followed. I heard him lock the secret door. We retraced our steps and reentered the Guardians' arena. The Captains waited with looks of concern. Their eyes darted between Spider and me.

I knew then my forgery of the seal was accurate, but the quandary was they all knew of the Emperor's passing. I bowed deeply and apologized for the dishonesty. In turn, I thanked each of them, "… for giving me the truth."

My training ended early that day. Between two guardians I was escorted to my quarters. My thoughts tossed in chaos. I called a maid to bring me tea and she returned with a letter from my brother. I shooed her way and opened the thin parchment. My stomach knotted, not sure what nature of news to anticipate.

Sister, I learned one of the officials who left to inspect the South Kingdom went by a common name. His real name is Ku

Cuixin. He had little recorded history beyond his grandparents. I suspect his documents were tailored because it doesn't match the handwriting of documents submitted around the same time. I'm following him, and will get to the bottom of this. Please burn this once you're done.

Stay safe, Winter

As I watched the flame consume the last of the letter, my door burst open. I stood. Frowning, I recognized Jin Su. Having been fraught over my father, I'd forgotten about him. It was a mistake. He'd been plotting against me.

"Arrest her! She's a murderer!"

Chapter Twenty-Six:
Torture

Jin Su had searched my old suite and found the bloody robes I wore the night Ting died. He convinced other Lords I was responsible for my half-brother's death. After my arrest, the imperial guards carted me to the dungeons. No Ying Guardians marched amongst them.

Instead of a cell, they chained me to a wall. I overheard an interrogator was on his way to persuade information. I knew what it meant—I was to be tortured.

I huddled and tried to keep my wits. Winter was away and couldn't help. Perhaps it was a good thing. He could be labeled a co-conspirator and thrown into the dungeon alongside me.

For three days no one fed me and only a few cups of stale water passed my way.

On the fourth day, Jin Su arrived with guards. I wrinkled my nose in disgust. He lectured me, but I inspected my nails indifferently. Something hard hit me on the side of the head. I snapped up in anger.

Jin Su's words were ice, "Pay attention you pig!"

I glared, vowing I wouldn't give him the satisfaction of losing my temper.

Jin Su waved and a guard brought in a bench. I heard screaming and a middle-aged woman was dragged in. "No please, I'm sorry! I'll never do it again!" she cried.

I eyed her suspiciously.

"This woman," Jin Su spoke, "was caught stealing from the home of a High Court official. She'd been at it for moons, but wouldn't admit her crimes. We're here to remind her."

Jin Su waved again and they plopped her on the bench. Three guards held her down and another grasped her leg. A fifth took her foot. "We are going to persuade her to confess. Hopefully this will convince you to do the same. Otherwise, we have no choice but to use the same methods on you," Jin Su snarled in threat.

He was wise to keep distance or I would've spat on him.

"Now," he commanded the guards.

I closed my eyes and looked away. A piercing scream filled the air as they snapped her foot. I heard more crunching and wanted to beg them to stop, but knew the words would be wasted.

And it'd give Jin Su satisfaction.

"How much did you steal?" Jin Su shouted.

"Ten silver coins! My husband's ill and I have small children," she wept. There was a pause before another cry.

Silently, I prayed for her.

"There were more than silver coins missing," Jin Su scolded. "Confess now or they'll cut your foot clean off!"

"Please sir! We have nothing! I will work as a slave to repay my debt!" Her words faded into a blood-curdling shriek.

My hands shook and bile rose in my throat. As I prayed she'd lose consciousness, I wondered if my maid and her husband had endured the same those years ago. I clenched my teeth and covered my ears, but nothing allowed me to escape the screams.

"Yes! whatever it is! I stole everything!" the woman wheezed in agony, "I will repay!"

I stole a glance and saw her foot hung at an awkward angle with black and blue splotches.

Sadly, fainting didn't spare her. They threw a bucket of water onto her face and rubbed strong herbs under her nose. Her eyes rolled open.

Jin Su intimidated, "Your kind is worth nothing." He gave me a smug smile.

Since her foot was broken, they used other tactics. The guards threw her to the ground and she grabbed her calf, wailing in disbelief. They tied her hand to the seat of the bench. No matter how hard she fought, she was no match against five men.

One retrieved a cloth pouch, and shook it to cause rattling. When he revealed the contents, I saw thin slits of bamboo. Horror washed over me. I looked to the woman struggling. In that moment, something inside refused to sit by. My fists clenched and my quaking changed to that of indignation. I weighed my options.

Spider and the Ying Guardians had taught me to gauge an opponent's ability. There were six men here. None with more than basic training. I saw a guard hold a bamboo slit lined under the woman's fingernail. She gasped in anticipation, as he picked up a little hammer to tap the bamboo into her flesh.

I stood. "Wait. I'll take her place." My tone was solid.

Jin Su looked me over curiously. "No," he spat simply.

"I'm the one you want," I threatened, "or are you too cowardly to torture a princess?" A look of hesitation flashed on his face. I continued, "It's no secret you've wanted me dead for a long time. If I know you, not many know you're with me now." I snickered, "You could kill me, and none would suspect a thing."

Jin Su thought for a moment, then shook his head. He didn't take my bait.

"Coward! If you only had half the guts of Gui Fengbi!"

"Gui Fengbi was a proud fool," Jin Su snickered. "And I know you cannot stand torture," he brushed me off, thinking he'd won.

"Guards! Prisoner escape!" I shouted at the top of my lungs. Jinsu wouldn't come near enough for me to grab, so I went to my second plan.

"Silence!" He shook a finger at me.

"Escape! Backup!" I screeched.

Two guards set their weapons down and approached with a dirty rag. I squirmed as they tried to hold me down. In the process, I felt their pockets and discovered none contained the key to my shackles. But one did hold a small knife. I kicked and fussed as a diversion, allowing them to gag me. Meanwhile, I picked the locks on my wrists—a trick I learned from the bandits.

With hands freed, I held onto my shackles. Once they backed away and lowered their defenses, I dropped the restraints. In two swift motions, I slit their throats. Sorrow resonated in my heart. These were sons of mothers. Yet I couldn't let the feeling distract me now.

Two more came at me with swords. I kicked the broad side of a blade and it flew from the guard's hand. My foot flicked a shackle into his face and he fell back, unconscious. I charged the other and pretended to leap. At the last second, I slid to the ground and slashed a deep cut in his ankle, severing tendons.

No longer needing the knife, I threw it at the last guard, standing before Jin Su. It struck his eye and he collapsed.

Amidst the carnage, Jin Su now shouted, "Guards!"

I heard running and grabbed a sword and a spear. I marched towards Jin Su who backed away with thinly veiled fear. On the way, I kicked the guard whose ankle I'd slashed. My foot landed squarely in his temple and he lost consciousness.

"How's this possible?" he muttered. Jin Su turned to dash.

I threw the spear and it wedged into the wall before him. He stumbled back and I lunged upon him in an instant. I grasped his collar, tossing him to the ground. I hooked my feet under his elbows and squeezed my knees. He howled as his shoulders popped.

I leaned forward and pulled back his hair. A grimace plastered his face as I pointed a sword under his chin, eying the throbbing vein. "Tell me," I threatened, "What part did you have in killing the Emperor?"

"Just kill me," he hissed.

"I'm not like you," I said through gritted teeth.

He chuckled, "Yes you are. And you're not getting out alive."

A mood of darkness gripped me and my blade moved on its own. His ear fell to the ground. Jin Su cried loudly. His shoulder twitched, trying to cover the bleeding on the side of his head. But his arms lay useless.

My action left me perplexed, but I needed to know if he had a hand in killing my father. "If you don't listen, you don't need ears," I warned sinisterly. I hardly recognized my voice, the one I once used to sing with my mother. "Maybe I should cut off the other," I yanked his head to the side.

"Yes!" he sounded just like the woman they'd abused. "We commanded a spy to poison the Tai wife!"

I could hear men calling in the corridors as they tried to decipher where the distress cry had originated. They didn't sound concerned. It was a large dungeon and sometimes trouble-making prisoners caused false alarms.

"Who is 'we' and why did you wish my mother dead?"

"Gui Fengbi. He wanted more power. There's another official whose name I do not know. He went to Lord Gui and asked for help. He said he wanted to overthrow the Emperor. He also wanted to remove the Tai name as well." Jin Su breathed heavily and voices in the hall drew closer.

Another thought dawned on me. "Does the Empress know any of this?"

Jin Su let out an evil laugh. A tingling in my spine suggested what I'd feared. "The Empress and this mystery man are lovers. The second son she speaks of is his," he cackled smugly.

Dread smothered me as my arms grew weak and knees numb. Before I could ask more, a sword crashed down on Jin Su's head. I leaped back in alarm.

The tortured woman had awoke. With one hand still bound to the bench, she beat passionately at Jin Su's skull, profanity spewing from her lips. I pried her sword away and cut her restraints. She continued to curse and spit at Jin Su.

I threw her onto my back and we ran through the dungeon. I heard shouts as we slipped into an open cell. I shut it and told the woman to lie quietly. As she shuddered in pain, I threw straw over us, listening intently until guards ran past.

Near our dim cell, one fretted, "We can't have another escape! One of us will be executed!" There was bustling for some time before the commotion died.

I peeked from the straw and saw no one outside the cell. I

shook the woman. She'd fainted again. Looking at her foot, I crawled to the corner and vomited. When I finally regained myself, I remembered what Hanming had taught. I surmised a foot in such a condition must be separated from the rest of the body. Since I didn't have tools to amputate, I would need a tourniquet.

I ripped my robe and found a stick strong enough to hold. Quickly, I set to work. As I applied the tourniquet, the woman panicked and tried pushing me away. I shushed her, "We're not yet out of danger!"

She pulled my hair and spat, I assumed from fear. I explained about her foot, "We need to get you to a physician."

She finally calmed and glared at me suspiciously. "Why are you helping?" she demanded.

It felt inadequate as I confessed, "I feel terrible how they tortured you." My words seemed weak.

She studied me up and down. In a haughty voice she agreed to come with me if I paid her. I stared for a long time, perplexed. Maybe she wasn't right in the head.

No. Those eyes glimmered with cleverness.

Did she even have a family? How much of what she confessed was true?

I finally understood what my mother meant when she once lectured, "Some people slip so far, they can no longer be helped."

I stood and went to the cell door.

"Wait for me," the woman called. "Don't forget, I want gold!"

I locked the cell with her inside. "Don't worry. I've bound

your ankle tightly. You won't die from those injuries."

As I turned to leave, she called after me, begging. When I didn't respond, she cussed loudly. Her words fell onto deaf ears.

My body ached, but my heart throbbed even more. If Jin Su's words held reason, then Hanming was the son of a traitor. The Empress was handing my father's Empire to another family. Nighttime chill settled in my bones as I stumbled in a daze. I trudged the familiar paths back to my mother's courtyard. Hanming's whisper before his departure came to mind and a shudder caused me to lose balance.

He wished to be a prince so he could wed me.

I didn't believe he knew what the Empress planned. Even so, I wondered painfully if I should've left Hanming in the dungeons to die. Then I wouldn't feel this agony now, torn between loyalty to my father and the desires of my heart. Fatigue ground into me. I stepped one foot automatically in front of the other.

Hanming did nothing wrong. He was merely born. Perhaps Jin Su gave false information. Why should I trust a single word of his?

As I cried, the clouds kept steady. Not a single star shone in the sky. Our Xin couldn't be seen.

Chapter Twenty-Seven:
Loyalty

I drifted to my old princess suite and climbed a tree. Sitting on the rooftop, I watched silvery moonlight peek between clouds. It cast lethargic shadows, remaining apathetic to my plight. I furiously slapped the leaves of a tree in tantrum. The courtyard had long been abandoned and I held no concern of being discovered. I wept soundly until daylight touched my skin. As I peered towards the light, I recognized no help would come. I waited all this time for my father to sort things, but he was gone. With no family left, the palace was no longer my home.

I snuck into my old chambers. Standing still, I soaked in nostalgia. The little bed where Hutu slept remained unkempt, the way he'd left it. My intricately carved cherry table sat lonely in the center. Silk curtains and richly embroidered sheets remained unchanged. Laughter with my sisters felt alive within the walls and echoed in my memory.

I shook my head and went to gather fresh clothes. Luckily,

my wardrobe remained too. Jin Su's people only took my bloody gown. I picked the plainest robes and removed my torn ones. I'd grown considerably over the years and had some trouble tightening my sash.

Not quite sure how to leave the palace, I bumbled about for a while, trying to devise a plan. I thought I was alone until someone cleared his throat behind me. I grasped a fruit knife left on my table and peered over my shoulder. In the doorway stood a man in guard clothing. His aura hovered, a gentle green.

As he approached, I recognized Spider. I watched him cautiously, remembering he served only the Empress now. "Why're you here?" I asked, knife clasped behind my back.

He replied calmly, "I should be asking you."

"How can I trust you?"

"Do you not see? If the Empress wanted you dead, I would've killed you by now."

I studied him, face unchanged.

Spider seated himself at my cherry table and patted the bench beside him. "Let me tell you a secret."

Guardedly, I inched forward. He waited patiently as I eased myself down.

"I protect the Empress because she *is* the Empress. Not because she's my sister."

My ears burned. This sudden information changed my view of Spider and left me befuddled. My knees tightened, should I need to leap away. "You let her conspire to kill the Emperor!

Where does the loyalty of the Ying Guardians lie?"

Spider shook his head. "She had nothing to do with the plot." Sincerity followed in the silence and I felt inclined to believe him. He spoke again, "My sister and I, our loyalty forever belongs to this Empire. If my sister were to step out of line, I would have no choice but to take her life. That's the price of the oath we have taken. One day, you too will need to make such a choice."

"What do you mean?" I narrowed my eyes.

"I've said too much." Spider shook his head, "I promise, you'll know in your own time."

I didn't press further. My head had no room for those thoughts that night.

Spider assisted me in sneaking from the palace. He hid me in a handcart fitted with a secret compartment. As the guards at the gates searched, they didn't check below. When we traveled through the markets of the lower courts, I heard startling news. The Empress planned to visit the newly ascended ruler of the Lan Kingdom in the north.

My mind ran in circles. I couldn't shake the feeling more happened than I knew. Despite Spider's confession of loyalty, I held reservations. Can I trust he'd truly take me out of the palace? Or is this a trap I'm hiding in?

My question was answered when he opened the false door. Before me a horse neighed, saddled and ready. We stood at the borders of Zhenxun. Spider handed me a sword and a gourd of water, "Be vigilant. Though you're stronger than average opponents, you haven't moved passed beginner's training with the Ying Guardians."

I thanked him and rode south.

Spider's words stayed with me. He'd taken an oath, and would kill his sister if needed. I shuddered as a terrible thought crossed my mind. What if I needed to harm Hanming?

Equally, I didn't like thought of him harming me. I rubbed tears away, squaring my shoulders, "There must be another explanation. Words of a traitor like Jin Su shouldn't be taken with weight."

It took three days of fast riding to reach the home of the tree bandits. I hoped they'd remember me.

I took the saddle off of my horse and hid it in a bush. With a slap, I sent him grazing. I positioned myself beneath a familiar large tree and whistled. Looking up at a barely visible platform, I heard soft murmuring.

"Who are you?" a deep voice demanded from behind. A cold blade appeared at my neck.

I beamed, "Elk, how are you?"

I heard shuffling as the large man shifted to see my face. Joy lit his eyes as he sheathed his weapon. He held me in tight embrace, "First your brother, now you!" Elk waved and the rope dropped down. I took a wistful ride on its loop and soon perched on a platform.

My brother greeted me with a grave expression. After a quick reunion with the bandits, Winter excused us to speak privately.

"I followed Ku Cuixin to the south territory. For some reason, he left to travel north. At least Hanming was assigned to travel with him. Though I cannot reach him, I feel better knowing he's on our side."

I bit my lip. Do I tell him about Hanming and the developments back at the palace?

Winter studied my face, "What is it?"

I decided not to say anything until I knew for certain. "Winter, the Empress is planning a visit to the new King of the Lan Kingdom."

Winter tilted his head, "On behalf of Father?"

I choked, "Our father passed away—but no one knows—the Empress has been acting in his place."

His expression darkened. "How can a woman like her run our father's Kingdom?"

"What do you mean, 'a woman like her?'"

"In the Nan Kingdom, EVERYONE knew she's an adulteress!" he struggled to keep his voice low. "How's no one in our Empire aware of her disloyalty!"

Elk poked in and motioned for us to keep quiet. I nodded and patted my brother's shoulder. My emotions knotted too. I thought of my father asking me to help the Empress despite her birthing Hanming as a bastard. Until recently, I'd kept faith in my elders, assuming they knew better.

Poor Father. How did he come to trust such a woman? My mind also went to Spider, the Empress' brother. Had he helped me leave the palace to be rid of me?

"We must follow them north," Winter lifted his head. I read determination in his eyes.

I finally understood why people withheld information from me in my youth. If given at the wrong time, knowledge could unleash brash actions with large consequences. Now, I felt the tables turned. I found myself holding dangerous secrets, and my brother the one acting hastily.

Yet, there was little I could do to stop him. I too wished for more answers.

~*~

We woke early and bid the tree bandits farewell. Elk asked, "Give Silk Deer and the others regards if you cross paths."

Winter and I agreed.

I hardly noticed the warmth of late spring as we rode. My concerns drifted back to the palace. With my father passed and the Empress gone, there was no one left to rule. It seemed Zhenxun hovered dangerously on the edge of collapse, amidst a den of wolves, each waiting to pounce.

"Winter, Father's dead. What are we fighting for?" I grumbled.

He glared, "The Empire is the legacy of our family."

"It's natural for Empires to fall. I don't see what's left to save. It's nothing more than a lot of greedy Lords, fighting over power."

Winter reined his horse to a stop and faced me. "What are

you saying sister? Have you lost yourself?" His eyes shone with exasperation.

"Winter," I tried to keep from whining, "our parents are gone. Our sisters are happily married away. We have nothing left there!"

His look softened, "I understand now. You're thinking of the palace as your home. What you fail to realize is that an Empire is much more than just us imperials. It's bigger than *our* family. The Empire is every single citizen relying on us to protect them." Winter's voice hardened, "Loyalty goes both ways. It's our duty to ascertain fair leaders to oversee the Empire." Realization sank into me as he stressed, "We cannot do this without the loyalty of our citizens. In return, we must be loyal to the people."

I conceded thoughtfully, "You're saying it's our duty to re-main—to protect the people from corruption in our own courts—even if it's to our personal detriment?"

"Yes," he returned his horse to a brisk pace. "Being an imperial is about more than power. You need to ask, 'from where does the power come?' One needs wisdom in choosing battles, courage to do the moral thing, and compassion to those who do you wrong."

I fell silent as I contemplated his words. Being a princess was more than a duty to our father. It was also a duty to our citizens.

After a moment, my brother continued, "When the Yao Emperor resigned to our ancestors, he did so because it was best for his people. They needed the leadership of *our* ancestor, and the cooperation of every citizen working in unison to tame the river. Without it, needless deaths would've continued."

Winter's tone challenged. "Now I pose questions to you: Do you think the Empress has the best intentions for the Empire if she's having affairs and stealing away to the Lan Kingdom? Do you think it's our duty to protect the Empire by exposing her treachery?"

He let the question hang. For the rest of the trip, I pondered Winter's lecture heavily.

Chapter Twenty-Eight:
River Crossing

When Winter and I came within view of the bandits' cave, a furry splotch lifted his head. Hutu scampered to us, slower than before. He'd grown thick, but still remembered me. I picked him up and was rewarded by a slew of kisses. He barked, asking how I've been. I ruffled his ears and told him, "I've missed you!"

The bandits came out to greet us and Silk Deer linked her arm into my brother's. When he didn't respond, a look of concern came over her face. She turned to me, "Is something the matter?"

I smiled dejectedly, "A lot has happened."

"Let 'em rest," An old woman came forward and took my reins. "There's time to talk later."

"Of course." Silk Deer took my travel pack. "It's good to see you," she whispered.

I sniffled, bobbling my head. I felt the same, but was too emotional to speak.

Hutu followed when they showed us our rooms. When Silk Deer left to give me privacy, he trailed after her, but first gave me a goodbye yip. He was her dog now.

I sucked in a breath of cool, cavern air. The musky odor relaxed me as I lifted my arms to stretch. Aches still pestered, from both the journey and recent events. I straightened my back and sat on a mound of furs. Taking in more of the calming air, I exhaled to push stress away. I closed my eyes and began meditation—a variation of Spider's healing technique I experimented with.

Hours must've passed before I heard in a silvery voice, "Summer, it's dinnertime!"

I opened my eyes and a pearly aura came from the other side of the animal hide. It was Silk Deer.

As I entered the kitchen, I blinked twice. Before me, a startling plethora of color moved in live mosaic. The bandits bustled, setting tables and carrying bowls. Friendly chatter filled the cavern and the hearth glowed warm. A fog hovered around each person, some brighter than others and pulsating to distinct rhythms. Sometimes when two people spoke, their rhythms matched. Except for pure blue, everyone exuded a unique hue.

"Summer? What're you staring at?"

I turned to Winter, speechless. His aura glowed plum, like our mother's eyes. "I—I—" I wasn't sure what to say, "Its nothing." He gave a quizzical look before taking me by the elbow. As he led me to a table, my mind sharpened and the colors receded.

The usually jovial bandits contained a serious side as well. As we ate, Winter updated all with the occurrences of our home Empire. They wore somber expressions and shared our concern with war against the Lan Kingdom. It meant thousands of soldiers marching through their territory.

"Tell me again why you're chasing the Empress and not organizing a coup back home?" an older bandit asked Winter.

"Our Empire's fragile. It's difficult to win a coup without outside allies. Not to mention, our armies are weak from conquering the Nan Kingdom."

Another asked, "What will you do once you find the Empress?"

"I'm not certain," Winter began, "First I'll demand answers. Based on her responses, I'll know whether she can be trusted. Then I'll figure out what to do."

"But how can a lower imperial like you approach the Empress?" one asked.

Winter paused, remembering he protected the bandits from knowing he was a prince. "Because she's traveling outside Zhenxun. I have a better chance of approaching."

"You must be careful," Silk Deer spoke with concern. "The Lan Kingdom has been hunting blood bandits, pushing them south. We've run into desperate ones. They're quick to violence."

"It's best not to go alone," a large woman agreed. "I can come along for the fight."

Winter shook his head, "Thank you, but this is something

I cannot allow you to risk your lives for. Besides, it would be easier to hide if I were alone. I can stick to the trees and move swiftly." Winter turned towards me. "Summer, you'll need to stay here. I'll try not to be gone long."

I gazed at him incredulously and opened my mouth in protest. If only I could tell him about the Ying Guardians.

His eyes stared me down. My heart filled with heaviness. I gulped, "I hear you, brother." Yet I knew I couldn't allow Winter to go on this journey without me. I recollected the viciousness of the blood bandits we'd encountered. If they were driven to desperation, they would be many times more dangerous. No matter how stealthy Winter could move, he remained vulnerable alone.

After dinner, I wrapped left over food in waxy leaves. I shoved it in a sack and stole a gourd of water. I hid the items under my dress as I returned to the sleeping room. Once there, I changed into a Ying Guardian training robe Spider left with me. I folded my dress and hid it behind a protruding rock. I pulled a large fur over my shoulders and dozed briefly before the expected sound of footsteps woke me. I felt Winter kneeling. A hand petted my head. I breathed deep, pretending to be asleep.

"Be safe, Sister," I heard him whisper.

I remained motionless, listening to his fading steps. Once they disappeared, I quickly grabbed the food and water. Slinging the fur over my shoulders as a cloak, I exited my room.

As I made my way towards the mouth of the cavern, I heard soft clicking. I froze as the sound drew near. A soft whine stirred my heart. I bent down and Hutu's wet nose pushed against my palm.

There was a soft striking sound and a lamp lit a few paces away. The sad face of Silk Deer caught the light. She approached with a sigh and wrapped her arm tightly around me. "Please be careful, and watch over your brother," she whispered. I nodded, accepting the long dagger she placed in my hand. I gave Hutu one last pat before I walked away. Silk Deer escorted me as far as the hanging vines.

"Summer," she paused. "Please tell Winter I'll wait for him. No matter how long it takes."

Silk Deer had always joked about romance and teased those who said they were in love. Yet, no one denied she saved herself for Winter.

I promised to relay the message.

Using moonlight, I took steps towards the sounds of the rushing river. I could barely make out Winter's tracks. He'd decided to travel on foot. It was a good decision. A horse would've drawn attention. With senses alert, I trailed in silence, careful not to accidentally stumble upon my brother.

Before long, light of a new morning appeared. By midday, I'd caught up with him but stayed a safe distance behind. It grew too warm for the fur so I rolled it and carried in across my shoulders. At night when he climbed a tree to sleep, I did the same.

Days passed and finally he reached the river. Winter avoided the bank and kept in the woods. Without rest, he turned upriver and moved west. I wondered how he planned to cross and if I'd be able to follow. I recalled years ago the powerful currents had nearly pulled me under.

Around this time, my food supply ran low. I set some traps for small animals, allowing Winter to pull a day ahead. At night I built a deep pit and cooked the meat. Once I replenished my supply, I hurried to catch up.

In this manner, we journeyed west for five days. On the sixth, my brother stopped when the sun was high. He climbed a tree and from where I hid, saw he gazed towards the river. He perched on the top limb until nightfall and made a bed in the branches.

The next day when I awoke, Winter disappeared. I dropped down and searched for tracks but couldn't find any. Baffled, I climbed the same tree. Peering out from the top branch I saw far into the distance. About half a day west was a sharp bend in the river. Several small islands of large rock jutted sharply. I shielded my eyes, squinting. It appeared thick ropes connected these islands, creating passage from one bank to the other. On the north side, I spied a plume of smoke rising from treetops.

I ducked out of the hot sun to a lower branch. By chance I saw bark missing from a nearby tree. I smiled. Winter must be traveling through the trees now. No wonder I couldn't track him.

I allowed myself time to rest and ate some berries. Once finished, I moved on. I kept my pace slow, not wishing to alert my brother. Though I didn't know exactly where he was, I felt certain he headed towards the rope bridge.

Shouts awoke me that night. I climbed higher into my tree and crouched, straining my ears. It did no good. I couldn't tell if the cries stemmed in anger or celebration. Undoubtedly it was the people I'd seen earlier in the day on the north side of the bank. They must've crossed the bridge. I wondered of my brother's whereabouts and prayed for his safety.

When morning came, I peered from the leaves, trying to ascertain my location. Pleased, I saw the rope bridge nearby. I searched cautiously for smoke plumes, pondering if Winter had crossed north. In debating on whether I should venture across the bridge, I took one of my mother's coins and flipped it.

"Crest side up, I cross." I slapped the coin onto the back of my hand. It was the crest.

I shrugged. Even if Winter were to catch me following, it was too late to send me back.

The shouts I'd heard in the night left me with uneasiness. I collected a bundle of sticks and rolled a sharpened piece of wood inside, along with my mother's gold coins. I made sure they were well hidden. I carried my dagger on top of the bundle, in the open. Then I tied the fur around my shoulders to hide my breasts. I put a bounce in my step, trying my best to appear a young man. I even hummed a tune as I marched to the rope bridge.

Once I arrived, I observed it hanging modestly above crashing waves. Before the merciless power of this river, I felt apprehensive. A thick rope ran along the bridge's bottom for stepping.

On either side ran thinner ropes to grasp for balance. Zigzagged sinews in between kept them spaced.

The river frothed angrily, crashing against the jutting rock islands. Up close, they seemed shaper than expected. It's as if an angry giant had thrown knives into the water. The river thrashed wildly as if rejecting the blades.

Forcing down reservations, I tightly grasped a side rope. Mist from the river peppered my calves and I feared slipping. "Focus. One step at a time," I coached myself. The bridge bounced and I reached for the other side.

Before my fingers could close, a force pulled me back. My heels hovered above the water for a moment and my heart skipped. I let out a cry as my back hit the ground. I heard laughter as a rough hand set me on my feet.

"What do we have here?" a voice snarled. Three men surrounded me with red bands on their arms.

"Answer, boy!" another commanded.

"Collecting firewood!" I welped, genuinely shaken.

The third pulled the bundle of wood off of my shoulders. As it came off, I pretended to stumble and secretly slid the sharpened wood into my sleeve. These bandits, distracted by my dagger in the open, didn't notice my sleight of hand.

"You need a knife for that?" one demanded.

"It's for cutting big chunks," I nervously made chopping motions, "into smaller pieces."

"You'll be lucky if I don't cut YOU into pieces! It's my knife now," the man ripped the dagger off of the bundle of wood. A sack was thrown over my head and my hands tied behind me. They searched my pockets for money but found none.

In a frustrated grunt, they lifted me by the collar and forced me to walk away from the sound of the river. I tried my best to determine where we were headed, but their jostling made me lose bearing.

After some time, I heard other voices and smelled a campfire. I felt myself pushed onto the ground. Someone joked, "What've you brought? This one's small enough for fish bait!"

"We can make 'im work," another dismissed.

Rough hands tied my ankles together. Without warning, I experienced vertigo and my head hit the ground. I spun wildly as blood rushed to my face. It took me a moment to realize I dangled upside down. Indeed, I felt like bait hanging from a line.

I heard rope grinding against bark and voices fade as murmurs of a hunting trip were tossed around. I waited a few minutes before pushing the sharpened wood through my sleeve. I rubbed it against the rope on my wrists.

"Hello?" I heard Winter's muffled voice. I froze—a child caught in mischief. "Who's there? Are you alright?"

I felt too sheepish to respond. The sound of mild struggling reached me before something soft hit the ground, next came creaking. At first I felt unsure what was happening and hid the sharp stick back up my sleeve.

Then, the sack flew off of my head and sunlight struck my

eyes. Before me, swinging upside down was Winter. He stared in disbelief, the sack from my head in his teeth. He'd swung over and pulled it off.

I let loose a nervous chuckle and gave him the biggest grin I could. His face glowed red. Although I'd like to think it was from being upside down, I suspected it was partially from fury. His eyes scolded, lips pressed tightly.

"Winter," I took the opportunity to speak first, "You can yell at me later, first let me help us escape." I pulled the sharp stick from my sleeve again and rubbed vigorously at the rope. When it weakened, I tugged hard and it snapped. Next, I reached towards my feet.

"Careful!" Winter warned, "We're high up."

I nodded, unfazed. We suspended at a height four times taller than me. My guess it was to discourage escape. If a captive didn't know what he was doing, he could fall to his death. Fortunately, Winter and I were comfortable with trees and heights.

I used skills obtained as a court entertainer. I reached past my feet and grabbed the rope. I hiked myself up and gave the rope some slack. Mustering strength, I swung my legs overhead and hooked my knees. Taking a deep breath, I repeated the process and climbed upwards.

It was more difficult than climbing wide silks. The narrow rope dug into my skin. When my arms buckled, Winter cheered me on. I bit my lip against tears of strain. Once I threw an arm over a branch, I sprawled for a rest, huffing in exhaustion.

"Hurry Summer, we don't know when they'll be back," Winter called. My shaking fingers found their way to the rope around my ankles. I used the sharp stick and rubbed through. Once my feet were free, I climbed down and lowered my brother. I handed him the sharpened stick to cut his ropes, then ran to my bundle of sticks. I dug around and found the pouch with my mother's coins. I replaced the cord around my neck and patted them in relief.

The bandits had taken my dagger, so I searched the camp for another. My penchant for beautiful things persuaded me to grab a sword with a blue-jeweled sheath. Winter found his blade and grabbed a bag of food. As we threw weapons and provisions onto our shoulders, voices approached. Winter and I exchanged a look to confirm we thought the same. We raced towards the river.

As we burst onto the bank, shouts followed. We saw the bridge and this time I couldn't afford to be afraid. Winter grabbed my arm and threw me onto the ropes. I clung as tightly as I could as the stepping rope bounced. I nearly slipped.

When we reached the first island, a whizzing sound flew past my head. Turning, I unsheathed the sword and struck an arrow in midair. Winter took his sword and hacked at the rope bridge.

"Assist me!" he shouted over roaring water.

I quickly joined in frantic cutting. We occasionally struck at soaring arrows. Some blood bandits traversed halfway across the bridge. I picked up a loose stone and threw it. It hit a bandit's temple and he charged in anger, but only a few steps. He slipped and fell into the waves, which made no work of dragging him below. The change in weight caused a violent bounce, slowing the others.

I saw Winter had nearly cut through the stepping rope. I swung my sword with all my might. A loud whack echoed as the rope snapped. The rioting tumults below swallowed the bandits.

Without dally, Winter and I continued to the next section of the bridge. We were too far to be hit by arrows, but it didn't stop our hearts from pounding.

Chapter Twenty-Nine:
Kingdom of Blue

"When did you learn to climb like that?" Winter panted.

"My time with the court entertainers," I wheezed, trying to calm my quaking limbs.

"You surprise me."

I took the words as a compliment.

Winter told me he had tried to cross the rope bridge the night before, but the blood bandits grabbed him. He proved himself useful by giving bits of information on the southern terrain. It convinced them not to kill him. He had been waiting for a chance to escape before discovering I was captured too.

As we continued north, Winter brooded. He scolded me for following him. I bore the reprimand, glad to have my brother alive.

Though we saw no more bandits, we remained vigilant. At night we slept in trees and covered our tracks thoroughly. By the third day we traveled through a forest of trees with thick bark.

They were unlike any back home.

My foot snapped a twig, and an echo sounded in the distance. An odd sensation tickled the back of my neck. Even Winter slowed his steps. I saw splotches of red and black haze through the trees. Someone's aura.

"Halt!" a voice shouted.

Winter drew his sword but I told him, "Lower it."

Soldiers dressed in heavy brown uniforms appeared, encircling us. I recognized their insignia. Until that moment, I'd only seen it in books. The imperial army of the Lan Kingdom.

We knelt and placed our hands behind our heads. Before I could react, they lifted me to my feet and bowed. Winter and I stole an exasperated glance. I shrugged and mouthed, "Play along."

"Prince Ku Rentu!" a voice sung. An affable man made his way through the kneeling soldiers. I peered around before realizing he spoke to me. I nodded in acknowledgment. "Prince Ku Rentu," he said again, dropping to the ground. "We're glad to find you safe and sound. Otherwise, your brother would have my head!"

"Yes. Of course." I cleared my throat, trying to make my voice lower. "What's your name?"

"General Hong, at your service!" he declared proudly.

"Yes! General Hong," I chuckled nervously. "Please escort me, and my servant back to the palace. We've had some unfortunate experiences and I'd like to return home."

"A thousand times yes!" General Hong motioned and a fine horse was brought forth. I made a show of mounting it before tossing my sword to my brother. It was my playful revenge for him scolding me.

Later, I discovered the sword I stole from the blood bandits belonged to prince Ku Rentu. Since I dressed as a boy and was around the same age, the General mistook me for him. Though safer to travel through the woods with their imperial army, I held concerns. Once we reached the Lan Kingdom, the royal Ku family would surely know I was a fake. The consequence could be deadly. Winter and I needed to weasel away before entering the imperial city.

~*~

We journeyed for two days before reaching the first village of the Lan Kingdom. There, we rested at an inn and resupplied. Winter mingled with the prince's soldiers and learned the palace was only a day away.

That night a cold wind rattled the doors and howled ominously. We pretended to sleep, waiting for the soldiers to settle. I felt hesitant to leave the warmth of the inn. But Winter said, "Such weather is common in the north. We won't find a better night."

We tiptoed past dozing guards and left through the back. Winter dressed as a solider and I a commoner. I left prince Ku Rentu's sword behind for fear it would attract more attention. General Hong and his men had been kind and I would feel guilty if they returned with nothing. The sword at least gave proof they came close to their prince.

As we snuck towards the stables, I stole a sword from a sleeping guard. Winter gave me a smirk, "You're learning the arts of banditry quite well."

Quietly, we walked the horses out of the village. When no longer in earshot, we galloped north. Icy wind cut my face and my fingers grew numb. The furs around my shoulders did little to keep warmth in. Overhead a crescent glowed weakly and the stars did not dance. Soft flakes of ice drifted as my breath bloomed in a pale gray cloud.

After a few hours, I begged, "Brother, we must stop."

We ripped pieces of cloth and wrapped them around our hands. I cupped my fingers to my face and breathed into them. Winter asked, "Are you alright?"

I nodded, "Let's keep going."

Despite the cold, it felt exhilarating to ride without a soul around. The vast plains stretched endlessly and the velvety night absorbed much of our noises. We took comfort knowing no wild beast could pounce from hiding.

By time the sun rose to our right, dark structures appeared in the distance. Golden rays painted the land and warmth returned. We fast approached the Lan Kingdom.

Our horses were spent as we trotted towards a village at the Kingdom's border. While still some distance away, we dismounted and took off their saddles. Wandering to a frozen pond, Winter broke the surface and the horses drank beside us. Once satisfied,

I lifted my head and smiled at the earth glistening with jeweled frost.

Winter and I left the horses and traveled to the village on foot. The sun rose higher and the frost receded as well as the chill. My mind pondered the task at hand. We would need to find a way to enter the palace. Once inside, Winter didn't plan to approach the Empress immediately. He wished to observe her and learn as much as he could.

I couldn't help but wonder about Hanming. Did the Empress tell him he was to rule my father's Kingdom? How would Hanming take the news?

We stopped in the market and bought two bowls of noodles. Winter used coins he found in his stolen uniform. Once we finished, he advised, "You must act as a traveler, Summer. Ask someone for the palace." He couldn't play the part wearing a soldier's uniform.

I approached an herbalist and shoemaker chatting in front of their shops. They seemed friendly and readily gave detailed directions to the palace's main gate. They even offered information that half their military lived within the palace. It struck me they were proud of their militia. If they lived up to the reputation, it would be bad for my Empire if we went to war.

Using their willingness for sharing tidbits, I asked if they'd heard of an Empress visiting.

"Oh yes," the shoemaker lit with excitement. "She's supposed to tour the marketplace today!"

"We've been working extra to make everything nice!" the herbalist chipped in. He shook his head and let out a proud laugh. "When she arrived two days ago, her servant stopped in my shop! He told me she was weak from the journey and needed medicine."

"Yes! My friend here carries the freshest herbs!" the shoemaker flattered. "All in the palace come to him!"

My ears perked. "Two days ago? On the road, I'd heard she left for here a while ago."

"Oh, you know imperials use the grand bridge of the west," the shoemaker explained. "They wouldn't use the rope bridge like us commoners."

It made sense. I thanked them and reported to Winter. My brother nodded, "There's a wide, sturdy bridge to the west of here."

"Does that mean she visited the Tangut Empire?"

"It's possible. Many claim the mountains have healing powers and the Empress is ill. Journeying from the south would've weakened her. It's reasonable she'd rest there a bit."

"Our sisters are there," I spoke as warmth spread through me.

"The Tanguts are neutral. As long as no one intends them harm, they'll help any who seek it."

Following directions, we found ourselves before the main gate of the palace. My eyes trailed up tall ramparts as my breath caught. A band of rich blue running at the top seemed to meet the heavens. Upon further study, I discovered these were fine porcelain tiles with intricate blue paintings. Some illustrated stories so lifelike I expected them to step out of the wall.

My brother tapped my shoulder and gestured. Following his gaze, my eyebrows arched. On a high hill behind palace gates, a pagoda proudly faced the sun. In the morning light, the building glowed in transcendent blue. The walls were as pale as an autumn sky, but the shingles dark, like the ocean.

The sound of a gong woke me from my trance. Soldiers rushed from doors in the palace wall. They ushered people away from the main gate and lined themselves, creating a secure path.

Slowly, giant doors creaked open. Unlike our palace doors, these opened upward. Lines of horses with Generals emerged. The gong sounded again and a court official appeared, clutching a scroll. He unrolled the parchment and read words in a booming voice. "Today we celebrate the return of a son of the Kingdom. Locked away in the Empire of gold and jade, he and his ancestors were dishonored. With the death of the Yu Emperor, he was free to return. I give to you, Ku Cuixin and his liberator, Empress of the Yu!"

Rows of *suona* trumpeters blared as a carriage pulled by painted horses emerged. Dark blue ceramic shingles matching the pagoda covered the roof of the carriage. Happy shouts rang through the crowd and drums played loud.

I looked to Winter for a reaction, but his face remained impartial. "I'm not surprised," was all he said.

We watched the procession of soldiers, acrobatics, and colorful banners. Grand horses with braided manes pranced, carrying royalty.

"I've read that everything in this Empire is blue." Winter turned from the hubbub to study the palace. It was like him to put aside political differences and marvel architectural design. I wondered how many scrolls he'd read about this Kingdom. To compare in person must be thrilling.

I glanced at the blue carriage and caught a face peering out. Her eyes passed mine before returning. They filled with recognition. "Winter," I tugged his shirt. "The Empress! She just saw me!" I spoke urgently.

He took my hand and we made our way from the spectating crowd. We turned down an alley but heard footsteps behind us. "Summer, let's separate. Hide here and I'll draw them away. Meet me at the pond where we set the horses free." Winter lifted a large basket and shoved it over me before I could utter an objection.

With knees tucked to my chest, I rolled my eyes. He's delusional to think I'd listen.

I made my own plan.

I waited until steps of about a dozen men rushed past before I jumped from the basket. I grabbed the last guard and threw him to the ground. My thumb found a pressure point, rendering him unconscious. Spider had taught me about pressure points, but this was the first I'd used the knowledge. I sighed in relief that it'd worked.

I took down two more guards before they captured me. "At least Winter got away," I mumbled.

The guards didn't restrain my hands or feet, leaving me puzzled. They asked me to follow them to see the Empress of the Yu Empire. Only when I tried to run did they hold a sword to me.

We made our way through tight, winding streets and I wondered why soldiers of the North Kingdom obeyed our Empress. It was the first of many questions I wished to ask.

We arrived at the back of an ornately decorated inn. The owner doted with concern as the guards escorted me through the lower lobby. It sat empty; the front doors barred against the crowded street. We climbed a narrow flight of stairs and made our way to a large suite. There, a soldier opened sandalwood doors, revealing the Empress seated at a porcelain table. It too was painted a pretty shade of blue.

Her face lifted as she waved to dismiss everyone. Only one man remained and I recognized him to be a Ying Guardian.

"Summer!" she approached, steps sluggish. "I'm happy to see you!" she gave my shoulders a squeeze. I kept my eyes blank, unsure if I could trust her. "Sit with me. We do not have much time."

"Your highness," I refused a seat, "I have questions."

"About Hanming, I know. I expected as much. You're a smart girl. But first tell me, what do you see when you look at me?" She gazed deep in my eyes as if we shared a secret.

Did she know the things Hanming told me? "I'm not sure

what you mean."

"My eyes. What color are they?"

I felt taken aback by the strange question.

"Relax," she advised. "Try to see my color." The Empress leaned away and took a breath, suggesting I do the same.

It did no good, I plowed ahead, not relaxed at all, "I don't understand. You said you'd tell me about Hanming. I want to know if he's truly a son of the Emperor. Is that why he's inheriting the throne?"

The Empress waved her hand to brush away these questions. She acted as if their answers should be obvious. "Let me share with you about your father." She leaned and spoke in a low voice, "It was he who asked me to conceive with the Ku house. When Hanming was arrested, your father had planned to use his execution to release Hanming into hiding. Interestingly, *someone* helped him escape." She eyed me haughtily in accusation.

My mind slowly pieced meaning from her words. If Hanming wasn't in danger at all, then I made a mess of things. I couldn't be sure how to feel. "So, Hanming *is* a son of the royal family in the Lan Kingdom?" I asked instead.

The Empress stood upright, soulful eyes wide. "Your father was a wise Emperor. He wanted peace with the south. That's why he agreed to send you, his favorite daughter into marriage. It was at the sacrifice of another plan, but ultimately he wished to unite all."

"What other plan?"

"Shortly after he took your mother, your father got the idea for me to bear a child of Ku." Her voice grew rich, "Can you imagine the child you would have, with three royal bloodlines?"

"What do you mean?" I frowned.

"Ah, I've skipped ahead," she waved. The Empress sighed, "You see, if Hanming were a girl, she would've been betrothed to your brother. Seeing how Hanming is male, your father and I discussed your hand to my son. Why do you think the Emperor urged for you and your brother to be named for the Tai house? Unfortunately, right as you came of age, disturbing unrest brewed in the Nan Kingdom."

The words didn't register immediately. I pulled away, eyes down. Was I hearing Hanming's secret fate from the person who held it? Most startling, did it involve us both?

"What about my sisters?"

"They were in line to be betrothed to Tangut princes before your parents ever met." She clutched my hand. "You were not, and a great blessing!"

I gulped, "Where's Hanming now?"

"Captured. In the Tangut Empire," her eyes crinkled. "A small misunderstanding, but I could do nothing. He aided some lunatic prince," the Empress shook her head at the silliness. "Unfortunately, he injured royal guards and is now held prisoner." She took my chin in her hand, "I only left because I caught a glimpse of the future. I knew *you* would be here. So, I'm asking you to use your relationship with your sisters to help him."

Skeptical, I couldn't help but blurt, "How does one catch a glimpse of the future?"

"Why, a tortoise shell, of course. I've long practiced the art of divination," she beamed. "I've foreseen you and my son's growing feelings for one another." Her voice warmed, "Your union can lead to wonderful things."

I stumbled and finally accepted the seat the Empress had offered. Speechless, I clutched the edge of the table. Did I hear correctly? "The fates foretold of me with Hanming?"

The Empress sighed, dipping her head. "Be warned, often times details are lacking in divinations. I know you and Hanming have the ability to keep war at bay, but I also see potential for great pain and loss." Her expression melted, "Tread carefully. If war proceeds, the Yu Empire could disappear like the Tai Empire." A soft glow emanated atop of her head in mournful amber.

"Gold." I resigned to trusting her. "Your color is gold. As should be for royalty."

She blinked sadly. "I used to be rosy. After practicing qigong during my pregnancy with Hanming, my body never returned to full health."

"I don't underst—why can I see color?"

She placed a hand on my arm. "Go to the Tangut Empire," she whispered. "There, most can see color. It was a trait many lost in breeding when their ancestors left home." The Empress breathed, "My divinations tell me this talent of yours will serve you well."

"Empress, where is your home?" It'd never occured for me to wonder before.

She smiled broadly. "An old kingdom in the far northeast. It would take two moons to travel on horseback. Sadly, it fell and my ancestors moved to the Yao Empire. After it was handed to Yu, we stayed as noble guests. Your father wed me to honor the past."

Truthfully, I wished to know more about Hanming, but feared discovering something that could eviscerate my emotions. Each question from my mouth masked my true desire. "Why did you lie and tell Zhenxun my father is alive?"

Her face fell, "I hoped you wouldn't discover the truth. I'm still hoping no one else back home knows. If the Yu Empire were to learn they have no ruler, it would collapse. Right now, only thin hope holds us together. The Ying Guardians are secretly guiding trusted Lords to hide the Emperor's death." Her eyes drooped. "Please, I've already lost one son in this century-old battle." Her eyes beseeched me, "Please save my other son. I'll remain behind and try and prevent war. I gave them Ku Cuixin. The Lan Kingdom should be willing to listen to me."

I wondered if she long knew my secret feelings for Hanming and said her words to cloud my judgment. I studied her contemplatively, thinking back to the time she saved me from practicing harmful qigong. Also, to when she'd found me in Zhan Ji's home and brought me to my father. If that weren't enough, my father's last words told me to trust and aid her.

My heart moved and I decided to hold faith in the Empress.

But I had one more question. "Empress, when you announced your second son would assume the throne, who did you mean?" I knew the answer, but needed to hear it from her.

"Hanming, of course. Don't worry, with you two wed, the Yu blood will be in the ruling seat for subsequent generations." She reached into her sleeves and pulled out a badge carved in lapis lazuli. "We can discuss more later. First you have business to tend." She handed it to me saying, "This was a gift from the Ku royals. With it, and the status of your sisters, you can bargain for the release of Hanming and the missing prince."

I hardly recalled leaving the inn. The Empress' words swimming in my head left me dazed. As promised, I went to the pond where Winter asked to meet. I didn't see him. Since I wasn't long with the Empress, I might've arrived before he found a way to sneak from the market.

After some pacing, I decided time was of the essence. I wrote a note, "Left to find Hanming, be back soon," and placed it under a rock. I tied my black and gold headband on the stone as a sign. I then filled my gourd and slung my stolen sword over my shoulder, heading west.

Chapter Thirty:
The Tangut Empire

Grazing by melting snow, I chanced upon a horse Winter and I had released. With a loose rope, I fashioned makeshift reins. When night fell and the air grew cold, the horse huddled against me. I threw my fur over his back and a few times—against my judgment—wished to build a fire. Each time the thought arose, I reminded myself of the dangers. I stayed up all night, fearful that if I slept, cold would sap my life away. Morning came with the relief of the sun's heat and we continued west.

On the second night, a lone wolf ventured nearby. Thin and weak, he stalked us for dinner. Yellow eyes flashed with an ominous growl. My horse whinnied and pulled at his reins.

Carefully, I watched the creature. When it pounced, I was ready and swung my sword. The blade sliced his leg. My frightened horse kicked at the same time, striking the wolf's skull. I ended up with enough food for the rest of my journey and another fur to keep warm.

On the third day, I spotted mountain peaks scraping the horizon. Each day's journey made them taller.

On the sixth night, a glow at their feet became noticeable. Long before I reached outlying villages, the palace grew visible, proudly wedged in the side of the mountain. Torches on battlements burned brightly at all hours. Bridges crisscrossed throughout structures built into the rocky face below. To the right of the palace, an enormous waterfall cascaded.

At an outlying village, I took a room at an inn. Using coins the Empress provided, I rented a stable and bought extra grain for my horse. He nudged me with gratitude. I gave the stable boy an extra coin to let my horse have a blanket. I then retreated to my room and slept like the dead.

In the morning, I peered from my window to survey the streets. The mountain stole all my attention. I took a long moment and admired golden sunlight dripping beautifully against dark crevices. I wondered what view my sisters had from the mountainside. When they wrote, Spring and Autumn only shared their children's names and daily activities.

I set off from the inn. Before nightfall I reached the marketplace at the mountain's foot. Taking dinner at a noodle shop, I observed people riding goats and yaks. They wore bright colored aprons and sang as they worked. The mountain Empire was simple and low in population compared to my Empire. Yet it remained powerful because none could lay siege. Armies could be seen from days away. It traded with lands west of the mountains too, so embargoes from our side would do it no harm.

I tucked this information away, should it somehow assist the future Emperor of my home. Zhenxun's idea of impenetrability was massive walls. Yet as I've learned, sometimes that kept enemies in.

That night I entered a nicer inn. After receiving a skeptical glance for my unusual garb, I sighed and laid out gold coins. The innkeeper's expression turned pleasant as he scooped up payment. After he showed me to a room, I asked for brush and ink. He brought it quickly.

I sat at the table and constructed a letter to my sisters, informing them, *I am in your Empire and need assistance.* I added where I stayed and asked, *Would you please send for me?* Without a royal summons, one couldn't enter a palace.

In the morning, I paid the innkeeper to find a royal messenger to deliver my letter. Happy to see more gold, he quickly obliged.

I then went in search of a tailor who carried royal silk. Once I found one, I paid him extra to not ask questions. I ordered a royal gown, fit for a princess. He raised his eyebrows and declared only royalty may wear such dresses. I showed him the blue badge the Empress had given me and told him I needed it the next day. He bowed in consent.

At the edges of my mind, the Empress' words about Hanming and me niggled. I feared giving them too much weight would lead to false hope, so I shushed them. With little to do, I wandered the marketplace. The air smelled of roasting lamb and the sound of bells tied around cattle echoed with guileless joy. A small coin bought strange fruit from a merchant.

"Freshly imported from the west! Its bittersweet juices will tickle your taste buds," he announced. And it did as it ran down my chin.

The time to myself was much needed. The clean air reinvigorated me. By the next morning, my shoulders sat a bit lower.

I returned to the tailor's to see my gown on a wooden frame. Its unexpected beauty made me pause. It contained a high collar and sleeves hanging past the wrists. Instead of a flowing train, then hem was of equal length around the bottom. The waist pleated, giving a wide girth.

"Notice along the seams! Embroidered images!" he boasted and held up a thick sash, which he promised would wind around my waist. A piece of decorative silk hung below.

I fingered the fine dress he'd lined with rabbit fur, appropriate for colder altitudes. Whenever my sisters visited the Yu Empire, they wore clothing of our home. I realized this must be what they wore regularly in the Tangut Kingdom.

The tailor brought out the headdress, a long rectangular piece of rich red silk decorated with colorful plumes of feathers and pearls. It was to be fastened by circles of silver pendants. Beads of semiprecious stone were displayed from top to bottom.

I thanked the tailor. "Have you clean sackcloth? I must wrap this dress to carry to the inn."

"Aiya! For a silver piece, I'll have it delivered!"

I obliged and he called an errand boy. The two carefully packaged the gown and the child followed me without a word. Once I reached my room, I paid him and he left.

I summoned the mistress of the inn and ordered a bath. She commanded workers to carry in a wooden tub. Buckets of steaming water soon followed. I locked the door before slipping off my clothes. I took time cleaning off grime from travels. Then I pulled my Ying Guardian robes into the tub and scrubbed those as well. When I could scrub no more, I stood and dried off.

Finally clean, I took to the daunting task of dressing. I should've asked the tailor for instructions. The bottom layers of the gown weren't too different from my usual robes. However, the outer fabrics appeared they needed to be wrapped in a certain manner or the silk ties wouldn't match.

After what felt like an eternity of foolishly draping, I spread the gown on my bed. I lined up the ties as one would solve a puzzle. Once I understood how they connected, I managed to clothe myself.

Next, I struggled with the headdress. I discovered if I were to put little braids in my hair like the village women, it gave the silver pendants something to clip into. After some exploring, I managed to look presentable.

I strode to the edge of the tub and peered at my reflection. I let out a giggle, hardly recognizing myself.

~*~

Two days passed before royal escorts came in the morning. I felt amused by the expression on the innkeeper's face when a princess stepped from the room he'd rented to a traveler. Gingerly, I entered the palanquin with the grace of any royal. I felt the sedan lift, and I was off to see my sisters.

The ride soon grew uneven, as if the carriers leaped. I stole a glimpse from the palanquin and my heart quickened at the view of sharp drops. I leaned away from the window. A hand clutched my chest. From a distance I'd seen the narrow paths cut into the mountainside and thought them picturesque. Traveling along them left me terrified.

When we bounced, I knew we crossed rope bridges. I braced myself and prayed my escorts were keen on their footing. My hand moved to my mouth, to keep down breakfast.

I lost track of time, spending most of it in cold sweat. When I felt the palanquin clack on solid ground, a rush of relief poured over me. An escort announced my arrival. Preparing myself for the unexpected, I exited to face the grandiose palace. Titanic steps extended left and right before changing directions, forming a diamond. They carved into the mountainside and at every few steps, either a fierce statue stood watch or a pit of fire gave light.

An escort approached and informed me the palanquin could travel no further. Being of lesser royalty, I needed to climb the steps on foot. I thanked him and ventured forth.

Before the bend in the steps, I stopped to huff. The air tasted thin and each step was taller than what I was accustomed to.

By the time I reached the top, the sun shined high in the sky. I gasped for air, admiring a large black door studded with spikes. It stood boldly open, as if challenging invaders to enter. I glanced the way I came with chancy steps. Surely, no one would be so foolish.

To either side of the door were lamps as big as a house, each with a pool of oil to keep them endlessly lit. Below them, a lower General and two soldiers waited. He bowed, introducing himself before leading me to a short flight of nine steps. I followed, still wheezing.

To my joy, we rested for a few moments as the General reported my presence to an official. He searched through royal papers, and I silently begged him to take his time. Once he found the approval form, he greeted me with a bow.

I followed the General through the gate. It took much of my will power to keep from gawking. Twelve decorative arches sat in open air, leading to a neatly chiseled cave. Another large door stood at the mouth; this one closed. I took a keen look at the arches. They were covered in carvings of deities, including the Three Sovereigns. Constellations decorated the backside of the columns. I realized in awe they must be used to track seasons.

The General stopped at a closed door, equally as heavy as the open one we'd passed. He announced me, and the metal groaned open, revealing a well-lit path. Excitement trickled through my body. This was the first time I visited my sisters.

The cavern turned into a grand hall; the walls painted with

beautiful colors. Startling me most was a halo hovering over each artful figure. Some eyes were replaced by precious stones shimmering in various hues, similar to what I witnessed in the tree bandits cave one moon ago. As my eyes moved to the ceiling, I saw another painting of the Three Sovereigns. From their fingers flowed lines of light, encapsulating the figures' halos. They'd gifted the ability to see colors.

A sense of belonging welled in my chest, filling in a hole I didn't know existed. Reading inscriptions, I saw "Eyes That See Auras" were a gift to those entrusted to guide humanity's future.

The General took a sharp right and I followed. My gown swished elegantly, stirring the air. The movement gave me a sense of presence. I grinned, thinking I could grow accustomed to their fashion.

We walked a short distance and birdcalls reached my ears. Baffled, my eyes searched. I spied a tree branch extending from a crack. As we continued, the crack appeared to be the entrance to a grotto. The neatly cut ceiling gave way to open air and light fell in. Bright berries and fruits ripened as songbirds chirped. I couldn't help but grin, happy for my sisters to live in such an astounding world.

We entered a little box and I stood facing a wall in confusion. The General called out a command and the box shifted. I held onto the side to keep my knees from buckling. Ropes groaned and we traveled upwards. It reminded me of the rope tree bandits used to move people onto their hidden platform.

I looked over my shoulder to the way we came, and saw rocks pass. Sometimes, other halls appeared briefly. I gulped, thinking of the drop beneath us.

The ropes groaned to a stop, lining up the box to a passage with walls painted gold. The General exited. I gave my skirts a ceremonious stir and stepped out. He led me down a short path to a beautiful sitting room. Tears welled in my eyes. It was decorated similarly to an imperial room from our home palace. Dressed like me, my sisters exclaimed sounds of joy. Autumn, the eldest, rushed to place her hands on my sides. "Why are you thin?" she cried, aghast.

"Why does it matter?" I chuckled.

Spring chided, "Youngest sister, your skin is dark and dry. Having you been staying in the sun?"

Overwhelmed by emotion, I clutched their hands tightly. I joked, "Oh, yes. How carelessly I've been treating myself! On purpose! So that you may dote on me!"

"You always do play too much!" Autumn frowned in disapproval. I could see in her eyes it was her way of showing she cared. "You still make us worry!"

"And so terribly you torture us!" Spring scolded, eyes moistening. "We nearly lost our minds to hear you and Winter died!" She ran fingers through my hair as Autumn dabbed my wet cheeks with a square of silk. "We're so relived it was a mistake!"

Speechless, I submitted as they fawned over their baby sister.

Chapter Thirty-One:
The Prince

Autumn waved to the servants and commanded a meal be served. She lifted my chin and gazed with stern but loving eyes. "What trouble have you and Winter gotten yourselves into?"

"Me?" I played innocent.

"Ah Autumn, you know she was always a peculiar one," Spring giggled. Her tinkling always reminded me of a babbling brook.

"I'm sorry to have caused you worry." I then tried to jest with a broad grin, "But Sister Autumn, you've always enjoyed the stories of my antics."

She gave a superficial disapproving frown, but her eyes confirmed my statement. They laced their arms through mine and led me to a cushioned seat. Spring poured fragrant tea as they chattered, filling the air with the warmth of home. I sat, unable to cease smiling, heart too full to speak.

We partook in stewed goat and vegetables I couldn't identify.

I'd missed the care we took, filling each others' bowls with the best pieces of meat. A part of me wished to never leave.

Once dishes were cleared, my rambunctious nieces and nephews spilled into the room with governesses in tow. The boys wore shaved heads with only a fringe in the front, customary for a Tangut.

Once Autumn cleared her throat, they lined obediently from eldest to youngest. "Children, say hello to your Aunt Summer," she commanded.

Starting with the eldest, they stepped forward and announced themselves with a bow. I recalled how my sisters and I were taught to do the same as children. Despite the lighthearted occasion, I was unable to peer long into their faces. They reminded me of my mother and father.

After the formal introduction, Spring dismissed them to their lessons. My sisters returned their attention to me. "How is Father after Mother's passing?"

The question caught me unprepared. Her innocent dark eyes in glowing pearly skin gazed with concern. It dawned on me the distance between us. The space wasn't measured by land or time, rather secrets and heaviness of the heart.

Some of the earlier levity effervesced.

My sisters didn't have an inkling our father had fallen ill. I wished to tell them the truth, but the Empress' warnings about our home lingered.

I sighed, and with jabbing in my chest, told a lie to those

dearest to me. "Father felt very upset, but he's fine now." I swallowed a lump in my throat.

Spring patted my hand, "Please send him our love."

I smiled weakly. For a moment I thought Spring recognized something was amiss, but Autumn spoke and the concern fell from her eyes. "By the way, little sister, what business do you have? Your visit is a nice surprise, but out of the ordinary." Autumn refilled my cup with tea. "Is something the matter?"

"Yes," I nodded. On my journey I had rehearsed a story. I recited it as pleasantly and apologetically as I could. "You see, there's a Prince from the Lan Kingdom. He, along with someone from Zhenxun, was imprisoned here due to a misunderstanding." Gasps and eager nods to hear more erupted. "I'm here at the request of our ambassador to the Lan Kingdom. To clear up this mistake before any more embarrassment happens."

"But little sister, why would they send *you?*" Autumn asked bluntly. Spring eyed me with equal interest.

I sipped the tea, searching my mind. "Because only I can authenticate their identities." At this my sisters exchanged confused expressions.

After some hemming and hawing, they nodded. "We can help."

Autumn drafted a short letter while Spring called for a royal guard to bring me to a magistrate. I followed to another level in the mountain maze.

The magistrate raised a brow at me as he read the letter. I

fought the urge to tap my foot as long minutes passed. Once he'd scrutinized the words to his satisfaction, he turned a serious eye to me, ready to listen. It was something his expression dictated he wasn't likely to do for just anyone. "What may we assist you with?" his lips pulled into a hard line.

I braced against the heated glare and spoke of the prince. The magistrate tapped his fingers on the desk and confirmed there was such a man. "But he made no such claim to be a prince."

"I believe he felt in danger and tried to protect his identity."

The magistrate considered my words. He then called to a guard and asked for the prisoner to be brought forth. Moments later, a man appeared in shackles. His eyes darted wildly, displaying intelligence bordered by paranoia. The magistrate confronted him. "Prince Ku Rentu?"

His eyes locked on the man behind the desk. "Who wants to know?" Hia shoulders hunched.

The magistrate flicked his hand carelessly at me. "This young lady."

"Good evening," I bowed. "Could you please describe to me your sword?"

His eyes scoured me from head to toe in search of harmful intent. Though his expression showed he still felt uncertain, he perhaps decided owning the details of a weapon could bring no harm. In a clear voice, the description of the blue-jeweled sword I'd found poured forth.

I turned to the magistrate and confirmed his identity. In minutes, his release was approved, with the magistrate ordering the prince, "You're forbidden to ever return to this land."

"Please sir, there's another matter!" I stopped him as he shooed us out. The magistrate scowled.

I brought up Hanming. Only after both the freed the Prince and I promised to take custody of him, Hanming's release papers were signed as well.

"Now get out!" the magistrate hollered.

The prince and I were escorted to an area adjacent to the dungeons. For hours, we waited for Hanming to emerge from the cells. The agitated young man kept peering over his shoulders.

When I tried to speak with him, the prince shushed me and whispered, "There may be spies about."

I imagined if Winter and Hanming showed their innermost fears, they'd act a similar way.

"How did you get arrested?" I asked.

He studied me once more. This time with a bit more trust, since I did get him released. "I mistook guards of the Mountain Empire to be blood bandits. I'd encountered some earlier on my journey and had lost my sword to them."

"And Hanming?"

"My altercation unfortunately spilled into your emissary's travel party where Hanming protected a woman. In doing so, he accidentally killed two royal guards."

"I see." My heart dropped to know Hanming met with such misfortune.

"He's a gentleman. We spent a lot of time conversing in the dungeons."

No sooner had he spoken, the jangling of shackles reached our ears. We stood simultaneously as Hanming appeared around a corner. While we were waiting, I had daydreamed of teasing him; once more I'd freed him from prison. But at the sight of Hanming, all words caught in my throat. My heart raced and I feared I might burst into tears if I spoke.

Hanming's tattered clothes dripped with blood. I could see fresh wounds through his ripped shirt. He'd been whipped recently and couldn't meet my eyes. My gaze could not be pried from his dirt-stained face. Such a sad shade of blue seeped through.

A guard announced, "Owing to this man's acquaintance with the Princess' guest, he is granted permission to be seen by a physician."

Prince Ku Rentu went with him.

I was escorted to my sisters.

They tossed a slew of questions my way concerning my relationship with Prince Ku Rentu. "Is he your betrothed?" They were equally mortified and fascinated in turns.

"Sister," Spring fretted, "There's a reason we're uneasy with the Lan Kingdom!"

"They're vicious and violent. Are you to marry him?"

Autumn shook her head. "This cannot be! Summer would be alone in that forsaken place!"

Spring countered with a thoughtful expression. "Still, a high-ranking Prince! If he were not a barbarian, what a great match indeed!"

I could hardly get a word in. Just as well, since I had nothing to say. Instead, I soaked in every minute of their attention. Neither cared about politics. It only mattered I found a good husband. For a moment, I entertained a thought. Could having a good husband be the only thing that mattered? How simple life would be then!

Spring brought me back to their chatter with a nudge. "By the way, who's the young man with the Prince? I'm glad his wounds weren't serious."

The question bounced around my head as I scrambled for the simplest of answers. The Empress' words pushed to the front and I nearly blurted, *He—not the prince—is my intended.*

"Yes, who is he?" Autumn echoed. "You vouched for him, but he can't be a mere lower court official, though his tattered robe were that of one." Her nose wrinkled.

"He," I paused, "He's a part of the ambassador's entourage who has important responsibilities."

My sisters shrugged. The answer satisfied them.

My heart ached, wishing I could reveal my true feelings for Hanming. To my chagrin, I observed an invisible wall rise, separating me from Autumn and Spring. I said little the rest of the night, the truth squirming uneasily inside me. How I wished I could share with them!

I felt relieved when they yawned. We curled in Autumn's suite to sleep.

At breakfast the next morning, a maid announced my travel companions were ready. I clutched my sisters' hands. The time I shared with them was too short, but Winter waited. I feared leaving him alone in an enemy Kingdom. We embraced farewell.

Tangut guards escorted us away from the imperial city. It served to ensure we caused no more trouble, and to protect us from bandits. We kept conversation to a minimum. Prince Ku Rentu's eyes were as fidgety as ever.

Once we reached the Tangut borders, their guards made camp with us. In the morning they offered us horses and saluted farewell. I didn't take one, instead retrieving the one I'd left in an outlying village.

As the three of us rode away, Prince Ku Rentu let out a playful whistle. His demeanor gradually took on ease. Beside me, Hanming rode quietly. Subsequently, Ku Rentu chuckled aloud as if he found something amusing.

In his neutral tone Hanming asked the prince, "What is it?"

"This is the woman you're in love with?"

My ears burned. Awkward silence followed. It continued until we stopped for our midday meal. Even then, the conversation centered on travel plans. I stole a look at Hanming. He appeared focused on starting a fire. The tips of his ears glowed red, though I couldn't tell if from embarrassment or cold.

It wasn't until we stopped for the night did the Prince speak again. "It seems as if I've caused tension." His tone softened, "What's wrong with loving?" Neither Hanming nor I responded and the question lingered over our small fire.

Our feelings had always been shared in private. We had no clue on the proper way to behave before a third party.

"Princess, you're unique." Ku Rentu said, taking the feedbag from my hands so I'd listen. "You don't settle like your sisters. You'd rather adventure." I kept my eyes aside, as he inched closer, teasing, "And you can't ignore me forever, or it'll be a long journey."

I gave a tired look, "It wasn't by choice. This life swept me away."

Prince Ku Rentu nudged his chin towards Hanming. "What about him? Has he swept you away?"

"We're old friends."

"Princess, all teasing aside, I know your type well. I know how Hanming feels about you. When he thought we were going to receive the death penalty, he asked if I were spared, to let someone know his feelings. He wanted me to tell you he was sorry he couldn't be with you." He cocked his head to the side. "So… why can't the two of you be together?"

Hanming approached, "Because I dread a dark destiny for myself, and I do not wish to drag her along." His eyes gazed deep into mine, as he stepped between us. "My feelings for you are no longer secret, Summer. But I truly believe you'd be happier without me.”

I wished to share the words his mother had spoken to me, but feared they were a dream. Instead, I said, “But our paths have crossed countless times. Why can’t you accept I’m already a part of your destiny?” I moved not a muscle. And let the declaration fall where it may.

Hanming spoke firmly, “You should understand since you’re the same as me. One day, I’ll be obligated into marriage. What’s more? I might need to take more than one wife. Even if by some rare chance we were to wed, I don’t wish you to live every day knowing you’re not the only one.”

Slowly, the prince backed away to the fire. Hanming and I were forced to face our words.

“Some nights, Summer, I pray you’ll be safely taken far away to live a happy and prosperous life as your sisters do.” He added, “You deserve to be surrounded by people who love you, and only you. Most of all, you deserve to be safe, and I cannot promise you any of those things.” The frigid air quivered his voice and crusting frustration built in me. A gauzy blue fog formed to remind us we were miserable.

Hanming’s rejecting words following so soon after hearing our Empress’ wish for us to be betrothed cracked the last of my resolve. I didn’t know what to believe and grew too tired to hope. I walked away and rolled into furs, shutting out the world.

They probably thought I’d fallen asleep or couldn’t hear through my covers. Prince Ku Rentu spoke apologetically, barely over the sounds of a dwindling fire. "I am sorry, Hanming. I was hoping by bringing emotions to the surface, to draw you two closer. I'm thankful you saved my life, my friend. I didn't know you carried such burdens."

~*~

We arrived at the Lan Kingdom without confronting blood bandits. I didn't tell the Prince my brother was in his Kingdom, still questioning how much he could be trusted. He wanted to thank Hanming and me properly and escorted us into the palace, advising, "It would be a good idea to hide your identities. There aren't many sympathizers for your Empire."

Hanming and I were announced as royal citizens from the Tangut Empire. We were already dressed the part, so it was easily believed. Prince Ku Rentu credited us with saving him from bandits.

I wondered about General Hong.

"Hanming," I whispered as we trailed the Prince. It was the first we'd spoken since our outburst. "Why are we trusting him?"

"The prince is a sympathizer to our Empire and I don't know who else can be trusted inside these walls." After a pause, "I'm going to find my mother and I think you should stay close."

Hearing Hanming refer to the Empress as his mother sent a chill down my spine. It reminded me of the reservations I still held about her plan to announce Hanming as the heir to my father's Empire. Did Hanming know?

The Prince escorted us to a mid-sized suite and told us to

leave the doors locked. He suspected his enemies would harm us if they could. He then left.

The idea of a locked door made me feel trapped, but Hanming assured me we could escape through the window if needed. We exchanged few words and mostly passed the time with pacing. I wished to speak more, but Hanming's manner seemed closed.

~*~

True to his word, Prince Ku Rentu returned that night. He ordered a meal prepared by trusted chefs and sat with us. He poured liquor for Hanming and me, then graciously raised his cup. The Prince thanked Hanming again for saving his life.

After the toast, the Prince put on a serious face. He suggested I might need to leave the room. Hanming shook his head, declaring, "I hold the princess in complete confidence."

The Prince studied Hanming for a moment before proceeding carefully. "I just spoke with your Empress." His eyes cut across the table. "She told me you are her son."

I felt disconcerted. Why would the Empress trust Prince Ku Rentu?

"Don't worry I know what she intends. Your secret's safe with me." The Prince paused before asking Hanming, "Do you know who your father is?"

Pain crossed his face. He asked in a voice so low it was barely audible, "Do *you* know my father?"

"Yes." His eyes softened. "Would you like me to tell you?"

Hanming gulped. He poured another drink and threw it back. His features twisted as he held his breath. It eventually came out in a long a sigh. I reached under the table and our pinkies linked. He did not pull away and calm spread across his face. "Please do."

The Prince leaned back and I sensed the air grow thick.

"Your father is my relative, Ku Cuixin. He's been in your Empire all his life." The Prince paused. Hanming's face remained impassive, staring intently at the center of the table. "I've said before, your mother and I both wish the Empires to be united. I made a suggestion to her that might repay my life debt to you. To my surprise, she'd already thought of it."

Silence filled the room.

"People revere imperial bloodlines because Heaven grants them the mandate to rule. The issue stirring discord is that each nation feels their ruler's blood is most deserving." The prince leaned towards Hanming. "You are a son of the Ku household. Princess Summer, of both the Yu and Tai houses. Together, you represent the bloodlines chosen by the Three Sovereigns."

Neither Hanming nor I stirred.

The Prince lifted a finger. "However, a union alone between you two would not work. If anything, it'd lead to revolt. I recommend a secret marriage." His nose twitched. "The key is a child. A child of the Ku, Yu and Tai bloodline cannot be denied. This child would unite all, creating a powerful alliance for generations."

A blanket of silence followed.

I found humor in how quickly my life changed. What was once forbidden became a suggested resolution for peace. A part of me rejoiced at the thought of Hanming and I being together. Another knew the road ahead would be filled with countless perils.

Did we deserve to be happy? After so many dear to us have lost their lives?

"I cannot do that to her," Hanming protested. His eyes firmed, but I recognized hidden longing.

I felt it too.

I abandoned reservations. "I accept. I will share his destiny."

Prince Ku Rentu gave a clap at my words.

"Summer?" Hanming asked cautiously. "Are you certain?"

"I have been… years ago."

Our pinkies unlinked and his hand grasped mine tightly.

Chapter Thirty-Two:
Seventh Day of the Seventh Moon

An old fairytale about a cowherder and weaver girl told of him belonging to the earth, and she in the heavens. They fell in love and she descended to the earth to be with him. With no one left to weave clouds, rain couldn't fall. Plants wilted and people grew parched as lakes and rivers dried.

The Mother of the Skies lifted the weaver back to heaven and set her to work again. In her loneliness, she cried day and night, filling the clouds with her tears.

The earth flooded.

The Mother of the Skies granted the cowherder access to heaven. Once reunited, the weaver became distracted by joy and neglected her work once more.

The Mother of the Skies pulled a pin from her hair and drew a silver river across the sky. She sat the weaver girl on one side and the cowherder on the other. By day, the girl must weave clouds. At night they may peer across the river.

Once a year, on the seventh day of the seventh moon, magpies formed a bridge. It allowed them to cross and meet. On this day, the heavens filled with the glow of love. It became an auspicious day for lovers.

~*~

I sent Prince Ku Rentu's private couriers in search for Winter. I wished for him to be at my wedding. Though I held reservations he might not approve, I hoped Winter would understand it was in accordance to our father's secret wishes.

Days passed and no one located my brother. I grew anxious, and my imagination wilder. I called another courier and gave him specific instructions to travel to Zhenxun. I hoped Winter might've returned.

As I waited restlessly, the Empress called for me. When I entered her chambers, I slowed my steps before bowing. She appeared different. Dark circles traced her eyes. Her skin had grown even more ashen.

"Summer, I haven't had a chance to thank you for bringing my son back."

I lowered my head politely, "It was nothing."

"Now to think, I will have you as my daughter. It truly warms my heart."

I braved a peek at her face. She appeared feeble, but her joy radiated pure. "Empress, I need to know something."

"Speak plainly, Summer," she squeezed my hand, her touch cold.

I held her in a steady gaze. "Where do your loyalties lie? Do you have intentions to use this marriage to usurp my Empire into the North's territories? I see a hundred reasons for your actions. But I need to be convinced you're not treasonous."

The Empress softened, "Summer, I've always told you the truth. I know for those looking from the outside, my actions label me a traitor. Yet I only wish for peace." She shook her head sadly. "I promise this with my remaining son's life."

A life she wishes to give to me.

By the color of her eyes, I knew she spoke the truth. I allowed myself to be comforted. Yet, my inquisitiveness still hungered. "Why can't Winter be the heir? If people believe Hanming's the Emperor's son, our marriage would raise legality questions."

"I contemplated the decision at length and nearly did announce Winter as heir. However, when word came about restlessness in the north, I knew what needed to be done. The Lan Kingdom would be less inclined to strike if they secretly knew one of their own sat upon the Yu throne." She huffed, face drooping. "We cannot afford another war. And as for you, we need to discuss changing your identity."

"But if they find out he's a Ku, he'd be deposed!"

"As long as I'm alive, there will remain enough dissention to protect him."

I lowered my head and accepted this information. With someone as powerful as the Empress, the plan might actually work.

"Oh, very important!" she clapped, remembering. "I told you I practiced special qigong while pregnant with Hanming. Do you recall? You will be with child from the bloodline of Lan. They have a unique qi. If you do not learn to practice this qigong during your pregnancy, your baby will have health risks." Her lips puckered, "But I must warn you, there will be consequences to your qi."

"I'm prepared," I nodded, feeling as if I this was an induction into a centuries-old tradition.

"You'll grow sensitive to the color blue and recognize a wide variety of its hues. You'll be able to feel Hanming's presence when he's near."

The thought made me smile.

~*~

The qigong practice was simple, but left me queasy. The Empress knitted her brows and said it was just the beginning. I grit my teeth and worked through nausea.

One day as we practiced, an agitated knock came at the door. Prince Ku Rentu marched in, mumbling. His hands kept wringing and occasionally flailed in different directions. After making sure the door secured behind him, he spoke directly to the Empress. "My half-brother, the King is mad! He's preparing to launch armies to retake the Nan Kingdom. He wants to kill all people in your Empire along the way!"

He spun around. "What's worse, when I tried to reason with him, he ordered guards to seize me. He says he'd kill anyone who opposes his plan. He let me go with a warning only because I'm his brother. But Empress," he faced her desperately, "you *must* be careful! He hasn't sent a kill order for you because he doesn't recognize you as a Yu. He still sees you as a daughter of another Kingdom." Prince Ku Rentu twitched some more, "Still, I think it'll be safer if you leave soon. I don't think I can protect you much longer."

The Empress gave a sympathetic look. "Just until the seventh day of the seventh moon. It's the most auspicious day for a wedding!"

Prince Ku Rentu seemed hesitant at first, his eyes jumped from my face to hers. But finally he agreed. I ended my practice and retreated to my quarters.

Not long after, a courier arrived with a letter. I read the response and felt beside myself with excitement. It came from a High Court official in Zhenxun who knew my brother. He informed me Winter was safe but asked I stay in the Lan Kingdom, since a power struggle ensued at home. He asked me to keep him updated.

I quickly pulled out brush and ink. My hand shook as I wrote two letters. The first informed my brother of my upcoming union. Though I wished for his attendance, I wrote him, *You'll remain safer staying away*. I sealed this letter carefully with a painting of an orange blossom, our mother's favorite flower.

The second I wrote to the High Court official, requesting he give the sealed letter to my brother only. I called for the courier and sent him off.

If only I'd heeded my mother's warning. By then, I should've learned to be vigilantly suspicious. Overwhelmed with pleasant thoughts of my wedding, I chose to see honesty. Never once did I question the authenticity of the letter I'd received. Following events changed the course of history—for more than just myself.

On the third day of the seventh moon, Prince Ku Rentu was imprisoned in his quarters and declared a madman. It wasn't difficult to convince others due to his erratic tendencies.

The following day, the Empress was summoned to the Lan King. The rest of our entourage was to remain behind, separating her from the Ying Guardians.

"Something's wrong," she murmured.

I sensed her edginess and found a maid's outfit from the Yu Empire. Without a word, I dressed and followed her. Royal guards escorted us up terraced steps much like ones in our Empire, except rounded, not square. I thought this no coincidence since it matched the cylindrical shape of the pagoda. As the first settlement of the Lan people, it made sense they used the shape of heaven to garner blessings. Our Empire, formerly the Yao Kingdom, used squares in its design to represent earth.

I thought to a childhood lesson. Earth fits inside heaven, but they must work in harmony. I found it mildly humorous as our Empire was far larger than the Lan Kingdom.

The Kings's grand hall for receiving guests sat in the base of the pagoda. Like the rest of the palace, blue paintings decorated the semicircular walls. These felt austere, as if they'd never reverberated from music or laughter prevalent in the rest of the Kingdom.

As we approached the throne, a guard stopped me. The Empress spoke kindly, "She carries my medicine."

The King waved, seeing no harm in a girl. His guards allowed me to proceed. We bowed in greeting as the grand doors shut with an ominous thud behind us.

Six guards stood around the King and two servants waited. He instructed the Empress to seat at a table a few paces below his throne. I remained on my hands and knees—as a maid should.

I stole a glance and discovered the King was a large man with powerful features, not much older than myself. His whiskers and glaring eyes reminded me of a wolf. I wondered of his life journey and how it might've carved cruelty into his face.

He lifted fingers and waved. The servants poured tea. The Empress tipped her head in gratitude but didn't reach for the cup. I knew her well enough to know she suspected poison.

"I know your Emperor has passed," the Lan King spoke in a booming voice, forsaking introductions.

My heart shook at the harshness, missing my father. I peeked again to see the King stroking his whiskers.

"I will not banter. I asked you here for information on your home. If you're willing to help, I'll make you a part of my court and you may live comfortably. Since you've brought back my cousin, Ku Cuixin, I owe you the courtesy." He shook a finger, "I must warn. If you refuse, your days will be numbered."

Her voice cracked in her reply. "May I have a few days to consider?"

I jolted, but remained kneeling. How dare she contemplate betraying our home?

The King huffed with displeasure. Silence fell, and with it the very room seemed to grow colder. Eventually he thundered, "You may have one day! I will summon you tomorrow."

The Empress bowed and the King stood, leaving swiftly with his guards. The brief meeting left us shaken.

Once in private, I glared at the Empress, "How could you consider his offer?"

She placed her hand on my shoulder. "Dear Summer, rest your heart for I have no intention of betrayal. I merely bought us time. You must marry my son tonight and leave before first light. I will go alone to the King and offer myself as a concubine."

"And if he refuses? What if he tortures you for information?" My hands shook.

The Empress raised a brow, "I will feed him useless bits, to buy trust. If he does torture me, my weakened body won't sur-vive long enough to offer anything of use." She took a shaky breath. "I must use the opportunity to assassinate him. As a young King with much to prove, he's known for ruthlessness." Her eyes emptied and her voice echoed sorrowfully. "He might spare me, but he made no such offer to my son, you, or the rest of our people. He plans to execute you all."

My throat went dry. The Empress was right. I scolded myself for not considering such facts. "I will accompany you tomorrow," I spoke firmly. "If you go alone, he'll grow suspicious."

She frowned and considered this for some time. "Although I don't like it, you are right. I'd prefer you leave with my son immediately." Then she gave a soft smile, "Enough talk. I must make arrangements with Ku Cuixin to have you two married tonight."

~*~

I hadn't set eyes on Ku Cuixin since we'd left our home. He took my hands and gave his blessing. Welcoming a daughter, he placed a bone-carved hairpin decorated with silver, gold and jade in my hand. He spoke in a soft voice, "This belonged to my mother." Soft grayish-blue floated about. I closed my fingers and thanked him, finally recognizing he was a gentle soul.

I prepared in the Empress' quarters as Hanming spent time with his birth father. She dressed me in a gown of the Lan Kingdom and personally wound my locks. I questioned wearing robes from a foreign land for our sacred ceremony. In the end, I knew a dress was merely a dress. Our hearts didn't change, already united in a heavenly constellation.

It took time to grow accustomed to sleeve fastenings at my wrists. Minute beads of numerous colors traced fanciful patterns. I took a red handkerchief and draped it over my head. It reminded me of the mock wedding with the bandits. Perhaps fate had teased then.

The Empress escorted me to the seating area of her suite where a holy man waited with Hanming. Since both of my parents had passed and Winter wasn't present, one of the Ying Guardians stood in place of my family. Amusedly, I thought this the reverse of the bandit wedding when Hanming's family was missing.

The holy man read scriptures ordaining duties of husband and wife. Together Hanming and I bowed, honoring our ancestors. The pomp and joyousness of our mock wedding was missing. Simplicity had taken its place and an amethyst hue charged the air.

When we took our vows to each other, he hooked his pinky with mine. The holy man declared us to be one and my veil lifted. I blushed when Hanming's hand grazed my cheek. Feeling weak, I gazed into his eyes. I saw them fill with sorrow and elation. "Now, my destiny is your destiny," he spoke tenderly, a bit frightened.

The Empress let out a sigh. Ku Cuixin looked on with teary eyes as the Ying Guardian stood dutifully.

After drinking ceremonial wine, we stole back to our quarters. Instead of staying in our sectioned-off corners, I joined Hanming in his bed. For most of the night, we laid quietly. At times he gently traced hands along my shoulders as we reminisced. Emotions ran high as we giggled over the good and comforted our pains.

"I never wished to make you feel ignored or hurt," he said when I shared my upset towards his cold behavior at times. "I began to love you in the palace. My feelings were too passionate for me to contend, so the only choice was to separate myself. Even now as I lie beside you, I cannot be sure this isn't a dream."

The words soothed my heart and all was forgiven. I kissed the corner of his lips. "Hanming, I love you," I spoke boldly. I felt his body shift as he returned tenderness. My fingers trailed along his neck as he wrapped me in his arms.

When I awoke the next morning, I found myself wedged against Hanming. A light snore stirred my hair and I closed my eyes to savor the moment before a knock came at our door.

We dressed quickly and admitted a Ying Guardian. "The Lan King has summoned the Empress," he announced with a frown. I stole a quick kiss from Hanming before leaving.

The Ying guardian and I traveled fast and light. We reached the Empress in no time. When she saw me, she leaned close, "How were things last night?"

I blushed, "All's well."

I quickly threw on the maid's gown. Together we made our way to the pagoda. The guards didn't stop me this time. "Long live the King!" they roared in unison.

I crouched behind the Empress in a subservient position. From the corner of my eye, I spied the King on the throne. The same six guards arranged beside him.

"Be seated," he commanded harshly. She thanked him and did as asked, returning to the table where tea sat poured. I sensed his eyes scrutinizing. "What's your answer?"

The Empress labored from her seat to kneel before the King. She spoke in a crisp, clear voice. "Your highness, since my husband's death, I'm but a lowly widow. Please take me to be your concubine so I may serve you. If you wish to conquer the Empire of Yu, I am willing to offer information as a show of loyalty."

I heard the King scratch his whiskers and shuffle as he rose. Solid steps lowered towards the Empress. "Stand," he commanded. I heard her move. "What information do you offer?" he asked in false interest.

"I can give you the names of Generals—" she began.

"—Useless!" he interrupted, "I need to know how to expediently get into the walls!" He took a step closer, forcing her to retreat.

Her voice shook. "You would need a disguise."

He continued to push her back. She was almost on top of the table when he spoke again. "How do you propose we disguise an army?" He threatened.

"I—" she swallowed, "—I don't know."

Without warning he grabbed her. The Empress let out a cry as I shifted weight to my feet. I lifted my head just enough to see him release her hair. The brute threw her to the ground. The Empress held up her hand as she stole a glance my way, warning me not to move. I remained huddled. My long robes hid indication of martial arts training from any who might be watching.

Maliciously, he spat, "Then what good are you to me?"

"Please, I can ask my son to help. He will be succeeding the throne." Her voice quaked, from exhaustion not fear. Blue appeared on her lips as her breaths grew shallow.

The King threw back his head, releasing a hearty roar. He picked up the teapot and smashed it to the ground. The Empress' skin blistered from where hot water touched her hands. "You lying whore," he grabbed her collar. "You think I don't know? I have people inside your palace!" In the cruelest manner, he taunted, "I know your precious Crown Prince is dead. What does that say to you as a mother? You're worthless, like your dead son."

It was heart-wrenching to hear the ruler speak of Yu Longjing as if he were a trifle. My half-brother had been one of the kindest souls in the world.

Yet, even I didn't expect the Empress to act as she did. An impassioned roar escaped her widened lips as an arm swiped in a flash. I didn't know she could move that fast. The King stumbled with a shard of teapot in his neck. His guards rushed forward as the Empress pushed her weight onto him.

"Do NOT speak of my son!" she shrieked, continuously stabbing, composure evaporated. She, who selflessly kept back pain for decades, had erupted. She'd done everything from mothering an illegitimate child to offering her body—all to keep peace.

When this violent man spoke ill of her beloved Yu Longjing, it consumed the last of her resolve.

My body responded and I intercepted two guards, catching them by surprise and striking pressure points. As they collapsed, I took their weapons and stabbed a third as he grabbed for me. I felt the blade sink into his heart as I went under armored plates. I cringed, eying the remaining three circling. Their eyes told me the Empress and I weren't allowed to leave alive.

So be it.

I adjusted my grip.

One lunged from behind. I blocked his weapon and dodged a kick. He retreated a few steps with a cut lip. They were strong, but nothing compared to Ying Guardians. They gauged my fighting ability and I read their postures too. I feared being the weaker but knew they could never guess the extent of my training. I held the element of surprise.

All three came at once. One pinned me from behind as two others grabbed my legs. My arm holding a sword was twisted and I dropped my weapon. I threw my shoulders into a narrow position, giving my hands leverage to grab my restrainer's wrists. From there I pushed my feet into the other two and vaulted upwards. Using momentum, I sent one of the trio flying sideways. The remaining pair still clutched my ankles and I found myself balanced in a split.

The guard I threw charged back with a sword. I ripped fabric from my dress and flicked it into the face of my attacker—a trick

I learned from the bandits. I wrestled the sword from his hand and slashed at a guard holding my leg. He'd been trying to pull me off balance. He jumped back, releasing me.

The remaining guard tried to drag me but I somersaulted in his direction. My blade caught his throat and he gasped with hands clutching his neck.

The last two charged together. I countered their attacks, but a kick to my hip brought me to my knees. I twisted to avoid one blade, but another left a cut on my forearm, causing me to drop my weapon. I remained calm, wrapping the fabric around my wound, as I rolled away. I found myself by the broken teapot and kicked shards into their faces. It did not slow them much, but long enough for me to grab the King's sword.

I cut a gash in the dead man's neck and flicked blood onto the ground. The guards stopped abruptly to avoid stepping in their ruler's sacred blood. Using the distraction, I moved unabashedly through the crimson. Before they could react, I stabbed beneath a guard's armor. Red stained his robes.

The last guard charged with added fury. I focused on his spinning blade and saw an opening. My sword struck into his helmet. As his body fell still, I turned to the Empress. In her hands a sword dripped with blood, having ended the guards I'd rendered unconscious. She looked to me with apathy. "No witnesses."

Without words, we shed our blood-soaked outer robes and threw them into a dim corner. We fixed our hair the best we could. The Empress struggled to breathe. She could hardly stand.

We couldn't afford time to rest so I propped her against me as we exited. She told guards outside the thick doors, "The King wishes not to be disturbed until he summons. You're to escort us to our quarters."

No one questioned why we were partially dressed. I assumed the King held a lecherous reputation.

On the walk back, the hairs on my neck stood. I expected blood-curdling screams or curses to follow as someone discovered what we'd done. With the limping Empress on my arm, it felt like decades before reaching her suite. Hanming greeted us and helped his mother into a chair.

Our expressions must've been grave.

"What happened?"

"Later," the Empress shook her head. "We need to leave, NOW."

In moments, we readied. The Ying Guardians stole Lan Kingdom clothing for disguises. We knew if we left in a large group it would draw suspicion. "We'll break into smaller packs," a Ying Guardian instructed, "and hide throughout the outer walls. When the gates open for food deliveries in the morning, we'll sneak out separately, through different gates."

The Empress added, "Once outside, we'll meet at our previously agreed location." This was something she and the Ying Guardians had decided before I came along. "Go now. Be quick."

Hanming and I would be separated. We exchanged a longing embrace and wished each other safety. The Empress was in the third and last group.

~*~

Before nightfall, we'd snuck far from our quarters. By then, rumors traveled that something had happened to the King. But no official announcement was made. Commoners speculated on him falling ill. Large squads of guards patrolled the palace streets, arresting random workers. My group and I stayed well-hidden and avoided light.

The next morning, palace gates didn't open. Two days later when complaints about diminishing food supply grew turbulent, small doors allowed in food. If the guards were in a good mood, they allowed a few people to exit, each having to endure a thorough search. Luckily, most of the guards didn't know who or what they searched for. None knew their King was dead.

One by one we were able to pass through.

Chapter Thirty-Three:
Fire Powder

My team of Ying Guardians acquired horses. I no longer cared if stolen or purchased. We rode swiftly towards the west where a broad bridge spanned the river. We would cross it to the south bank. An old trading route would then take us to our meeting point with the Empress and Hanming.

Anxiety made my hands numb and the reins kept slipping through my fingers. The violent murder of the King played continuously in my mind, driving me mad. I couldn't forget the Empress' face. She'd degraded to nothing more than a woman destroyed. Her amber energy held flashes of black as she wept in violent abandon.

It occurred to me then that she had never mourned the death of Yu Longjing, forsaking her emotional needs. The illness of the Emperor and finding a new heir demanded all her energy. The tense situation must've been aggravated when she received word that the Lan Kingdom prepared for war. In the midst of it all, she rushed to retrieved Ku Cuixin from the south and returned him to his people to attempt peace.

Then, she fell under my scrutiny—the princess who should be her ally.

Spider's words became startling clear. He and his sister have put the Kingdom before their own needs. Could I say the same for myself?

I felt as if I were in a river, being rushed in a predetermined direction. Would I end up trapped in an eddy, or manage to flow free to the sea?

Despite sympathies, I felt the Empress' breaking point couldn't have come at a more inconvenient time. The Lan Kingdom would surely stop at nothing until our imperial city lay decimated. My brother was there and could be in danger, regardless of the Ying Guardians' presence.

It became urgent that we needed an Emperor to reestablish order.

When we stopped at night, I couldn't sleep. I kept my eyes trained east, looking for my new husband and his mother.

"Princess, you need rest," a Ying Guardian reminded.

"I'm fine." My heart wouldn't ease until I knew Hanming was safe.

We'd wed on a fourth day. I feared all the inauspiciousness of that number. The number that brought me into this world as the fourth born to the fourth wife, and it kept reappearing. What did fate have in store for me?

Two days of traveling brought us near the river. It flowed steadily and I found comfort in its familiar sight. Passing the outskirts of the Tangut Empire, we slowed our pace for the horses' sake. I glanced repeatedly over my shoulder, searching for clouds of dust to signify galloping horses. To my disappointment, nothing appeared.

By nightfall we approached the bridge. Some Ying Guardians wished to head south but I felt uncertain. I suggested we camp on the north bank. "There's no knowing what lies south. We can cross at first light." They agreed it would be safer since we knew the way we came was free from threats.

I stayed awake, staunchly facing east. I looked to the stars and found the Xin Hanming and I shared. To the heavens I mumbled, "Our life together has just begun. Please don't take him away."

I fell into uneasy sleep.

Morning came and it was time to move. Rushing water made our horses nervous so we led them on foot. I sighed with relief to see this bridge was far sturdier than the rope one. Made of wood and bronze, this one allowed four horses to travel side by side. Reinforced beams secured deeply into the shores. "What an amazing feat!" I exclaimed.

A Ying Guardian informed me the bridge had taken a generation to construct. "And many lives were lost during flood seasons."

Another added, "Back in the days of Tai Empire, traders used this bridge. When the Tai Empire fell, the bridge saw less use until it was ultimately abandoned."

A third warned, "We must tread carefully, some areas are crumbling."

An idea struck me, "Is this the only crossing south?" I asked.

"No, there are two more bridges," he responded. "A rope bridge lies to the east. Then, half a moon's travel further is a wider bridge. It's also in poor condition and sits on the northern outskirts of the Tai Empire."

I frowned, "How does the north expect to mobilize an army to the Yu Empire if there are only two inconvenient crossings?"

"It's believed since the war began in the Nan Kingdom, they've slowly sent troops south. Their excuse is to push blood bandits from their region, but their troops don't return. We believe they're gathered in the forests. Our Empire has been too preoccupied to dispatched troops on this issue."

I shuddered, remembering the confidence in the Lan King's eyes when he declared war on my home. "How great are their numbers?"

"There's no certainty. That's why the Empress went north, to try and prevent war."

The Ying Guardians and I arrived at our meeting location. I felt disappointed to see we were first. There was nothing to do but wait.

The Ying Guardians and I set our horses to pasture, and hid saddles. We climbed a tree and once safely obscured, I whispered, "I've been thinking. We need to destroy this bridge. If the north cannot cross to deliver messages, they can't mobilize to attack."

"What of the rope bridge and the eastern bridge?"

"My brother and I cut the rope bridge. The other is far and still buys us time."

"Destroying a bridge like this wouldn't be easy," another spoke.

I grinned. "I have an idea." I shared with the Ying Guardians how I broke Hanming from his cell. "My sisters' Kingdom is nearby. I can be there in one day's travel and procure fire powder."

"This plan would need to enact quickly. The Lan Kingdom should be in chaos over the death of their ruler, but it won't last forever."

"I wouldn't act until the Empress and her son are safely across," I reminded astutely.

"How much fire powder do we need?"

I tried to remember the explosive power of half a pouch. "I believe about twelve barrels."

"Transport would be difficult," the first Ying Guardian commented, but his eyes agreed with me.

"Yes," I nodded, "We'll need a wagon."

Hiding in the treetops, we formulated a plan. One of the Ying Guardians would come to the Mountain Empire with me. There, we would see about purchasing fire powder. The rest would wait for the others.

Hesitantly, I touched my silk pouch filled with what was left of my mother's gold coins. Parting with them would be heart wrenching, but as an imperial, I had my Empire to consider.

Timing was of the essence. We couldn't bring the fire powder to the bridge too soon or we'd need to hide it from blood bandits. "If they were to ambush us, they would undoubtedly take the powder," I reasoned. "Such explosives would be dangerous in their hands."

"However, if we're too late, and the North Kingdom sent messengers across, then destroying the bridge would be inconsequential," a guardian echoed.

Once we decided on a course of action, a Ying Guardian and I dropped silently from the tree. We called back two of the horses and rode towards the Tangut Empire. Crossing the bridge was done without incident. On the other side, I looked east. To my joy, I saw a small group on horseback. I turned to the Ying Guardian, "I want to see if they're our people."

He appeared hesitant. "If they're Lan Kingdom soldiers, it could be dangerous."

"If they are, then we would need to stop them from delivering a message south."

The Ying Guardian knew I stood correct.

To our relief, it was the Empress. We recognized her robes from a distance. As she approached, my concern grew. She slumped and her face held no color.

"Empress, you're not well," I gasped.

"Where's my son?"

"He's not yet at the meeting point, Empress. You need to worry about your health. We can bring you with us to the Tangut Empire. They have medicine and a quiet place to rest." I turned to the Ying Guardian who accompanied me. "We need to change our plan."

"What plan?" the Empress asked.

"Once our people are south, we aim to destroy the bridge."

She nodded, "Don't change it for me."

"Please, your health—" I began.

"We have time," one of the Ying Guardians with the Empress spoke. "As we left the Lan Kingdom, the high council was in discord. Some are saying they should release Prince Ku Rentu. Others argued to mobilize troops immediately. My guess, we have approximately four or five days before they come to an agreement."

It was decided.

The Empress and a Ying Guardian were to enter into the Tangut Kingdom and seek refuge. She warned, "I don't wish to notify the Tangut royals, it would complicate things by turning my stay into a diplomatic visit." Instead, once there, we found an inn and pretended to be travelers.

The Ying Guardian left me to tend to the Empress as he searched for fire powder. I found rice liquor and patted her face as I'd seen her do before. She grew alert and wrote a prescription from memory. I sought out an herbalist and bought her medicine.

Once I returned to the inn, I asked a girl in the kitchen, "Please infuse these herbs in tea."

Young and eager to please, she did so with a smile. I carried the pot gingerly to the Empress' room and she thankfully drank the brew. Within the hour, color in her cheeks improved. Unfortunately, it did little for her spirits.

"What have I done?" she sobbed pitifully. "I've murdered the Lan ruler!"

"He planned to wage war." I tried to comfort.

She shook her head. "I took a life with these hands." As if trying to wipe away blood, she wrung her fingers against a handkerchief.

"Empress, you're upset. Everything in your life is the for the sake of your Empire. You feel you've lost your way because, for an instant, your pain losing Yu Longjing became more important."

She placed a hand endearingly upon my cheek, "Thank you, child. But each death is possibilities lost and hearts broken. It's never right to take life. Just think. How many of your dear ones have been taken?" Her golden aura grew dark. "Let me mourn. If I do not, I cease to be human."

I said no more. I put her to bed and excused myself.

Standing in the busy streets, I peered into my heart. Her speech astounded me. How many lives have I taken? Have I become less than human? I shivered as my mother's words returned, about good people performing evil deeds to survive. I looked to the heavens. "Mother, will I be forgiven?"

My father once told me, "Alchemists stumbled upon fire powder while searching for gold." At first I mistook his meaning for the metal. Then he explained it was the gold inside our soul, "The alchemists sought immortality. When elements of fire powder are separate, they are ineffective. Once mixed, they hold explosive power."

Was my soul like fire powder in its separate state?

Perhaps it's why I felt limited remorse. I'd experienced outrageous events and had yet to come to terms with them all. Once I do, might I mourn as the Empress does?

I hoped so. It would mean I remained human.

Though bedridden, the Empress used the opportunity to teach me more of the Lan meditation. Onset of nausea returned. "That's normal," the Empress reminded. Then added with a smile, "Or, you're with my grandchild."

My face grew hot.

A soft knock came at the door and I felt grateful for the interruption. "Princess Summer, may I speak with you?" I recognized the voice of a Ying Guardian. I lowered the Empress' silk curtains and went to him. "There are no merchants who carry fire powder. Its use is highly restricted. The only reserves are in royal storehouses."

My frown deepened, despite feeling relief at the prospect of keeping my mother's coins. For a moment I played with the idea of asking my sisters to assist in procuring this fire powder. After we destroy the bridge, I could claim it an accident.

I quickly discarded the thought. Accident or not, it would put them in a compromising situation.

"I'll find a way," I sighed. "But we're running out of time. I need you to take the Empress south and get her to safety."

"Princess Summer, I can't leave you behind."

I held up a hand, "You forget, I'm also a Ying Guardian."

He gave a nod of respect.

I affixed a sturdy gaze. "Now. Where are the royal storehouses?"

~*~

The medicinal tea improved the Empress' health and I felt confident she could make it home. Her intelligent eyes warned me. "If there were not such pressing issues back home, I'd never allow you to be left behind like this."

"I'm not being left behind," I smiled, "I'm choosing to stay. Besides, with the turmoil in the Yu Empire and the murder of the Lan King, I'm safest away from it all!"

She appeared amused, "Rationalize it however you wish, but don't forget you owe me a grandchild."

I bid them farewell and turned to the task at hand: finding the royal storehouse.

The Ying Guardian had said, "It's visible from the base of the waterfall. Four guards regularly patrol the area and the steps are inconveniently steep." I wondered how I could possibly carry twelve barrels on my own.

I paced for hours, unable to formulate a plan. Eventually, my stomach grumbled. Perhaps food would help with concentration.

I trudged to the marketplace and seated myself in an open-air noodle shop. I called my order to the attending boy. I couldn't set aside my frustration. Time dwindled and I needed a way to destroy the bridge.

I stared mindlessly at the crowd of passer byers, studying their features as a distraction, noticing how they differed ever-so-slightly from mine. My eyes drew to a man with a familiar gait. I set down my chopsticks, unable to believe my eyes. His was a face like mine. It was my brother!

I leapt from my seat and called out. Winter's eyes beamed with joy but his expression twisted. "Summer, you're still here? Our sisters said you left weeks ago."

"I did, but now I'm back," I frowned, "What're you doing here? Weren't you in Zhenxun?"

"No, I haven't ventured south since destroying the rope bridge," he responded.

A sickly heat filled my stomach. "You didn't receive my letters?"

Winter shook his head. "I got your note under the rock and was on my way here when I was ambushed by blood bandits. Luckily, a group of Tangut guards chased them away."

"You—you've been here the entire time?" Cold sweat formed

between my shoulders. To whom did I write in Zhenxun?

"Yes, I had a deep wound on my leg and when I announced myself to be the brother of princesses Spring and Autumn, they brought me to the palace. Royal physicians tended to me and this is my first day on my feet. I was preparing to return to the Lan Kingdom tomorrow…"

"Don't go back there!" I exclaimed, struggling to keep my voice a low volume.

Winter frowned, "What's happened?"

I pulled Winter into a small alley. In a hushed voice, I told him how the Empress had murdered the Lan King. Horror filled his eyes. I explained it bought our Empire time. I didn't tell him about Hanming's relationship to the Empress and my marriage. I wished to inform him under better circumstances.

"Winter, someone wrote to me as you from our home. In those letters, I gave sensitive information. The Empress and Hanming are headed there now. They're not safe. We need to go after them!"

"What information?" he asked.

I gulped wanting to tell him Hanming was the Empress' son. With respect to their friendship, I felt it best if Hanming told him. When I had sent the letter to my brother, I assumed he was already in Zhenxun. Winter would've heard about the Empress and her second son. Now didn't seem the appropriate time to spring this information upon him.

"There's a lot, and it's complicated," was all I said before changing the topic, "But I'm glad you're here. I need your help."

I told Winter about the plan to destroy the bridge. At first he narrowed his eyes, questioning my sanity. After I explained the North Kingdom had been slowly sending troops south, his eyes changed. He told me the plan seemed reasonable. I sighed, "Yes, but I don't know how to get the fire powder."

Winter grew thoughtful. "I have an idea. I'm still a guest at the royal palace. I can 'borrow' their seal and forge an order. The royal store house guards can load it onto a wagon for you."

"What about our sisters? Would this compromise their lives?"

Winter shook his head. "If no one discovers where the order came from, they have no reason to suspect our sisters."

~*~

True to his word, the next day Winter found me at my inn. He handed me the forged document. "Summer, I can't go with you if I'm to keep the blame off our sisters," he said with distress. "If I leave, they'll suspect me. If I remain and appear oblivious, our sisters would be free of scrutiny."

"I understand. I can take care of this."

"Summer," Winter clasped my arm in concern, "Have you no one to help? Where's Hanming?"

My heart dropped, "I don't know where Hanming is. We were separated while escaping." I lifted my chin to bolster strength, "Rest assured brother. This deed shall be done. There are great soldiers from our home accompanying us."

Winter looked at me with some hesitance. He didn't know of

the Ying Guardians. I wished to tell him, but it would make little difference. My big brother would always dote on me. Instead, I asked, "Winter, you'll be stuck on the north bank for some time. When will I see you again?"

He shook his head, "I don't know. Perhaps remaining behind will be a good thing. I can keep my eye on the Lan Kingdom and thwart them if I get a chance… Even if I must to persuade the Tanguts into action."

"I'll miss you, brother."

"I'll miss you too. My regret is I can't keep you safe in the foreseeable future." His eyes grew large.

"Have faith in me," I patted his hand.

"I do, youngest sister." It warmed my heart to hear those words. He sounded like our mother. He pulled me into an embrace.

"Winter, Silk Deer has a message," I whispered into his ear. "She'll wait for you."

His arms tightened before he pulled away, steeling his wavering expression. "I care for her too. But first, we must take care of the Empire."

I nodded in respect before saying farewell. I watched his shoulders disappear into a crowd.

I tossed my few belongings in a pack and stole a man's outfit. My bandit days proved far more useful than my princess ones. I changed and headed for the royal storehouse.

My feet scaled the steps with aim as guards peered down.

Curiosity wrote on their faces to see me out of breath. I handed over the document without a word; mostly to hide the fact I could hardly catch my breath. They studied it for a moment before nodding. I was dressed as a noble's servant, so they might've thought I ran an errand for the palace.

Four guards carried the barrels of fire powder with nimble footing. I watched in awe as they skipped playfully down dicey steps. After twelve were loaded onto a wagon, they called for a horse. They waved goodbye and didn't suspect a thing.

On my way out of the imperial city, a random guard stopped me. He asked about my exceptionally large wagon and royal horse. With nervousness, I felt my pockets for something to bribe him. My fingers closed on the lapis lazuli badge. I showed it instead, declaring royal business for the Lan Kingdom. He bowed and granted passage.

Once out of earshot, a sigh of relief escaped.

The lone horse pulled slowly. He wasn't meant to travel this distance with the heavy barrels and I felt badly. I hummed a tune and it seemed to lift the creature's spirits.

I kept my eyes peeled for blood bandits, but fortunately didn't encounter any. Still, I didn't wish to think luck was on my side until after I'd completed the mission. I feared it might jinx me.

I reached the bridge by nightfall and wasted no time crossing. On the other side, two Ying Guardians dropped from trees. I learned Hanming and the Empress were headed back to Zhenxun. A knot formed in my stomach. Whoever responded to my letter meant for my brother knew the Empress and Hanming's secrets. They were in danger. We needed to catch up as soon as possible.

Wiping a hand on the fire powder barrels, dampness came away. I frowned. It likely came from the waterfall near where it was stored. It was clever of the Tanguts, to prevent accidental combustion. However, it proved a problem for us.

I ripped a cloth tarp it into small squares and packaged fire powder into sacks. We hung these in trees, allowing wind to dry them expediently. The sacks held only the quantities in three barrels at a time. We tested small samples by striking flint, cheering every time the powder lit.

Once we dried all the powder, we prepared the second step by setting the barrels against the struts of the bridge. At the first, I added kindling. Leading to it was a thick braid of dried grass.

I looked at the Ying Guardians and they nodded. I took out flint and prepared to strike.

A jarring pain struck my shoulder and the flint flew from my grasp. A Ying Guardian grunted as we ducked. I peered to see an arrow in my shoulder. A Ying Guardian moved his hand from his side, revealing a gash.

We quickly drew swords and moved to hang beneath the bridge. We stood on the struts and clung tightly as rushing water stirred the air. Voices in the blood bandits' dialect shouted above. My left shoulder winced.

"Listen," a Ying Guardian called over the sound of the river.

"How many voices do you hear?"

"At least six," I answered.

"I hear seven," the other said, "Plus rustling in the distance. My guess is ten or eleven together. We can take them."

"It's getting dark, we'll be able to move in stealth," I agreed.

"No Princess. You make sure the fire powder destroys this bridge. The two of us will take the bandits."

They were right. If I could get the powder to explode, the blood bandits would be scared off.

In diminishing light, two Ying Guardians climbed along the struts, one with blood dripping down his side. Above us, the bandits continued to holler in a dialect I didn't understand. I grit my teeth, bracing against shoulder pain as I climbed back onto the bridge. I hid behind a low pillar, listening for sounds of Ying Guardians drawing attention.

Sure enough, a few minutes later, the bandits' shouts changed to a tone of panic. Clashes of metal led me to peek cautiously around the pillar. In low light, I hardly saw the commotion, only twisting shadows. I felt confident I couldn't be seen either.

I scurried to the first barrel, barely visible in the dark. I reached over, feeling for the kindling and gasped as a sharp branch cut my thumb. I didn't pull back, continuing to trace my hands in search of the grass braid. It wasn't there. I searched frantically. Perhaps in the confusion it'd gotten brushed away.

The sounds changed and the blood bandits drew nearer, their shouts more rage-filled. I reached into my pocket and pulled out tiny pieces of flint. I grasped them tightly and struck the sparks directly into the kindling. After a few attempts, a loose piece of grass caught flame. I ripped my sleeve and gently blew on the sparks, adding fabric. The kindling caught and my form illuminated.

Arrows whizzed past me. Too dangerous to remain by the barrel, I waited no longer than to see the kindling start to blaze. I dashed to the edge of the bridge. Without a second thought, I dove into churning waves. Behind me, a loud explosion reverberated. The force catapulted me into cold water. By some stroke of luck, I didn't strike hidden rocks. Any relief it afforded didn't last long as the river swept me away.

I thrashed madly to keep my head above the froth, groping for anything solid. My foot struck a rock and I cried in pain. The motion swung me around and I faced the bridge. I watched as the barrels of fire powder exploded in succession. I wanted to cry out in victory as the bridge crumbled, but my mouth gasped for air. Despite my predicament, a smile tugged at my lips.

Soon the burning bridge disappeared from sight and my strength waned. I tried many times to paddle towards shore, but the current kept pulling me away. Numbness spread from the cold as desperation filled every breath. Sputtering, I cried for help, praying for someone to hear.

Consciousness began to slip when I heard shouts from the south bank. I forced my eyes open and peered in the distance. Dark figures rushed into the water with ropes around their waists.

I was being swept midstream, too far for them to reach.

I summoned the last of my strength and told myself I couldn't give up. I needed to warn Hanming and the Empress. I pushed with every last ounce of my being, my injured shoulder lagging. As I swept past the dark figures, a grip closed around my wrist. I recalled a sense of gratefulness before dark engulfed my senses.

~*~

When I came to, I found myself half-stumbling, half-dragged inland. The sound of water softened to a hum. Two men held my arms draped around their shoulders. I mumbled in gratitude as a pain in my ankle made me wince.

Not much later, I slumped before a fire. Eagerly my hands reached forward to soak in heat. A blanket landed around me and I was instructed to get out of my wet clothes.

Still dressed as a Tangut boy, I braved a look at the men's faces to see if they could be trusted. I jolted to find myself surrounded by troops of the Lan Kingdom.

Chapter Thirty-Four:
Espionage

"Prince Ku Rentu!" The voice startled me and I jerked my head. A face wrought with concern hovered in the firelight. I recognized General Hong. "Where have you been?" he asked, coddling. "We were returning you to the palace as you requested, but then you disappeared!"

Hairs rose on my neck. The dunk in the river left my wits disorientated and I feared saying something that would give me away. My throat cleared to buy time, before answering in a strained voice, "Pressing matters demanded my attention."

"Forgive me for asking, but how did you end up in the river?" General Hong waved the soldiers away. They hovered nearby, leaning against trees, peering with interest.

Fatigue threatened, but I needed a lie to keep me safe for the night. I felt fortunate to have met the real Prince Ku Rentu and could emulate him on some level.

I gulped before imitating his lilt. "I was headed to the Yu

Empire with royal delegates when we were attacked. Blood bandits destroyed the bridge and I escaped by diving into the river. I commend you, General Hong for saving me."

"Of course your majesty, but let us get you out of your wet clothes." He didn't ask why I dressed in Tangut garb.

"I'll need privacy," I ordered.

"Of course, your majesty!"

As he led me from the fire, I braved an important question. "Have you returned to the palace?"

General Hong shook his head. "We were forbidden to return without you."

I relaxed knowing they were unaware of recent events.

The soldiers erected a large tent and stood guard. Inside, I removed sopping clothes and quickly donned a princely garb. The silks warmed my skin, invigorating me. I allowed a soldier with basic physician knowledge to extract the arrowhead from my shoulder. The rest had splintered in the river. As he bandaged me, I fretted over the Ying Guardians and how they fared in the skirmish.

Once alone, I seated myself on a pillow and closed my eyes to meditate. As I listened to casual banter, I discerned this platoon had little combat knowledge. Their main objective was to search for the Prince. I heard mention of "other soldiers" and could only surmise they meant Lan troops south of the river.

I faced a difficult decision. I could trick this platoon into escorting me to the Yu Empire. I could also take the opportunity and have them bring me to other Lan troops as Prince Ku Rentu. The latter ran a great risk of me being recognized as an imposter.

But how much information on the enemy could I gather before then? If General Hong mistook me for the Prince, it would be reasonable to assume others would too. I could survey the soldiers and get an idea of the threat.

The first option enticed me more because I needed to warn Hanming and the Empress as soon as possible. The platoon would offer safe travel. However, once we reached Zhenxun, the risk of being recognized grew exponentially.

I could always ask General Hong about the troops and their numbers. He appeared eager to please and would gladly tell his Prince anything he wished to know. Yet, I could see he was not an experienced General. He likely wasn't privy to vital information. I wanted to assess the troops myself, with eyes trained by the Ying Guardians.

I gnawed on my lip and rebuked my carelessness for sending the letters to the Yu Empire. If I hadn't, this decision would be easy. I felt greatly disturbed not knowing who read my private thoughts. Not only did I pour out my heart, but included scandalous information. If the letter reached the wrong hands, a coup would occur.

"Prince Ku Rentu," General Hong called from outside the tent.

"Come in," I spoke in a low timbre, trying to match the true prince's voice.

A flap lifted and General Hong stooped inside. Behind him followed a handful of servants. One brought in a low table as others carried dishes of food. My stomach grumbled at the sight. I'd forgotten to feed myself that day.

General Hong took it upon himself to test the food. Once he ascertained it was safe, a bowl of rice and chopsticks were set before me. I lifted the utensils like a nobleman. As I ate, General Hong informed me of recent events. "Upon hearing your report, we sent scouts to inspect the bridge. I'm sorry to say it's truly demolished and we can't bring you home. We have been using Lan Kingdom camps as bases of operations, occasionally breaking away to search for you. Tomorrow, we plan to stop at one and replenish supplies. Then, we will head to the east bridge."

I nodded without glancing up, "What rank are the Generals at the base? Are they my friends or foes?" I assumed with Prince Ku Rentu's dissention towards his brother, their court was divided.

"My prince, I'm but a humble General, lower ranked than others. I don't know if they are your friends."

I frowned, juggling risks once more. I hoped I was making the right decision. "Then I do not wish to waste time. I have business at the Yu Empire. You must take me there."

General Hong bowed, "I'm sorry, but we don't have enough provisions to travel the distance. We need to visit a base first."

I didn't want to seem as if I had anything to hide. "Very well, but let's make it swift."

My hands sweat profusely and a lump formed in my throat. I reminded myself this was an opportunity to scope troops. Yet, I still feared being discovered.

I lost my appetite and set down my bowl and chopsticks. General Hong ordered servants to clear the table. He bid me goodnight and left.

I thought nervousness would keep me awake, but I slumbered heavily until sunlight splashed across my eyes. I remained under the covers, anxious about what lie ahead. The pain in my shoulder subsided to a dull ache. Outside, soft voices prattled as they packed up camp. One said we were to leave as soon as the Prince was awake.

The tone in the camp changed suddenly. The soft clanging went silent. I slowly reached for a sword and clutched it to my chest, ears straining. Soldiers' boots shuffled as if being coerced. One man asked another to calm down. He was surrounded with nowhere to escape.

"Where is she? Her tracks led to your camp," Hanming's voice demanded coldly.

A surge of excitement lifted me to my feet. I quickly pulled on my boots and threw aside the tent flap. I stepped into the chilly morning air to see Hanming at the center of a circle of soldiers. General Hong stood beside him, Hanming's blade glistening at his neck.

When my husband caught sight of me, his eyes grew puzzled, running up and down my princely robes.

"My friend!" I said jovially. I made a show of setting down the sword and walked towards Hanming. The soldiers called for me to stay back. "Nonsense!" I chided affably, "This man will not harm me." I caught Hanming's eyes as I said those words. A quizzical blue danced across them. I reached forward and removed the sword from his hand.

General Hong quickly moved away and shouted, "Seize him!"

"Stop!" I commanded, barring the soldiers. I spoke in a reasonable voice, "I apologize on behalf of my friend, but I assure you this is a misunderstanding. He's saved my life and I owe him. No one shall bring him harm. That's an order."

"Yes, Prince Ku Rentu," General Hong bent at the waist.

"Prince Ku Rentu…" Hanming repeated.

"Yes, it is I!" I exclaimed, giving him a strong embrace. "Play along," I breathed into his ear. He gave the slightest of nods.

"My apologies," Hanming said dipping his head to General Hong. "I was searching for my companion."

"It's quite alright," General Hong responded amicably. He rubbed his neck where the blade was pointed; sweat beading all over his face. "My head is still on my neck and any friend of the Prince's is a friend of ours," he chuckled nervously.

"General Hong, I am appointing my friend as my personal bodyguard. He's to remain by my side at all times. Is that understood?" I demanded politely.

"Yes, your majesty," he replied with dedication. He was the kind to blindly obey his master. I could see he felt relieved there would be no skirmish that morning.

"Good, now let's continue with our day."

The soldiers resumed clearing camp and I waved for Hanming to follow into my tent. Once in private, I turned and wrapped my arms sheepishly around him. Memories of our wedding night stirred. His hand found its way to the back of my neck, cupping me to his shoulder. We remained embraced in silent celebration, my heart fluttering like a hummingbird.

"Where's the Empress?" I whispered.

"I escorted her in sight of Zhenxun before turning back. She's with the Ying Guardians. I couldn't bear the thought of leaving you behind," he said gently." The words chased away the morning cold. I planted a kiss on his lips.

He chuckled nervously. "So, Prince Ku Rentu, huh?"

I blushed, "It's a silly story. Winter and I ran into General Hong when we first arrived in the north. I had Prince Ku Rentu's sword and they mistook me for him."

Hanming gave a playful scoff. "How did you plan on getting home?"

"I've asked them to escort me to the Yu palace," I winked at my cleverness. Then added solemnly, "But first they're taking me to a base camp for supplies. I was going to use the opportunity and sum up their troops."

"Summer, that's reckless!" he gasped. "How many people do

you think will recognize you're not the Prince?" His tone bit into my pride.

"I know," I replied stubbornly, "But I would've thought of something!" I didn't want him to think me less clever.

"Then tell me, what?" he asked desperately. "I care for your safety."

"Well," I searched my mind trying to pull an idea. Then it struck me. "This," I reached into my robe, pulling out the lapis lazuli pendant. "I could admit not being Prince Ku Rentu, but a royal decoy. This badge is from the royal family. They would *need* to believe me."

Hanming appeared impressed. "That *is* quite ingenious."

~*~

As my tent was packed, I resumed my role as Prince Ku Rentu. A decorated horse appeared and I climbed atop. There were nearly fifty men in General Hong's search party—more than enough to discourage a blood bandit attack. Also enough to end Hanming and me if we gave them reason. We dared not speak with each other. Instead, we listened to conversations around us, hoping to glean information. Nothing of use came up.

Before nightfall, a soldier rode on ahead to announce my arrival. He returned shortly after dark to say we neared our destination. By time we arrived, the moon hung high as pieces of light filtered through trees.

I was shown to a decorated tent furnished with furs and silks. Hanming entered with me. Since I was royalty, we were given privacy through the night. We huddled tightly but didn't relax, speculating on the size of the Lan troops surrounding us.

"They must move regularly to avoid detection," Hanming frowned. "They must also break into smaller troops. The tree bandits stick to their usual trails so it's easy to avoid them."

"The woods are vast," I commented. "Winter and I didn't stumble upon any Lan militia when we traveled north. I shuddered to think how many soldiers we could've passed."

"I'm worried for you. What if they do not believe you're a decoy?"

"Hanming, you are fretting over trifles."

He kissed the top of my head. "I cannot help it." The words left sweetness in my thoughts as I drifted to sleep.

In the morning, I awoke to an empty bed and my mind raced. Did someone arrest Hanming in the middle of the night? Was he drawn into a trap? I looked around desperately for clues.

Then I noticed a familiar shadow on the outside of my tent. I peeked through the flap and saw Hanming standing guard. I sighed in relief.

The breath quickly caught in my chest as I peered past him. Hundreds of Lan Kingdom soldiers busied with chores and moved like clockwork. Some sharpened weapons as others shined armor. They moved silently, reminding me much of the tree bandits.

Thinking of the tree bandits made me look to the branches. There, soldiers perched with arrows trained on the surrounding land. Focusing on one, he appeared highly skilled with acute movements. In his hand was a looking glass. I'd seen one before in my father's study. It allowed one to peer great distances.

I turned my attention back to soldiers on the ground. Their uniforms indicated they were standard foot soldiers of average training. I let out another sigh. Hanming must've heard and glanced over. I pulled back the tent flap and he stepped inside. "Did you rest well?" he asked.

I nodded but moved to more important matters, "You must've been watching the soldiers all morning. How many do you think there are?"

"My guess? Three hundred in this garrison. I overheard them talking about others."

"A Ying Guardian told me they've been sending troops over the last five years."

"Yes, I've heard that too..."

I chewed my lip. "Hanming, there's something I need to tell you." I had held off on the information, having been exhausted and unable to mentally contend with it. "We need to return to the Yu Empire as soon as possible." I confessed about the letter I wrote to Winter. Tears streamed as I grew upset with myself. From memory, I recited the contents.

Hanming's face paled. "The Empress has returned to the palace. We need to move immediately."

"I know, Hanming," I said, "But General Hong's troops couldn't take me until we stopped here first. Let's take advantage of this opportunity and learn about the enemy."

Hanming's eyes hardened as they trailed to the ground. He nodded sharply with a clenched jaw. In an edgy voice, he announced he was going to mingle with the soldiers and learn more.

"Hanming, are you upset with me?" I asked tearfully.

His eyes softened, "No, my love, not you." A steady hand reached forward and his thumb gingerly traced my lips. "You couldn't have known it wasn't your brother. I am angry at the people who wish us dead." His words brought me comfort and he gave me a lingering kiss before exiting.

General Hong and his servants brought breakfast. "When are we expected to leave?" I asked.

He bowed, informing politely, "We will stay overnight and set out first thing in the morning. It's two days travel to the next base."

On a whim I asked if there was a pre-ordained rotation for base camps. He nodded and happily confirmed.

"Could I see a map of the rotations?"

He shook his head apologetically and said the information was reserved for top Generals.

I bit back a frustrated sigh. "Thank you, you're excused."

I plotted to get my hands on a rotation map. Our military would then be able to anticipate the Lan Kingdom's troops. I estimated they would soon discover the western bridge's destruction. It would take well over a moon for them to return and re-dispatch to the east bridge. If I arrived home in a few days and miraculously stabilized our government, we could have time to prepare defenses.

Yet, the letters I sent Winter still gnawed at me. Was it too much to hope an ally intercepted?

Hanming returned at nightfall. A man dressed as a Lan Kingdom soldier accompanied him. To my relief, I recognized him as a Ying Guardian with me at the bridge. I asked him about our friend. He reported the other Ying Guardian didn't survive. I felt saddened and it must've shown on my face.

"I assure you, Princess, there's no higher honor than dying for the imperial family."

"The words bring me no consolation, but thank you regardless," I spoke humbly, thinking about the Empress' words on valuing life.

The Ying Guardian informed me he'd been amongst the troops for days. "From what I gather, there are twenty thousand soldiers in these woods. With those numbers and our decreased militia, they can easily push through our defenses." His brow bent in agitation.

"What about our southern territory? Can we pull troops back?" Hanming asked.

The Ying Guardian shook his head, "The stability there is precarious."

I listened to the two converse, but my mind was elsewhere. When the discussion lagged, I turned to the Ying Guardian. "My friend," I spoke gravely, "I must send you on a mission." I informed him of my letter. "It will place the Empress in danger. Do what you can to see it destroyed."

He nodded, "It will be done." He turned on his heel and disappeared into the night. Disquiet took hold and I looked to Hanming. His eyes sank a deeper blue than before, the corners drooping.

The next day, we left base. I thanked my stars no one recognized I wasn't Prince Ku Rentu. We journeyed for two days as General Hong had informed, and arrived at another base. Judging by the position of the moon, we neared our home.

A General ranked above General Hong greeted me. His face appeared reverent and there seemed to be no suspicion of my identity. After some time, I braved asking to see a map of military rotations. He hesitated, but showed it to me. I stared long and hard at the parchment, memorizing as much as I could.

That night I took sticks of burnt wood and redrew the map onto a piece of cloth. I kept it close my body. The next morning, we set out again.

"Prince Ku Rentu," General Hong said on our way, "You'll be happy to know, I learned we'll be passing through a base run by your friend, General Wen."

"Oh yes, how nice!" I choked, stealing a glance at Hanming. His lips pressed in a firm line.

When we stopped to camp, Hanming and I stole uniforms. After taking provisions, we mounted horses and rode quietly into the night. I couldn't help but felt badly for General Hong. Once more he lost custody of "the Prince."

"This way," Hanming whispered after climbing a tree to study the stars. We were far enough south not to worry about blood bandits. We didn't sleep and rode through the night, determining it was safer to travel under the cover of dark. At dusk, we set the horses to graze and napped in trees until the sun dropped.

When we woke, we lowered quietly and called for our horses. They didn't return.

Hanming and I frowned and called again.

Nothing but stillness answered. Hanming grew tense and waved for me to follow. We dashed into the brush and headed east towards our home Empire. We didn't get far before he stopped in his tracks. Hanming held an arm to bar me. I peered over his shoulders and saw soldiers from the Lan Kingdom. They surrounded us. Though we dressed like them, I couldn't help but feel the cold grip of fear.

"What do we have here?" a voice called, "deserters?" A General approached on horseback. I blinked to make sure I wasn't mistaken. Like me, the General was a woman disguised as a man. I could tell by the graceful slope of her chin. Behind her, our horses were led by their reins.

An idea struck and I stepped from behind Hanming. I bowed before the woman. "General Wen," I guessed at her identity. "Permission to speak in private."

Silence hung in the air as she considered. I sensed catching her by surprise. She granted permission. Soldiers escorted us to her base. Hanming gave me a look asking what I plotted. I returned a reassuring nod, hiding the uncertainty I felt.

When we arrived, General Wen allowed us into her tent. Hanming and I bowed until she asked us to rise, asking about our business. The wheels of my mind turned as it concocted a partial truth. "General Wen, we were sent here in secret by Prince Ku Rentu. He asked us to trust no one but you since you are old friends," I began. I recalled the Prince's words to me when we left the Tangut Empire. He said he knew my type well. Could he be referring to General Wen?

"He has been imprisoned by the Lan King, because Prince Ku Rentu wished to stop the war against the Yu Empire. I'm but a humble maid who served the Yu Empress. He asked me to deliver a message to the Yu Empire in hopes of negotiating peace. Please, will you assist us?"

General Wen studied my face for an agonizing minute. I hoped she would release us if not aid us. Her expression remained impassive, but with a hint of curiosity. It wasn't everyday women impersonated men and I could sense she felt a bond.

"Do you have proof of your words?" she finally asked.

"Yes. Our departure was blessed by Ku Cuixin, Prince Ku Rentu's cousin who was returned by the Yu Empress." I reached into my robes and presented her with the lapis lazuli pendant. She took it into her hands and subdued shock flitted momentarily across her features. General Wen ran her fingers over the pendant before returning it to me.

"I will personally escort you to the outskirts of Zhenxun. Prince Ku Rentu has always been an advocate of peace and I'm glad you're assisting his cause," she responded.

I stole a glance at Hanming whose face filled with relief and admiration. Even I flabbergasted myself. I never guessed I could be such a capable liar. My mother had always taught me to speak the truth because the heavens judged integrity at all times.

Perhaps I merely followed the Empress' example. She lied to our Empire telling them the Emperor was still alive to protect it from tearing itself apart. If my brother and the Empress taught me anything, it was that imperials could not live for themselves. They lived to serve and protect their people. Even if it cost our integrity.

True to her word, General Wen and a handful of soldiers guided us to the outskirts of Zhenxun. She bid us good luck on our peacekeeping mission and rode away.

Hanming marched towards the village but I remained frozen. After General Wen disappeared, my legs gave out. Hanming rushed to my side and placed his arms around me, desperately asking where I hurt.

"It's nothing," I said with respite. "I'm merely overcome to finally be home."

Chapter Thirty-Five:
The Heir

I'm often hounded by sins I've committed. During my time in the world, I've stolen, lied, and murdered. Am I truly fit to be an imperial? What made me morally superior to where I could pass judgment on the crimes of others? Is it possible to live a life of complete innocence?

~*~

Hanming and I stole peasants' clothes and quickly did away with our Lan Kingdom disguises. We strode towards a modest inn and I looked over my shoulder with a sense of amusement. Not far off, sat the inn where I'd spent my first night out of the palace. It seemed a lifetime ago when I left for the Nan Kingdom as a betrothed Princess. Now, I was fortunate to be married to the one who held my heart.

I took his hand as we entered the establishment.

In the small hours, a gentle knock came at our door. Hanming and I grabbed weapons as he peered cautiously through a crack.

His shoulders relaxed as he opened the door for Ying Guardians. Their faces bore long expressions.

"What of the Empress?" Hanming asked. I could tell he braced for the worst.

"She's inside the palace and we've taken her underground," a Ying Guardian reported. "Spider is protecting her. However," he paused to find the right words, "the letter Princess Summer wrote has been brought to public light. It spoke of the Emperor's passing and details you as the Empress' illegitimate child with the enemy. Coupled with her previous declaration to place her second son as the heir, the imperial Lords have charged the Empress with treason."

Another Ying Guardian added, "Most of the imperial family in the palace has fled south, but I fear they'll not be safe for long. A battle for the throne is coming."

The Ying Guardians were careful with their tone, not to blame me.

But I hated myself.

I felt foolish. I had no right to jeopardize everyone with carelessness. I wanted to wallow in misery, but it wouldn't solve a thing. I brushed aside my pride and sat quietly until I could contribute.

"What's happening inside the walls?" Hanming asked.

"The Lords and top Generals are amassing personal armies and bribing for loyalties. I fear they aim to disband Zhenxun and loot it for all it's worth. The Emperor's cousins in outlying territories are sending troops, but I fear they won't arrive in time."

"And the Lan loyalists?" Hanming asked.

"Some are conspiring with the troops in the surrounding woods. We're able to intercept most messengers, but a few have gotten through."

Hanming lowered his head, deep in thought. "If it's known I'm a son of the Lan house, would Lan supporters aid me to ascend to the throne? I could try to stop war from there."

"It's difficult to say," a Ying Guardian answered in a frown. "Your mother's the Empress and they deem her untrustworthy due to her actions against the Yu Empire."

"Hanming, you must try," I said in a sad voice. "We need an Emperor, someone who the majority will follow. I will stay by your side and support you."

"Princess," the Ying Guardian spoke, "With all due respect, I am going to speak bluntly. The palace sees you as a fool for sending the letter. If Hanming were to somehow take the throne, it would be best for you stay in the shadows or disguise yourself. To have you by his side as Princess Summer would decrease his credibility."

I swallowed a lump in my throat as my ears burned. I couldn't deny the Ying Guardian's logic. We needed to garner support and I would damage Hanming's image.

Hanming patted my hand to let me know he didn't blame me. "Perhaps Summer in the shadows can work to our advantage. She's proven to be resourceful and outwitted many." He turned to me and asked gently, "Show them the map you copied."

I nodded, happy to have some remedy for my catastrophic position. I pulled the cloth from a deep pocket and spread it before us. Details of the Lan soldiers' rotations and dates were shown. I spoke meekly, "My brother said imperials do what's needed to the protect their people. The Yao Emperor surrendered to my ancestors. What if we surrender to the Lan Kingdom? Their armies can stop unrest within our government."

Hanming shook his head, "High officials of the North Kingdom would be in rage that our Empress murdered their ruler. If they do take over, it will not be peaceful. Furthermore, neither one of us officially represent the Yu Empire. A surrender will have no standing."

I looked aside dejectedly. The situation seemed hopeless.

The Ying Guardians exchanged a look. I could see they'd discussed something before approaching us tonight. I grew anxious and asked them to speak their mind. "Princess Summer, your face bears remarkable resemblance to your father…" Suggestiveness hung in the air, all eyes upon me.

"I don't understand."

"The dissidents inside the palace are outnumbered by your father's supporters. Right now, those supporters are wavering in their faith of the Empire because of the letter you sent. In order to secure our Empire, we need to reestablish their loyalty to the Emperor. To do so, we need to present a legitimate heir to the throne."

"What are you saying?" I frowned.

"We believe you should replace Hanming as the second son to the Empress. With your striking resemblance to your father, there'd be no question of lineage. Only then can you dispel the damage done by the letter, claiming it to be mere fabrication from the disloyal."

"Are you saying I should ascend as Emperor?" I exclaimed, petrified by the idea. "I cannot! It destroys the balance of heaven and earth to have a woman take the mandate of heaven to rule! Besides, I don't have the formal education of an imperial son!"

"Princess, it's for the sake of the Empire. There's no true divide between men and women where wisdom and judgment are concerned. The other things you can learn."

The words washed over me; their heavy pull erased all I'd been taught about a woman's propriety.

Hanming took my hand. "Summer, they're right. It doesn't matter who sits upon the throne. What matters is it's someone your father's followers will listen to."

My heart fluttered as the idea overwhelmed. I pulled away from the group and stood against a wall. How odd. My conscience stepped in at this moment, making me uncomfortable to lie. I had flaunted fabrications to get through Lan troops. Now amongst my own people, they asked me to commit the grandest farce in all of history. And I found it impossible to accept.

Soft steps approached and a familiar hand traced down my arm. "I would like to say this decision is yours alone to make, but it's not," Hanming said. "Our whole lives, we've been taught to put our interests on hold for a greater destiny. I'd been willing to sacrifice everything, and pushed you away." He linked pinkies with me. "Years ago, when you told me you weren't afraid to let our destinies intertwine, I felt as if I were cheating you out of a happy future." Hanming's lips brushed my ear. "I now firmly believe your destiny intertwined with mine because *you* were meant to rule. And *I* am here to support *you*."

Tears brimmed as Hanming's words shook my soul. I took a moment and quieted my emotions. I knew the Ying Guardians were right. The only way to save the Yu Empire was to rally my father's supporters—and quickly. The Lan troops hid just outside our gates. Winter couldn't take the task because if he were to try and discredit the letter, it would appear as if he were trying to hide guilt.

The only option was to present the courts with a son removed from scandal.

I turned to the people in the room. My nerves braced, "I'll do it."

~*~

Disguised as High Court guards, we traveled through the palace gates without question. The Ying Guardians had arranged our summons ahead of time. By the end of the sixth day, we set foot in the High Court.

Spider met us underground. There, the Empress lounged on a stone chair propped by pillows, smiling in greeting. Hanming rushed forward and placed his hands on his mother's shoulders. He asked if she were alright.

Her fingers trailed feebly over his cheek and told him not to worry. She then looked to me. Hanming turned and gave me his hand. "Mother, Summer has agreed to be your second son in my place. With her resemblance to the late Emperor, she'll be accepted."

"But son, what about you?"

"I wish to remain by her side. I'll see to your desire to unite the Kingdoms."

The Empress looked to me with hesitance. "How could she father a child? The Empire will eventually demand an heir!"

"Let us first concern ourselves with reestablishing order. Enemy troops are at our doorstep. When it comes time for an heir, we'll find a solution."

The Empress grasped my hands and beamed. "I should've thought of it myself. You do look *so* much like your father."

Hanming turned to the Ying Guardians, "We need to present the heir through a trusted source. Who has the most followers in the High Court at this time?"

Spider looked agitated as he spoke, "Gui Fengbi."

I snapped my eyes, "Gui Fengbi?" I repeated incredulously. "He's still alive?"

"Yes. In the High Court he holds the most sway."

"What about my father's loyal subjects?" I asked.

"I only know one man we can trust and is still respected by

the High Court," the Empress spoke. "Lord Zhan Ji. We'll need to send for him in the south territory."

I nodded, "He will need to be careful on the return trip with Lan troops scattered throughout the woods. I have a map of areas to avoid."

Hanming chimed, "The tree bandits will likely leave you alone. However, if you run into trouble, give them my name." He looked to me with a grin, "and tell them Summer's too… They've grown fond of her."

Spider assembled a team of Ying Guardians within a few hours and left. Hanming and I couldn't rest with revolution on the brink. Instead, we walked the Ying Guardian's tunnels and listened through walls. What we heard didn't inspire confidence. The Lords held differing opinions on what was to happen with the Empire. Some bribed Generals for protection, with promises of the imperial treasure or new territories.

Others believed the Yu Empire would fall and Zhenxun would return to the Lan Kingdom. They claimed allies in the north promised loyalists high places in the new era. If they joined the north, they could easily wipe out the rest of the Yu's presiding over distant suzerains.

My father's followers fumed over the Empress and her deceptiveness in trying to establish a son of the Lan Kingdom as the heir—damage done by my letter.

Through eavesdropping, I learned who was a true ally and who pretended to support my father. I made it a priority to weed out those who harbored dark intentions. I devised a plan and shared it with Hanming.

"Summer, it's risky," he chided, but I could tell he felt agreeable towards the tactic.

"Oh, Hanming," I shrugged, "Everything I wish to do, you deem risky. Is there anything you'll allow that's not?" I half-teased.

"Either way, I can't stop you, Emperor's heir," he said with a cautious smile.

I took his hands, "Who knew all those years ago when we first met, we'd be standing here today beneath the palace, trying to save the Empire?"

"Never forget Summer. You're the one to save this Empire," his tone grew serious.

"But one day I shall have your child," peered lovingly into his face, brushing a stray eyelash from his cheek. "Then the blood of three Empires shall finally be united. Perhaps then, we can live truthfully, and I can proclaim I'm a woman and your wife."

His lips touched gently to my brow. "As long as we know our truth, it's all that matters to me."

~*~

Zhan Ji's return happened sooner than expected. When news reached me of his arrival, I paced about. I didn't feel adequately prepared to step into the light as a man. I held my hands before my face. They quaked visibly. "What if no one believes I'm my father's *son*?" I closed my eyes and swallowed. "What if my most convincing isn't good enough?" I detailed in my mind how I would speak and carry myself. I would emulate Winter to be a boy, and the Empress for noble posture.

I thought sadly about my mother and the conversation we held concerning the Empress. I'd assured my mother she was the first and most important woman in my life. She'd appeared so happy hearing those words. Now in the public's eye, I was to claim the Empress as mine and forever forego my birthmother. A part of me felt thankful she'd passed. She would've been devastated.

The Empress selected my new name, Yu Taikang. I should've expected her to understand a mother's heart. I thanked her graciously for allowing me keep a part of my birth name.

She gave a weak grin, unable to respond. She had grown incredibly frail and no amount of rice liquor helped. She waved me on my way. I gave a lingering glance as I prepared to exit the tunnels.

I arrived in Zhan Ji's house dressed as a guard. There, Yang Hengyan took me to a private room and revealed princely robes. Her eyes filled with admiration as she cupped my face. "Don't be afraid," her voice spoke, rich with hope, "Your father would be proud."

I thanked her, hiding my fears behind a calm exterior.

We got to work. Yang Hengyan bound my breasts tightly before wrapping layers of silk around my body. A thick sash held everything in place. Then came the outer coat of bold black and gold.

Finally, she fastened a crown to my head that once belonged to my half-brother, Yu Longjing. I invoked his image to mind, hoping to invite his spirit as well.

When finished, I walked in large strides, practicing manly confidence. I stopped before a looking glass and studied myself. Princess Summer was gone and a prince peered back.

"Are you ready?" Yang Hengyan whispered. I gulped, dipping my head.

I exited the chambers and entered the private courtyard where Zhan Ji and Hanming waited. Eight Ying Guardians stood dressed as High Court guards. I looked to Hanming for support and he offered a loving smile.

"Now, young Prince," Zhan Ji spoke softly, "You can no longer be caught making eyes at my son. Tread carefully and always be weary of your surroundings."

"Yes, my Lord," I began to curtsy, but caught myself. I lifted my nose in the air and cleared my throat. "I am ready."

~*~

Zhan Ji called a meeting to discuss issues of the south territory. Respected by the majority of the courts, they assembled despite disagreements. Gui Fengbi sulked about with his supporters. He couldn't afford to miss the meeting lest he lose face.

As I entered with Zhan Ji, hundreds of eyes burned into me. Murmurs filled the air, but I kept my head high and eyes forward.

I strutted to the front of the room.

Zhan Ji stopped short of the throne and bowed to me. I continued forward as gasps arose.

Nostalgia struck me as hints of my father's radiant hue lingered around the imperial seat. I envisioned him nodding in approval. I turned and faced the room. On cue, Zhan Ji dusted his sleeves and bowed low. "Long live the Yu heir!" he declared. The Ying Guardians dressed as High Court guards knelt behind Zhan Ji and echoed his decree.

Before me, Lords and High Court officials alike dropped to their knees in disjointed confusion. Some let their eyes linger over my face before knocking their foreheads to the ground.

"Long live the Yu heir! May he live ten thousand years!" sounded throughout the space, barely in unison.

Despite the grin of triumph, I shook terribly. I locked my hands behind my back so none could see them tremble. "All rise," I called, remembering to keep my voice a low pitch.

The mass shifted to their feet, their eyes remaining on the ground.

I called on Zhan Ji. He stepped forward, but kept his head properly bowed. "I want to know why I wasn't summoned when my father and elder brothers passed," I demanded.

Zhan Ji nodded and turned to the room. "Yu Taikang, the second son of the late Emperor and the Empress, wishes to know why he wasn't sent for at his father's passing, and at the loss of his brothers."

All remained speechless. Finally, an official I recognized as a supporter of my father stepped forward. He bowed to the ground and spoke humbly. "Your majesty, I apologize on behalf of the High Court. We didn't know of your birth. Had we known the Emperor and the Empress had a second son, we would surely have sent for you."

Gui Fengbi stepped forward unexpectedly and knelt. "Pardon me your majesty, but do you have proof that you're indeed the son of our late Emperor? I'm only asking because after your elder brother, Yu Longjing passed away, the Empress tested your half-brother's from the Emperor's second wife in order to find an heir. The real question is: why your own mother didn't summon you."

I could feel the air in the room changing as the thought infected others. Gui Fengbi challenged my authenticity. I secretly felt pleased. I'd wanted to call him out and deface him, but now he offered himself.

"Have you not looked upon the face of the young Prince?" Zhan Ji scolded. "He wears the same face as the Emperor!"

"It's quite alright, Lord Zhan," I help up a hand. He glanced to me in surprise. I was going off script. The crown heir never lowered himself to explaining. Others always defended on his behalf.

I marched to Gui Fengbi. My glare bore down. "The question's fair," I said, careful to keep my voice level. "There's a reason why my mother and father sent me away. You see, I was raised in the Tangut Kingdom because they're peaceful. I have a condition and my mother felt it would be too much stress for me to succeed the throne."

"I'm sorry, your majesty," Gui Fengbi bowed, "I didn't know you had a health condition." I could hear joy in his voice. I suspected he plotted to assassinate me and blame it on this condition. "One more thing your majesty," though he kept his head to the ground, he spoke for many to hear. "Can you please address the issue of the letter that's surfaced? The one Princess Summer wrote to her brother from the Lan Kingdom?"

"Princess Summer has been visiting me and our sisters in the Tangut Kingdom. She hasn't been to the Lan Kingdom *at all*. Therefore, this letter couldn't have originated from her." I turned to the room. "Have any of you questioned the authenticity of the letter? Did you not think it possible to be forged by those who wish to sabotage the Yu Empire?"

No one dared speak. I single handedly reversed the damage my careless letter had caused.

I challenged, "Are there others who deny my lineage to the late Emperor?"

All remained silent.

Zhan Ji stepped forward, "Let it show on the imperial records that Prince Yu Taikang has returned to assume the throne. I move for his coronation before the end of this moon!"

Throughout the room, the majority of Lords and officials proclaimed their support to Zhan Ji's motion. Even Gui Fengbi put on a false face and uttered backing.

I nodded satisfactorily. The first stage of the plan completed and I had garnered support of my father's High Court. Next, we needed to obtain stability within the lower courts and round up troops. The Lan Kingdom had most likely dispatched messengers to the east bridge by now.

Before dismissal, the Lords and officials approached me and offered their blessings. Many snuck peeks over sleeves, studying my features. I didn't budge, knowing I was my father's child.

In private, Zhan Ji said he couldn't stay for the coronation. He needed to return south and prepare our Generals for return. I encouraged him to leave quickly before the Lan Kingdom could mobilize. He wished me best of luck and went on his way.

Chapter Thirty-Six:
The Emperor's Secret

In the days leading to my coronation, I spent most nights in the Ying Guardians' lair. Spider even allowed me into tunnels once forbidden, saying they now belonged to me. They led to private residences of the Lords and High Court members.

Despite discomfort, I eavesdropped on private conversations. Mostly it was casual banter, but some nights I stumbled on plots against me. A seed of darkness took root in my heart. Sometimes I became infuriated to where I wished to stab through the walls and kill them.

"Don't take it to heart," The Empress told me. "They've lost themselves and can no longer see people as living beings with a life flame. They only see game pieces."

"That's sickening."

"Yes," she nodded, "But at times you've done the same and you must know you'll continue to do the same whether you wish it. Your soldiers exist for you to dispatch," She waved a finger, "but always remember they're alive. Don't force them to lose their life unless there are no other routes."

A vein throbbed in my temple. "Empress, I've lied and murdered, but can still live with myself. Does this mean I am losing myself?"

"Help me to my room," she commanded weakly. I lifted her to her feet, alarmed by how light she felt. We shuffled to a simple dirt cave with a wooden door. A scent stirred the air and awakened sentiments in my chest. As we entered the Empress' sectioned-off quarters, I noticed a vase of orange blossoms. I couldn't help but stare longingly at the out-of-season flower. There was only one place she could've gotten them from.

"I always loved strolling by your mother's courtyard," she beamed. "I asked Spider to pick some sprigs for me."

My mother had kept a small house where the trees were tended to year round. It touched me to know someone still cared for them.

I lowered the Empress onto a seat beside the table and she broke off a branch. She held the petals to her nose and inhaled deeply. She turned and soft amber filled her eyes. "We never survive without a few sins. It doesn't mean you're losing yourself." the wrinkles at the corners of her face deepened as she handed the flowers to me. "Always remember your innocence. It'll lead you to make proper decisions."

I thanked her, gazing wistfully at the petals. Orange blossoms symbolized innocence. If they could persevere in the harshest conditions, so could I.

The short walk left the Empress tired and she wished to rest. I retreated to my quarters and changed into princely robes. As I exited the arena, four Ying Guardians dressed as imperial guards immediately fell in step. With them accompanying me, I strolled to the garden by the library and glanced around. The stones, trees, and water didn't change. Autumn approached and the leaves took on the hue of flames.

Yet… the energy of the garden felt stagnant, as if changing seasons drained it of vitality. I eyed a large stone I used to climb as a child, fathoming it to be a mountain. It had seemed so large then. Having seen the Tanguts' mountains, the stone was now merely a pebble.

"Maybe I'm the one who's different," I mumbled under my breath.

I continued to meander and passed my mother's courtyard. I slowed my steps and fought the urge to peek inside. I didn't know if anyone watched, but I needed to pretend that I had no connection with her.

I felt my heart twist as her place fell behind me.

Before returning to the Ying Guardians' arena, I went to my princely chambers to take dinner; for appearances. I watched keenly as servants tasted my food. For the first time in my life, I genuinely felt concerned someone might poison me.

When the food proved safe, I ate to keep my strength. But as I chewed, thoughts plagued me. I didn't know what to expect after being crowned Emperor. Somehow, I needed to unite my domain and push back enemy troops. One wrong move and countless lives could be lost. But how was I to do all that?

My appetite left. I set down my chopsticks and ordered the dishes to be taken away.

Alone, I sprawled upon the ornate bed and stared at the carved canopy. Surrounding all four sides were embroidered silk curtains drawn by rich cords. Once, I used to admire beautiful things. Now, all I saw was endless wasted hours of carving wood.

I tossed for a while, finding the bed uncomfortable. I'd grown accustomed to sleeping on the ground or in trees. A few moments later, I gave up with an irritated sigh.

A knock came at my door and I called out, dismissing the intrusion. I thought with amusement that I was becoming quite a spoiled prince.

The door opened and I sat up with great annoyance. To my surprise, Hanming entered. He closed the door silently and placed a wooden bar to lock it in place. I walked towards him as my heart quickened. Without another word, he took my face in his hands and kissed me passionately. My body turned to water as his breath flowed into me.

"I've missed you," he said woefully.

"I've longed for you too."

"I'm sorry I couldn't come sooner. We've been watching some suspicious Lords to ensure your safety," he explained.

"We're alone now. Some of the Ying Guardians are standing guard to protect your privacy."

"Do we have the night?" I asked, afraid to hope.

He smiled, "Yes. And my mother's blessing." Hanming took me by the hand and led me to my bed. We sat side-by-side, bashfully.

"Do you think it's strange I am dressed as a man?" I asked self-consciously.

"Summer, I've seen you wear many outfits. Let it be bandit furs, Tangut garbs, or a Lan soldier's uniform. It doesn't matter how you're clothed. When I look into your eyes, I know you're the girl I fell in love with in our youth."

"Hanming, why do you love me?" I asked, heart open and vulnerable.

"Love needs no reason. I simply do," he kissed me. I slid my body closer as he reached around my waist. Hanming removed the heavy sash holding my robes and I untied his uniform. We moved deeper into the bed as I pulled the silk curtains closed.

A halo of cerulean encapsulated us.

By my coronation day, I'd laid to rest reservations towards ascension. I'd grown into my identity as Yu Taikang. I climbed the steps leading to the highest terrace and seated myself upon the throne. Hundreds of officials knelt in reverence. If they knew I was a woman, I would instantly be executed.

Fortunately, Princess Summer had been gone from the palace

long enough no one remembered exactly how she appeared. All they saw was Yu Taikang's resemblance to my father.

I opened the coronation with a prayer, giving thanks to the heavens for my mandate to rule. Before a massive stone carving of the Three Sovereigns, I lit sticks of incense and bowed, "Please bestow graces upon the Yu Empire."

A crystal bowl of liquid set on a silk square appeared before me. I pricked my finger and deposited a drop of blood. I did not know the specific recipe to the fluid, but if I did not contain the blood of a ruling line—blessed by the Three Sovereigns, the drop would've turned black.

My blood beaded at the bottom, a rich carmine. I caught a few slouches of disappointment.

Next, the Lords recited memorials. As rote droned, I kept a sincere expression, but my thoughts went to clandestine conversations I'd overhead. It took much control to keep my features still when those who plotted against me moved within striking range.

The memorials completed in half a day—a sign many held reservations against me. Out of respect, the recitation of memorials should've have taken days.

Finally came the accession edict.

The edict did not take as long as the memorials. With the *ruyi* placed in my hand, I became Emperor. Fanfares burst all around and a celebratory procession commenced. I stepped into a golden sedan and it lifted me high. Court performers danced and entertained. Officials remained bowed, but all I saw where hiding snakes. I imagined the scowling features of some and trembled with anger. I warned myself to be careful. I could inadvertently slip into paranoia like Prince Ku Rentu.

My mother once told me a tale of a little fox crossing an ice-covered pond. He became overly excited as his eyes roved the distance. He didn't watch what was immediately before him and stepped onto thin ice. He crashed through. It reminded that while I watched people and events around me, I shouldn't forget to watch myself, lest I make a mistake.

The procession brought us to the banquet hall where a lavish feast appeared. Court performers continued to entertain. The past hailed when I laid eyes on Tomato and Red. But they didn't recognize me.

Lords and members of the High Court made toasts wishing for my health. I graciously raised my tri-legged cup and sipped fragrant liquor. We drank in tense celebration.

After my cup emptied, I drew eyes across my subjects as the ruler of my father's Empire. Now, my Empire. How many were a threat?

~*~

In the days immediately following my ascension, much business needed attending. First, I pardoned the Empress. The joy of having her council was cut short when I noticed her further diminished health. Days of hiding took its toll. The need to slow Lan Kingdom troops demanded from me and I could do little besides send the best physicians to her.

I took a gamble and ordered my most loyal Generals to take top troops out of the palace. I gave them a copy of the Lan troop's rotation map and instructed them to sabotage bases. They weren't to kill unless necessary. If the opportunity rose to negotiate peace, I didn't wish to have slaughtered people on my hands.

With many trusted Generals gone, I was left vulnerable. I turned to the scheme I'd devised before my coronation, to contend with those who bore me ill will.

I called a meeting of the Lords, informing them I wished to address my health. I knew many were eager to learn of my weakness. Rumors had circulated, speculating on the condition that initially removed from the imperial line.

I entered the grand hall and seated myself upon the throne. Ying Guardians hid amongst imperial guards, watching attentively. As a child, I'd often peaked past the gates, into the imperial chamber. I'd seen my father speaking bold words. The throne had seemed so far away then. Now as I found myself upon it, it was too close for comfort. My words and actions would become law. I couldn't be too vigilant.

During formalities, I dabbled and spoke eloquently addressing affairs of the Empire. I sensed rigidity. To the souls bowed before me, I was an unknown. My actions were unpredictable and they didn't know how to leverage me. Even my father's allies twitched warily.

"When Lord Zhan first introduced me, I mentioned a condition of mine," I addressed when the formalities finished. I looked to Gui Fengbi with his head hung low. "Some of you assumed this is a medical condition. I promise, my health is in good order and I shall not be leaving this world before my time." I caught the subtlest of trembles as edges of robes flicked from jerking wrists. I waited, letting uncertainty stew.

Once satisfied, I continued, "I have a rare condition… I can hear evil thoughts of men. Since youth, I knew dissonance festered within our palace. The loud and ominous voices of those who wished to harm my father terrified me and I was sent away. After extensive training, I've learned to control this ability."

Agitation rose in the room, and I caught glimpses of stormy colors. The officials who wished me dead became most anxious. Despite skepticism, many were troubled by the chance I spoke the truth.

"If a court is filled with traitors, then what need do I have for them?" I challenged.

Gui Fengbi stepped forward and bowed with pomposity, a feat I didn't know was possible. "Powerful Emperor, no one here is traitor to you!"

Other officials followed suit and knocked their heads before me.

I slammed my ink stone on the table as I'd often seen my father do. The room went silent as trepidation filled the air. I took my time, rising deliberately. I remained on the pedestal but paced with slow, angry steps. I let the officials tremble. The longer they feared, the more open to suggestion they'd be.

When I felt satisfied no more outbursts would occur, I lowered onto the throne once more. I picked up the ruyi scepter. "Official He Rinsi, you have conspired with magistrate Mang Pao to bribe three Generals in the Middle Court to pledge you their troops. You're waiting to see where I stand politically before instigating a coup."

The two men I called threw themselves to the ground and denied allegations. I'd overheard their conversation through Ying Guardian tunnels. These men didn't have the worst intentions for the Empire. The troops of three Middle Court Generals could hardly cause a coup. Regardless, I stripped them of rank and ordered them to be taken to prison on the charge of conspiracy. I relied on their distress to spread to the more challenging culprits.

I swept my eyes across the room. "General Bin Geng, you have secret agents in the south working to destabilize the government. You've also been sending messengers to Lan Kingdom troops hidden in the woods. You're informing them of our numbers and the divide in the High Court." I lowered my head. "You dared to inform them of my father's passing."

"Please!" General Bin Geng dropped to his knees, "I'm sorry!" A gasp tore through the crowd as they witnessed what they believed was a heavenly power.

"I'm not finished! General Bin Geng, you conspired with agents in the territory to murder my half-brother from my father's third wife. Such an act against imperial blood is punishable by death without trial."

"No! It wasn't me!" he pleaded.

"It WAS you!" I shouted. "Did you not share this secret with Official Man Keshen? You even suggested I should've been handled the same way if my existence was known."

General Bin Geng paled.

"Guards!" I called.

"At your service, Emperor!"

I took my time lifting the brush. On a vertical slat of bamboo, I wrote, "Beheading," and tossed it to the ground.

General Bin Geng stared in stupor. When soldiers moved to take him away, he peered to me with hardened eyes. "You and your bloodline aren't fit to rule!" he spat in my direction. "Consider yourself lucky. If you didn't end my life today, I would've surely taken yours!"

I narrowed my eyes, hiding terror. "Take him outside." I commanded brusquely.

Imperial guards dragged General Bing Geng away. He continued to challenge with a cold stare. Unrelenting, I held his gaze, refusing to concede.

For Ting.

Soon, he was out of the grand hall and I heard an imperial guard announce his sentence. I gulped as the sound of a blade reached my ears.

Though greatly disturbed, I wasn't finished. I needed to eliminate the largest threats, so smaller ones would be frightened into rethinking their stance.

"Your majesty!" Gui Fengbi knocked his head to the ground once more, "How can you issue such a sentence in your first days of ruling? Forgive me, but do you not question if you have all the facts?"

I ground my teeth. I'd wanted to save him for last, but he was always so troublesome. "Official Gui Fengbi," I addressed. "General Bin Geng wasn't alone in his plot to assassinate my half-brothers. Would you like to share with the court who assassinated Yu Ting? Or shall I inform them of your treason?"

"Please!" he begged, "Let me stand trial! I was coerced into evil things by Lord Jin Su! The thoughts you read in my head aren't my own! They were planted there!"

"Yes, please let him stand trial!" another mortified official spoke.

I turned to him. He'd been in my sights too. "You harbored a plot to murder my father. Were you not one to conspire with his consort, Feili?" I'd heard his confession through the walls.

"No!" the official gasped, his eyes revealing all.

I lifted my brush again. The officials held their breaths as I dipped it in ink. It was the brush that decided their fate. Its wielder felt unforgiving. Another bamboo slat slid into my hand. In sweeping strokes, the characters "Beheading" appeared once more.

I tossed it before the official who spoke in Gui Fengbi's defense. He looked to me with large eyes, unable to comprehend his fate. The imperial guards dragged him away. My stomach churned; but the darkness in my heart felt justified.

"Official Gui," I turned back to him, "If you wish to have a trial, I'll grant it to you as a show of mercy. However, be warned. All your sins shall be revealed."

"Yes, thank you!" he knocked his head on the ground.

"The trial shall begin in two hours," I declared.

"Your majesty!" Gui Fengbi exclaimed, "That's not adequate time to prepare my defense!"

"I can take away your privilege," I glowered.

He fell silent.

"Dismissed."

Gui Fengbi lefted disjointedly.

Over the next hour, I gave four more executions, eliminating the most dangerous of my enemies. Two more had conspired the murder of my mother and father. Another two actively colluded with the north and south, pushing for the overthrow of Zhenxun.

"I know there are more with ill wishes. It's because you haven't acted that I've spared you. Just remember, moves against he Empire will not be tolerated."

I released the court, instructing them to reconvene for Gui Fengbi's trial. With quavering hands and ashen faces, they retreated from sight.

With the convincing demonstration of my "condition," I knew some believed heaven truly did ordain me to rule. Others likely feared me to be a demon sent to bring the Empire's downfall. It didn't matter what they thought as long as they believed I could see into their minds.

I thought fear could be used to control them. Unfortunately, I'd gone too far. I could only execute those who had confessed ill deeds while I eavesdropped. The most dangerous kept their secrets unspoken. Men far more nefarious than those that I'd executed grew restless. They saw it imperative to contend with me before I could read their thoughts.

I ambled in the imperial gardens, wishing to be alone before Gui Fengbi's trial. I ordered my guards to follow at a distance and entered a walled off area filled with decorated brush. The guards looked on from the entranceway.

I bent down and picked the autumn bloom of an imported dahlia. I took a moment and sniffed deeply. The petals tickled my cheek and in a feminine motion, I tilted my head, drawing the flower over my lips. I thought of Hanming, hoping pleasant thoughts would chase away the morbidity of the executions.

A heavy footfall startled my reverie. I tossed the flower aside and straightened my body to stand like a man. I turned to see a blade at my chin. At the other end stood the angry pock-marked face of Gui Fengbi. "I can't allow you to take away all I've worked for!" he hissed.

"What have you worked for?" I demanded coolly, "A promotion to governor? What good will it do if this Empire falls?"

"It doesn't matter," he seethed, "Even if this Empire falls, I will take a chunk of its wealth!"

I was in no real danger. Gui Fengbi handled the sword awkwardly. He let out a laugh and poked my neck. I placed two fingers against the blade and held it at a distance. "Tell me, Emperor-who-can-read-my-thoughts, what am I thinking now?"

I gave a coy smile and dipped my chin like a lady. "You're thinking I am Princess Summer," I used my woman's voice.

Confusion crossed Gui Fengbi's face as he stumbled back. He opened his lips to cry out. Before he could utter a sound, I moved in a smooth motion and disarmed him. Using his sword, I cut out his tongue with a swift flick. I slapped it into the pond for the fish with the tip of the blade. As he howled, Gui Fengbi moved his hands to his mouth.

In another swipe, I cut off his fingers.

He would live. But the secret of my identity remained safe, torturing him to the end of his days.

"Guards!" I shouted. "This man has made an attempt on my life. Take him to the prisons. He's waived his right to trial."

~*~

Later that evening, the Ying Guardians expressed their disdain with my actions. Even Hanming said I'd gone too far. I didn't falter as I explained I didn't wish to for anyone to suspect I was a woman. So, I acted boldly as a man.

"A man's actions aren't measured by hard-handedness," Spider explained with a frown, "It's about knowing when to give and take. Summer, you've made yourself countless new enemies, *and* revealed you can fight.”

“I thought if they feared me, they’d obey,” I said, perhaps more dismissively than I’d intended.

Spider shook his head in disappointment, “Fear only works to serve the weak-minded. With intelligent and educated High Court officials, fear motivates the opposite way. They’ll stop at nothing until their interests are protected.”

“Can I not execute all those who oppose me?” I asked glumly.

Normally a tranquil person, Spider’s face reddened at my words. He openly scolded, “Have you forgotten the value of life?”

“The people who plot against me are no longer human because they cannot value life,” I responded in impudence.

“Are you hearing yourself?” he demanded. I folded my arms. His eyes softened. “Are you sure you’re not acting from fear?”

The words struck a chord and I stuttered. I felt color drain from my face.

Yes. I have been terrified all this time!

Nothing comprehensible left my lips.

Spider must’ve read my emotions. He suggested perhaps it was time the Emperor “caught a fever.” What he meant was I should disappear for a few days and set aside my duty as Yu Taikang.

We finally agreed on something and I changed from the Emperor’s robes into the dress of a common maid. During this time, I tended to the Empress and informed her on all that’d transpired.

Her face grew distraught and in a gentle voice disciplined me for being foolish. She agreed with Spider. Even with the Ying Guardians watching, my life would be at greater risk.

There was nothing I could say to comfort her. She fell asleep blubbering. I felt guilt at causing her restlessness.

That night I stayed with Hanming in his private room near the Empress' chambers. It was small and the walls thin, but I didn't mind. I curled beside him and listened to the music of his heart. His arm clutched my shoulders as if I'd fly away if his grip loosened. We chattered quietly about nothing in particular for a while.

"Hanming, was I wrong to execute those men?" I asked eventually.

"Yes and no," he responded. "I don't wish you to bear the burden of ending their lives. Such a display of power from the Emperor can only have one effect and that's to push hidden enemies into the open. However, sometimes drastic actions must be made."

"It sounds like you don't agree," I mumbled miserably.

"My mother told me about your encounter with the Lan King. It seems you're behaving like him, with much to prove." He squeezed my shoulders. "I swore to support you. If you believe your actions were justified, then I won't question them. But perhaps you're trying too hard to act the way you think a man should. Consider approaching situations more as yourself."

His words gave me much to ponder. Coupled with Spider's

suggestion that I acted from fear, I slowly came to see the root of my behavior. Still carrying bitterness from the loss of my father and mother, I'd used my position to exact revenge.

I sighed and buried my face into Hanming's chest. "Reproach me please, so I may find some redemption. What I did wasn't for justice, but for me," I refused to admit fault to anyone but him.

He kissed my neck. "My mother once said women were made to celebrate life. Men don't have this instinct, which is why we go to war. Perhaps a woman's touch is what's needed to end conflicts."

Little did I know, it was too late to change tactics. My enemies mobilized.

Chapter Thirty-Seven:
Abduction

When I returned to the post of Emperor, the Empress paid me a visit. She entered with slow steps, leaning heavily on a maid. I asked if she'd seen the physician and she dismissed my words.

"I've heard things," she said in a low whisper. "There are people plotting to move against you soon. They fear your ability to read thoughts. It's imperative you call back your loyal Generals." Her eyes hardened. "You need them to protect you, and you must ask Zhan Ji to come sooner. We are on the brink of revolution, and you're surrounded by those who don't trust you."

I took her advice and sent two groups of Ying Guardians to deliver messages. The first returned in a few days reporting that my Generals in the woods had successfully sabotaged many bases and were on their return. They also informed me of Lan Kingdom troops ordered to mobilize against Zhenxun. Additional platoons of over ten thousand soldiers were headed in from the east bridge.

My sabotage of the west bridge only bought a little over a moon.

This new information caused me to waver. Wary of an attack on the palace, I needed support at the outer walls. I couldn't dispatch Generals whose loyalties I questioned. The best decision would be to keep trusted Generals posted outside the palace.

This would leave me still surrounded by enemies during a critical time.

Ultimately, I recalled Spider's words about those who were honored to die for me. Why should I not risk my life as well?

So, I gambled and sent word to my trusted Generals to remain at the outer gates. The militants left in the High and Middle Court were unpredictable. It seemed likely I had a few allies within them, but enemies lurked for certain.

I thought back to an idiom my father once used. Our Empire had become like a sagging ridgepole. Strong on the outside, but the center threatened to break.

The days passed agonizingly for me. Time in the High Court seemed frozen. All spoke in soft voices, sensitive to the impending battle.

The breaking of the ridgepole.

~*~

Days passed and news reached of the outer walls. My loyal troops were being slaughtered. It reminded me how poorly prepared I was to be Emperor. Unlike my brothers, I was never educated on war strategies. I felt overwhelmed to say the least.

The Empress offered a solution. She spoke with Hanming and me in private before addressing the Ying Guardians. Hanming objected adamantly.

"Son," she said sternly, "I must surrender myself as the murderer of the Lan King. If I don't, the slaughter of our troops will continue. Summer's in danger and she needs her trusted Generals to remain alive. I'm not long for this world anyway and this is a fair trade. My life for the lives of thousands."

"Mother," he stressed.

Seeing him hurt choked my heart. The Empress was only in this position because of my brash actions.

"Stop it, son," she scolded. "This isn't about you or me. I've already made my choice."

Hanming clenched his jaw but accepted her decision. The Empress turned to me, "Summer, don't look so perplexed. I know you must feel this is your fault, but in truth, I'm the one who assassinated their ruler. Sooner or later, I would need to pay the price."

Her words rang true, but I didn't feel better. What price would I pay for my deeds? What were the Ying Guardians thinking, placing a girl like me on the throne?

Tearfully, I nodded. The Empress squeezed my hand. I left her alone with Hanming to say farewell and sequestered myself in the Emperor's chambers. I remained there for days, refusing to take food or company.

When word reached me that the Lan Kingdom accepted the

Empress' surrender, I brought a hand to my mouth. Sobs tore through me as I acknowledged losing one of my closest allies.

There was no method to discover what became of the Empress. Perhaps the north put her out of her suffering. I wished to believe she was freed from earthly pain.

I couldn't bring myself to seek Hanming; and he didn't come to me. I secretly felt grateful, too afraid to face him. How could I offer comfort if I was a part of the reason she'd offered her life?

Dismay filled my heart as I questioned whether he despised me.

As I distressed over Hanming and the Empress, High Court officials held a banquet to celebrate the easing of Lan Kingdom attacks due to her surrender. I didn't feel it appropriate, but feared the consequence of not attending.

With a long face, I sat through the meal. Imperial performers entertained and Tomato presented me with a young dancer who was to keep me company for the night.

Without looking, I prepared to dismiss the dancer, but a familiar, pearly hue flashed forward. My breath caught as my eyes darted to her face. Silk Deer knelt before me! Myriads of questions danced on the tip of my tongue, but they needed to wait until we were in private.

Silk Deer performed an act with climbing and balance, something she excelled at from living in trees. Afterwards she was seated behind me. I glanced continuously her way, but she kept silent, head down. Some officials joked they were learning what type of women held my interest. I laughed along, feeling awkward.

After the banquet, we were escorted to my private chambers. The Ying Guardians began to lead Silk Deer away but I called a stop. They studied me for a moment and I reassured them. Hesitant, they left Silk Deer.

No sooner did the door shut, I felt heavy hands on my body. I found myself flipped to the ground with Silk Deer pinning me, a thin knife at my throat. Her eyes threatened, "You're not a legitimate son to the throne. Who are you?"

I couldn't contain exuberance. I guffawed and Silk Deer's face crossed with consternation. Her body remained tense as I tried to cease laughter and speak. The relief wouldn't let up. She slapped my face and it stunned me momentarily. "Silk Deer," I finally gathered my wits. Her eyes filled with disbelief that I knew her name. "It's me, Summer!"

"Summer?" She reached forward and loosened my robes until she reached the bottom layer. She saw my breasts tightly bound. "Summer!" she echoed with joy. She squeezed me as I shushed her, reminding that my identity was secret.

She nodded, now her turn to laugh hysterically.

We stayed awake chatting. Silk Deer told me about the tree bandits fixing the rope bridge. On the north bank, they found Winter. She felt overjoyed to see him alive. However, he was agitated, saying he needed to return home as soon as possible. He'd learned of a civil war brewing in the Lan Kingdom.

Winter then finally confessed to Silk Deer his identity as a son of the Yu Emperor. She didn't believe him at first and played along for amusement. Only when they reached the palace and Winter shared plans to sneak in did she suspect he told the truth.

"Where's my brother now?"

"Stuck in the Middle Courts with Elk. He warned me that the current Emperor is an imposter and should be assassinated. We never imagined it was you!"

"How did you make it into the High Court?" I asked.

"Winter told me you used to train with imperial entertainers. I auditioned, saying you recommended me. Your cousins Tomato and Red immediately accepted. They've treated me very well." The look on her face changed. "Oh, I almost forgot," she said. "Winter asked me to give you this letter should I run into you. I always hide it on me for safekeeping."

Silk Deer reached into her robes and pulled out a small envelope. She handed over the paper as she shook her head, still marveling at me being the Emperor. I opened the letter.

Summer, I left the Tanguts after hearing news of the Lan civil war. Half of their Kingdom wishes to coronate Prince Ku Rentu, the other wishes to respect the late King's decree that Prince Ku Rentu is a madman. The one thing they agree on is attacking the Yu Empire for assassinating their King.

Silk Deer, Elk and I have managed to infiltrate the lower courts in Zhenxun. My instinct tells me you're in the High Court, but I cannot find information on you. I'm wondering if you're hiding.

Do you remember the chest we found in the ruins of the Tai Empire? I'd left it with the tree bandits. During my latest stay with them, I opened it. Inside are journals like the one Mother used to read. These were kept by Tai royals too. Some detail the fall of the Tai Empire. In the last few weeks, I've read vigorously and am almost done. Some information is disturbing.

According to a younger brother of the last Tai Emperor, the Yao of the Lan family had a large population in the Tai Empire. They systematically poisoned the Tai with false medicines, betraying their trust. They also barricaded the Tai on the east coast even though the Empire foresaw the ocean rising.

Afterwards, they drove the Tai out of the land so they couldn't rebuild. It's the Yao who became blood bandits. The journals weren't clear if any of the Yao remain in the Yu Empire, but one thing can be certain. If the Lan can give rise to people like the Yao, they cannot be trusted.

I'm sure by now you've discovered the Yu Empire has selected a new Emperor. This person is supposedly a second son by our father and the Empress. I know you trust the Empress, but I have reservations. There's no other brother of age in our family to become Emperor. There's a terrible lie in our home and I need you to be careful. If anyone discovers we're children of our late father, our lives will be lost.

Until I see you dear sister, protect yourself.

"Silk Deer, have you read this?" I asked.

No response came. I looked over and saw her breathing deeply, eyes closed. I tucked the letter deep in my robes and snuggled beside her. I suddenly felt tired, and finally safe. Discussion could wait as slumber glided over me.

~*~

In the morning, sounds of servants bringing breakfast woke me. I quickly tightened my robes to hide my womanhood. Silk Deer started and looked around as if she didn't recognize her surroundings. Once she saw me, her face relaxed.

I dismissed the servants and they bowed out respectfully. Silk Deer jumped to her feet and grabbed a steamed bun.

"Wait, don't eat that!" I warned.

"Why not?"

"It could be poisoned!"

"Oh," she looked disappointed but tossed the bun back. She laughed, "My, what an exciting life you're living!"

"Silk Deer, did you read the letter my brother gave to you?" I asked, picking up from last night. She shook her head. "Did he tell you about the Lan and Yao family?" I tried again.

"Yes," she said slowly, "He said the Yao are the now blood bandits. He also said to kill any Lan the moment I discover their identity."

"I'm afraid my brother doesn't have it completely right. Not all people from the Lan family are bad. It appears it's just the Yao sect."

"I really had no idea what he was saying," Silk Deer shrugged. She frowned and rubbed her stomach, "Can we get something safe to eat?"

I smiled, "Sure."

After Silk Deer was fed with the servants, she returned to the imperial entertainers. I promised to keep in touch.

~*~

Despite cordial appearances, I could sense something amiss in the High Court. Auras alerted me. The colors coming off many officials seemed foul. I felt unsure if they birthed from anxiety or ill intent.

When I found a free moment, I summoned Quan Bao of the Ying Guardians. I informed him of my brother in the Middle Court and asked him to locate Winter. I also told him about Silk Deer and Elk as my allies.

Quan Bao nodded and went on his way.

I wanted to give him a message for Hanming too, but wasn't sure if I felt ready to see my husband. Instead, I returned to my duties as the Emperor and didn't retire until late in the evening. I dismissed my servants and barred the door.

"Summer?" My body tensed to hear Hanming's voice in the dark. I turned apprehensively and saw him exit a hidden corridor. Mourning darkened his eyes.

Words escaped and I could only stand in shame.

He stopped a few paces away and neither of us spoke; the air a heavy gray.

"Do you hate me?" I finally blurted.

"No. Do you hate me?" he asked. "I'm sorry I haven't come

to see you, I've been sulking."

"Don't apologize!" I rushed to place a hand against his chest.

Hanming shook his head, "My mother was right. Her surrender was a necessity. Even if our Empire is strong, the Lan wouldn't have stopped until she gave herself." His words grew tearful and I knew he suffered.

I lifted my fingertips and touched his cheek. Wetness came away. I led him to my bed and seated us on the edge. Finding a silk handkerchief, I dabbed his tears. No words were spoken as Hanming laid his head in my lap. I cradled him as he wept.

We fell asleep and awoke shortly before sunrise. With lamps burned out, a musty glow filled the room, matching our dense mood. He promised he wasn't upset with me, but I told him it didn't matter. I was upset with myself.

"Would the rest of our lives be like this? Stealing moments here and there?" I asked.

"It's better than never having you."

"Is it selfish to wish for more?"

"I don't know, Summer. But I too wish to come home to you every day without worries of losing our lives."

"Hanming, Winter's in the Middle Courts. I've asked Quan Bao to find him," I said, hoping to brighten his mood with good news.

"That's marvelous!"

"He has a distrust of the Lan family, especially the Yao bloodline. I think you need to tell him about your father," I said.

Hanming nodded, "As soon as Quan Bao finds him, I'll speak with Winter."

We heard servants shuffling, preparing to serve breakfast. Hanming left swiftly through the secret passage and I dressed myself before unbarring the door.

Little did I know, the night I shared with Hanming was the last peaceful moment I'd have for a long time.

Servants tested my breakfast and I waved them away. I preferred eating in private. It allowed me to organize my thoughts for the day.

As I lifted rice to my lips, discomfort settled in my chest. At first, I thought it was lingering irritation from damp night air. I finished half my bowl before realizing the subtle sensation had spread.

Then it struck me. My routine was predictable. I always dismissed my servants after they tested my food. Poison would've shown symptoms immediately, a blue hue on the lips or darkened fingernails.

Slow-acting paralysis powder didn't present signs.

An unsuspecting taste tester could be stricken up to an hour after leaving my chambers. My enemies didn't need poison to kill me. They merely needed to render me helpless.

I tried jumping to my feet, but crashed to the floor. Only a low moan sounded when I tried calling for help. My eyelids grew heavy as extremities lost feeling. The last thing I saw were blurry figures approaching, their auras an ominous sanguine.

Chapter Thirty-Eight:
The Number Four

The number four. It sounds like "death." Born as the fourth child to the fourth wife, even my wedding day fell on the fourth. The number four: a dreaded number most wished to avoid, appeared ceaselessly in my life; demanding I become intimate with it.

I felt swaying, indicating I moved. My consciousness wavered as I sensed woven reeds around me—most likely a large basket. Would the culprits drop me in a pond and let me drown?

I tried to strike, but my limbs wouldn't obey. I opened my mouth, but only gargling sounds emerged. I should've been terrified, but instead felt indignant. I refused to let this basket be the end of me.

As my vision gradually returned, I noticed specks of light. The basket contained a covering with holes for breathing.

How courteous.

The specks disappeared. We'd entered indoors.

A jolt shot through me as I felt myself dropped to the ground. Numbness dulled any pain as air rushed from my lungs in a muted grunt. The top of the basket came off. I wished to lift my head, but couldn't budge.

Rough hands pulled me out. Through blurred vision, I identified menacing auras. After some shuffling, I found myself in a box. A slat of wood held my neck in place and my hands secured before me. Once my captors felt confident I couldn't escape, they poured a foul-smelling mixture down my throat. Someone held my nose and I swallowed in reflex. When cloudiness of mind receded, I discovered myself alone.

The mixture burned in my stomach and I assumed I'd been finally poisoned.

Moments later, sensation returned to my fingers. It appeared they had fed me an antidote. Once able to move my neck, I looked around to see I sat in a storage room. I called out, challenging the kidnappers. There was no response and no footfalls.

Using the opportunity, I studied the prison box. It was the same type that had transported my maid, Lin San and her husband years ago. The slat across the top was latched on the side. My protruding hands were bound at the wrists by leather.

I found amusement in my situation. Carelessness placed my maid and her husband in a box like this.

Now here I was.

I rotated my wrists trying to loosen the leather. Using fingernails, I picked at the knots. It was no use. I couldn't angle my hands enough to gain leverage.

Next, I shoved against the slat holding me down. I studied the latch and an idea occurred. I threw my weight to one side, trying to knock the box over. After many attempts and a bruised shoulder, I found my face in the dirt.

I kicked the box, forcing it to scoot. The latch caught in the ground and it opened. Bracing my knee against the inside, I leveraged my body and pushed it open.

My victory didn't last long. Three large men dressed in black entered. The box was set right-side up and latched once more. Because they appeared to have extensive martial arts training, I didn't resist. The bottoms of their faces remained covered, so I studied their eyes, committing every detail to memory.

If I lived, I swore to hunt them down.

Two stepped aside as one brought out a scroll. He read a message from an unidentified High Court official. It challenged my relation to the late Emperor and demanded I relinquish the throne.

I analyzed the situation. The unnamed official must fear that I could read his thoughts, which was why he sent cronies. He must want something other than me stepping down. Otherwise, the men would've killed me.

"What does he truly desire?" I demanded. "How about you bring him to me so I can read his mind?"

"Is that your response?" the large man asked.

"Tell him to make his intentions known or kill me. Don't

waste my time," I shot back.

Two men left. The third stayed to keep watch. He stood with his back to the door, arms folded. His umber aura told me he was capable of killing. Yet, unlike the other two, this one held a hint of compassion.

"Were those your friends?" I asked in a neutral tone.

"You can read my mind. You know the answer."

"I can't read minds," I said with a sigh. I saw the slightest of twitches. I couldn't be sure if he'd scoffed or felt nervous.

I used an idea inspired by my meeting with the Lan Kingdom's General Wen. "You see, I'm not the Emperor. You've made a mistake." I heard a soft breath from his chest. "I'm a decoy for the true Emperor. He's hiding. Watching the High Court." Then I gave a laugh, "But this doesn't matter since I'm to be killed."

"I don't believe you," he said. "You're the Emperor."

I shrugged nonchalantly, "I'm to be killed, so I see no harm in asking: Please relay a message to the person you're working for. I have family in the Middle Court. If your master can guarantee my people's protection, I'll tell them where the true Emperor's hiding." I gave the man a downcast look, attempting to persuade him.

He turned away, but I could see my words had manipulated him. I didn't speak more, but obediently kept my head down.

It wasn't long before the others returned. They were gone for about twenty minutes. This meant whoever ordered my kidnapping stayed nearby.

One of the men held a scroll. I turned my head away. He kicked my box trying to get a rise out of me. When I didn't respond, the other man grabbed my head and turned my face towards the first.

"What's your connection to the Lan Kingdom?" the first man asked.

"None," I answered.

He made a mark on the scroll with a piece of charcoal. "Why did you allow the Empress to surrender to Lan Kingdom?"

"To stave the invasion." I put on a show of cooperation for the third man, hoping to convince him I wasn't the true Emperor. If he believed me, then he could persuade the other two. If word traveled to the official who ordered my kidnapping, it could instigate his appearance.

"Are you an agent from the Lan Kingdom?"

I hesitated, astonished by the question.

Perhaps the hesitation saved my life. I saw the man make a mark.

"No," I answered slowly. I paid closer attention to the nature of the questions.

"When were you born?"

I answered with Winter's date but two years after.

"Where can lapis lazuli be found," came the last question.

I hid a smile. "In the north."

It became clear. My room must've been searched and the

lapis lazuli pendant found. Whoever ordered my kidnapping must be aligned with the Lan Kingdom. They didn't kill me on the small chance I was a secret agent. Since I'd executed their comrades, they were being careful. When I tried to convince the third man I wasn't the Emperor, it unknowingly played to my advantage.

The two men left again. The third followed and I heard muffled voices. A moment later, the third returned to stand guard. I kept silent, patiently awaiting my captors' return.

My knees had gone numb and my mood soured. I thought it odd I could feel irate. There was little fear in me. I wondered if this was a new side of me I was uncovering. Or perhaps I'd gotten used to my life constantly being in danger.

Nearly an hour passed before the door opened again. This time, an older man stepped in wearing plain clothes with a handkerchief over his face. He dismissed the guards and they left us. By his posture, I could tell he was a High Court official. The third guard must've convinced the others I wasn't the true Emperor.

Cautiously, he moved forward and I observed a sandstone aura. I recognized him as an official I didn't feel certain about.

"If you can read my mind, tell me what I'm thinking," he said.

"I know your name. You're magistrate Fang Yumeng."

Panic flashed through his eyes but he pulled it under control. "Tell me what I'm asking."

I was caught in a difficult position. "I cannot," I finally said. "My ability isn't consistent. Some days I hear thoughts stronger than others. Today, if you wish to know something, you must ask with words." I waited as a drop of sweat fell from my brow. Would he be able to tell I was lying?

He raised a brow, but nodded, "Who sent you?"

"You know who sent me," I responded coldly. "You found his lapis lazuli badge when you searched my room. The Lan King gives his regards." I hoped he didn't know the Empress murdered him. The High Court was only told she was surrendered as a token.

"Why do you look so much like the late Emperor?" he asked.

"I am one of his illegitimate sons, forgotten and deemed useless." I felt pain in my heart to say those words, but the situation demanded I somehow escape. If I could make Fang Yumeng believe I acted from victimization, I could convince him to trust me… just a little.

"I lived outside the palace as a thespian, wanting nothing more than to be my father's pride. When Lan agents found me, they taught me to behave like an imperial and moved me into the palace." I gulped, "I am here, waiting for heavenly affirmation from my father. Until then, I live to serve my master, the Lan King."

I felt disgusted. What was I not willing to do or say to save my skin? How was I to make this right so I may leave this world with honor?

My words visibly moved Fang Yumeng. He opened the door and ordered the men to take me out of the box.

The cronies cut the leather binding. With creaky knees, I found my way to my feet. Tingles prickled as blood returned to my legs.

Fang Yumeng asked about the timing of the invasion. My ears burned.

What invasion?

I told him I'd been out of contact. He should fill me in.

"That's partially our blame," Fang Yumeng said. "We've been actively cutting off outside contact to you."

"So, the invasion's commencing?" I asked, a different tingling settling.

He nodded, "Today. Lan Kingdom troops will be pushing into the palace, but we don't know when."

Bile burned at the back of my throat.

He continued, "Ideally we'd time the High Court coup with the arrival of Lan troops to the Middle Court, but it's difficult to get messages across." He rubbed his chin. "We had intended to begin the revolution by midday. You were the last step of our plan." He blinked hesitantly. "We held suspicions, unsure who you really were. You executed two of our most active leaders. I can see now, you did it to gain the trust of the High Court."

"If you're planning the coup at midday, then you best fill me in on details now."

Fang Yumeng nodded. I could sense he held uncertainties and

wouldn't tell me everything. But anything now would be useful.

When exiting the small room, I saw it was a pantry in an abandoned courtyard once belonging to a concubine. When my father passed, many had fled the palace.

If Lan troops attacked, my trusted Generals would be stranded at the outer walls. I needed to swiftly eliminate as many traitors as possible to maintain power. I wanted to ask Fang Yumeng for the identities of those who opposed me, but feared too many questions would lead to suspicion.

Fang Yumeng and his three cronies took me to a neighboring courtyard—also deserted. We entered an old bedroom where a dozen or so officials sat around a table. They gasped upon seeing me and demanded answers, leaping to their feet.

"Calm yourselves," Fang Yumeng said. "I've ascertained the 'Emperor' is an agent of the Lan Kingdom. With his help, we can easily surrender the Empire."

The reaction was mixed. Eleven officials glared at me with venomous auras. Two more cronies stood guard near the door, neither of them militiamen. This could mean the Generals who stood against the Yu Empire were waiting elsewhere with troops.

"About the coup," I demanded as if it were my business to be informed, "how many soldiers do we have?"

The expressions on the men's faces varied further and I sensed doubt escalating.

A tiny movement caught my eye. My glance darted as the group deliberated. A door had opened in the ceiling. The Ying

Guardians found me.

"Why do you need to know?" an official narrowed his eyes.

"I don't trust him," another piped.

"Fang Yumeng, why did you expose us? Now he knows our faces!"

"I knew we shouldn't have sent Fang! He's senile!"

A man with a commanding persona pointed to me. "Kill him."

I wished to learn about my enemies, but it seemed I wouldn't get the opportunity. Rust color filled the air as the cronies by the door charged me with swords. I ducked between the legs of one and sprang to my feet. Grabbing his arm, I twisted. A cry of pain followed a snap and I took his sword as he fell.

I blocked the second man as the other three rushed. I cut down the first two and the officials in the room let out a gasp.

Fang Yumeng raced for the door. I threw my sword into his leg and he crashed to the ground. The officials huddled against each other, shouting in fervor. It was foolish of them to gather together. But they couldn't have known about my training.

I took another sword and faced off with the last three cronies. Behind the officials, Ying Guardians dropped. Spider and Quan Bao came to my assistance, slaying two men stronger than me. The last was the man with the hint of compassion. I sparred to move in close. Then struck a pressure point. He lost conscious-ness, saving his life.

I looked up to see officials kneeling before Ying Guardians. I blocked the only door. Marching to the huddled, I crouched low. "Tell me, where are your Generals hiding?"

"It's too late," an official shook his head. "The plan's in action and you'll die before sunset."

"That remains to be seen." I stood and pointed dauntingly with my sword. "Those of you who desire to keep your dogged lives, tell me what I wish to know."

"We'll never tell you anything," an official surnamed Wai cussed.

"No, I want my life!" another cried.

Discord expanded as they argued. I watched, calculating the intensification. When I felt satisfied the group was adequately divided, I lifted my sword. Official Wai fell to the ground.

Dead.

A gasp tore through the group as they scurried from me. I waved and the Ying Guardians blocked the windows, preventing escape.

"How is it an Emperor takes blood with his own hands?" a young official asked in disbelief.

"That's not the correct question," I sneered. "You should be asking how many will be executed until you inform me where your Generals hide."

"Please!" the young official begged. "There are troops in the second consort's abandoned quarters!"

"Silence!" an official struck the young man in the face.

"How many?" I asked.

The young official held a hand held firmly over his face as blood gushed from his lip. "Maybe a few hundred."

His response sent the group into fury. Shouts rose and fists flew. I lifted my hand signaling the Ying Guardians not to interfere. I observed with pleasure, the officials tearing into each other like beasts. Some pulled hair as others used dropped weapons and hacked aimlessly.

Spider came to me, whispering, "Summer, this is wrong. Give them a swift death or imprisonment."

"No," I shook my head. "I want them to experience what it's like to be torn apart by their greed."

"Sounds as if you're seeking retribution."

"Yes," I choked, thinking of my mother. The last days of her life were miserable.

"Be careful my friend," Spider spoke. "The road of vengeance is not one of return."

"When I became Emperor, I was prepared to never return," I whispered darkly.

Control over my rage slipped and emotions dragged me along as if torrents of a river. Painful howls came as the officials drew more and more blood. Unable to organize and come at me, I watched pathetic bodies beat against each other.

The young official who had offered me information begged to be spared and ran towards me. He grasped my golden robes and pleaded for life.

"Why did you join the enemy of the Yu Empire?" I asked.

"I was foolish, cowardly, greedy, and all unsavory things a man could be! Please I just want my life!"

"If you are those things, is your life worth saving?" The words echoed through my hollow form, sending chills down my arms. Glaring at the pitiful man, I caught a glimpse of myself. Unlike me, he admitted the things of which I was equally guilty. Did I hide behind the visage of Emperor, using the excuse of protecting the Empire to behave heinously?

Another official pulled the young man into the fray. I watched as a silken belt went around his neck. He floundered for some time before lying still. Murdered by his ally.

"This is wrong," Spider hissed in my ear; this time a warning.

"Are you questioning the Emperor you swore to protect?" I glared from the corner of my eye.

"My duty is to the Empire," his voice cut through me. "You're allowing personal sentiments to rule and not displaying characteristics of decency."

"What will you do? Kill me?" I challenged, facing him.

"Remember our conversation about loyalty?" His eyes grew severe. "I'd take my sister's life if she were to commit treason. Don't think as Emperor you're exempt."

Pride surged, not allowing me to show shame. I averted my eyes and they fell on the young official's trampled body. I wished to feel remorse, but couldn't.

Was it because I saw myself in him and knew I deserved similar?

One official gathered his wits and ran towards me with an arm raised. I sighed and my sword stole his breath with a simple slice. The motion galvanized me and I made a decision. The officials slaughtering themselves barely noticed my approach. I executed them, making their deaths swift and merciful. A red fog of desperation billowed and something sinister set into me.

Only when my traitors sprawled dead did I see I had tasted bloodlust. Morbidly, I thought it might have to do with the number four in my life.

I cleaned my sword. "We need to deal with the troops in Second Mother's courtyard." I turned to leave through the door where Fang Yumeng slumped unnaturally.

I must've been catatonic.

Quan Bao stopped me, "The Emperor shouldn't be seen like this." I blinked before looking down. Not an inch of me was spared of crimson.

We barred the door and I left with the Ying Guardians through the ceiling. In the arena, I changed into a fresh Emperor's robe with uncharacteristic composure.

If only I knew. Trouble had just begun.

Chapter Thirty-Nine:
Sacrifice

Dressed in clean robes, I stood mute in the Ying Guardians' arena. Spider dismissed the others and took tea with me. He sat me at a stone bench beside a table protruding from the wall. His usual calm demeanor returned. "Summer, if you're not well, it's best you remain here where you're safest," he placed a warm cup in my hands.

"It's nothing. Just effects of the paralysis medicine," I mumbled a lie all too easily.

Spider couldn't be fooled and gave a scolding look.

I shook my head, "The Empire needs strength now more than ever. How would it appear if the Emperor hid?" I said those words more from a sense duty than what I felt. "Where's Han-ming?" I asked tiredly.

"He's been searching for you since you went missing. He'll likely check in soon. Would you like to wait here?" He wanted to keep me under control.

"Yes." I could use the respite.

No sooner I uttered the word did a Ying Guardian rush into the arena. He called in an urgent voice. The Lan troops had pushed into the Middle Courts; a part of my enemies' coup. My loyal Generals were holding them back, but could not for long.

The hairs on the back of my neck bristled.

The Empress gave her life for nothing.

I set the cup firmly on the table. "Hanming will have to wait. I need to return to the throne."

"Summer," Spider said firmly, "You're on the verge of becoming unhinged. You were thrust into this role with pressures you're unaccustomed to. If you need to step back for a short time, we'll not blame you."

"Now isn't the time for me to rest," I said despite exhaustion.

I marched towards an exit. Behind me, Ying Guardians followed closely.

I entered the throne room and sent for my father's two most loyal Generals. They'd returned to the High Court to give reports.

When they appeared, I ordered them to search Second Mother's courtyard and kill all hidden troops. They hesitated and I sensed distrust.

I cursed to myself. Even my father's allies suspected my legitimacy to rule.

Bravely they voiced the error of killing without proof of guilt.

"General Hou Yi," I addressed in a low voice, "Our Empire's on the verge of falling. The Yu rule could soon be over... Why do you serve the throne?" I felt curious for his answer because I was no longer sure myself. Winter's words about serving the people sounded like rhetoric and ceased to move me as it once did.

"Your majesty," General Hou Yi began, "I know times are bleak and victory seems hopeless. However, this land is our home. Our ancestors are buried here. The blood and tears of those who came before built this Empire. There will always be an enemy knocking at our door, and there will always be those who disagree with the way things are conducted." He softly cleared his throat. "Evil men exist to do evil things. It's not our duty to eradicate them. Rather, we keep them at bay and maintain balance. This humble servant asks your majesty to show mercy. It is only through forgiveness and compassion that life can flourish."

General Hou Yi bowed lower. "These are words your father taught me."

"My father?" I echoed.

"Yes, your majesty."

I gulped, "Have you lost someone?"

"Three brothers in the war with the Nan Kingdom. I stand before you as a testament of my family's loyalty and our faith that the Yu Empire shall not fall."

Seated before a man I hardly knew, I heard my father's words and remembered his kindness. In that moment, it dawned on me the Empire wasn't merely about power like so many officials believed. This land was the legacy of those we loved before us. We fought not only for the future, but the past as well. I championed my ancestor's right on the throne. I realized then, I fell guilty to the greatest treason. I didn't place faith in my Empire, nor myself.

"General Hou Yi," I spoke gently. "You are right and I am wrong. Your words of wisdom will remain with me for years. If my actions have proved brash and poorly calculated, it's because I lack experience."

"Your humble servant doesn't deserve such praise," he dipped lower.

"Please, rise," I commanded. He climbed to his feet. "Our time runs short. I've learned this morning there are legions of troops hidden throughout the High Court, waiting to begin a coup. That's why I ordered you to slaughter the soldiers." I breathed through my nose. "Because of your words, I will reconsider my command. Do not slaughter the soldiers. They are only following the orders." I softened my voice. "Find the Generals conspiring the coup. Arrest them."

"Yes, your majesty," General Hou Yi bowed. A bright yellow aura of relief blossomed around him.

After dismissing the Generals, I called forth the remaining Lords and a dozen questionable High Court officials. As they entered, I sat upon the throne with my eyes closed. I recalled a time when I stayed with the bandits in their cave. I had practiced a meditation that enhanced my ability to see auras. I breathed deeply, performing the same routine and lost track of time.

"Your majesty?" a voice called in the distance.

I followed the voice and slowly opened my eyes. As expected, I observed a palette of colors. It faded fast, so I focused in on the ominous shades.

I nodded to the official who spoke. He exuded a pale, earthy aura. Harmless. I cleared my throat and called the names of people who harbored ill energies. I dismissed the rest and ordered them to close the doors.

They complied.

Left standing were two dozen officials and Lords. Their heads remained bowed and I couldn't study their eyes. "I believe it's accurate to say you hold treacherous thoughts towards me?"

Silence came as the answer. One didn't need to see auras to sense deadly intent. I found myself in a dangerous situation.

"The Lan Kingdom is beating down our walls and there are troops hidden, waiting to ambush," I announced.

Once more, no response came. The officials could've been made of stone.

"Official Hu," I called. He answered but kept his eyes to the ground. "Tell me, why do you continue to serve the Yao even after they've surrendered this land to my ancestors?"

There was a long pause before he responded in a growl, "My people of the Lan house existed for over six hundred years. Our bloodline is blessed by the Three Sovereigns and we alone have the mandate to rule."

"What of Ku Cuixin? I know he believes differently. He recognizes all three bloodlines."

"That traitor doesn't speak for us!"

"Is that why you held him prisoner in the High Court and blamed it on my father?"

"We've prevailed in taking down the Tai house on the coast. Now, it's time for the Yu house to fall. This Empire shall be returned to its rightful rulers!" As he spoke, dark blue seeped from his head. It flowed sluggishly to the ground, writhing like a snake. It slithered on top of my ornate desk, reaching for my face as if it wished to choke the life from me. I waved. Some of the blue dissipated, but cold air lingered.

I opened my mouth to speak, but didn't get the chance. A horn sounded in the distance and the officials lifted their faces. Their eyes bore hatefully into me, sending chills down my spine. They climbed to their feet like the dead rising.

"It has begun," Official Hu announced.

Panicked shouts mixed with cries of pain and clashing metal came from outside. I tightened my grasp around the hilt of my sword. The officials continued forward, unaffected, possessed by their desire to see the Yu Empire fall.

I wondered if this was a perversion of loyalty. Their ancestors were buried in this land as well. Was this the dark side of the same devotion General Hou Yi displayed?

"Stand down," I ordered, rising. They ignored me and I drew my sword. Several retrieved daggers hidden in their sleeves. Though none were as youthful or well trained as I, their numbers were great. I searched for a tactical advantage.

Doors to the throne room burst open. Soldiers of the Yu Empire poured in, striking each other. General Hou Yi's men had found the hidden troops, disguised as our own. The officials were pushed towards me in the fray. Many lunged with their daggers.

I cut them down in defense.

More followed and I kicked my heavy desk off the pedestal. A half-dozen officials were knocked over by the weight. Others swarmed around.

I did my best, but with soldiers pouring in, I knew I couldn't hold them off for long.

To my relief, Ying Guardians appeared from a hidden door behind a screen. Hanming raced forward and blocked a sword. An official stabbed him in shoulder and Hanming let out a cry. I rushed to disable him. Moving in a continuous arc, I did a six-step sweep and fended off attackers.

Hanming stood close, poised, "How do we tell the soldiers apart?" he eyed the oncoming mob.

"General Hou Yi's men are on our side. Check their uniforms."

The Ying Guardians surrounded me, fighting off any who dared approach. We progressed towards the hidden door. The remaining officials were dragged into conflict and I lost track of them.

As I prepared to duck into the secret passage, I caught sight of a familiar plum hue. I looked into the distance. My heart skipped to see Winter.

Then, I noticed he drew a bow towards me.

A second later, an arrow shot forth.

I jerked to the side, feeling air press against my cheek. The arrow stuck the wall behind me. With strong hands, Ying Guardians ushered me to safety.

I felt shaken. My brother just tried to kill me. I could only assume Silk Deer hadn't reached him yet. I comforted myself, saying it was a misunderstanding.

"Did you see Winter just now?" I asked Hanming once we reached the arena.

"No, and I haven't been able to locate him," he said.

"He shot at me," I breathed.

"He's in the imperial court?" Hanming's brow furrowed.

"Yes. He's fighting amongst our enemies. I fear for his safety."

"I will go to him," Hanming spoke.

"I want to go too," I said.

"You cannot," Hanming turned to me sternly, "Your safety is imperative."

"Hanming—"

"You told me he shot at you! I need to clear things before you show your face, lest he tries again!" His eyes went wild with concern. "I cannot lose my wife! And we cannot lose another Emperor!"

With difficulty, I let him go. "Don't forget to tell Winter about your relation with the Lan family. He has a distorted view and I believe you can help him see truth," I choked.

Hanming planted a kiss upon my head. After a lingering look, he grabbed his weapons and headed down a tunnel with a dozen Ying Guardians.

Alone in the arena, I sat clutching my upset stomach. Overhead, people died for and against me. If I were to die, the Lan Kingdom would gain control. The Nan Kingdom would also rise, and the legacy of the Yu and Tai houses would forever turn to dust. Everything hinged on my life and I wished to shake myself of the pressure.

"My place is by Hanming's side. I was his wife before all this," I whispered sadly. It was much simpler than being Emperor.

I huddled against my knees, fathoming the death cries of my allies. I feared at any moment, my enemies would come crashing into the Ying Guardians' arena. A shiver ran through my body and I thought to find a cloak.

As I unfurled, I blinked in confusion. I'd never been able to see my aura before, but a distinct hue hovered around me. I lifted my hands and moved them through the fog. It appeared similar to Hanming's blue… but a shade off.

I looked around, wondering if he'd returned. Finding myself alone, I studied my body and noticed the color strongest around my midsection.

Realization dawned that the color came from my womb.

I sucked in a breath filled with joy and apprehension. I carried a child of the Lan bloodline!

Trepidation clutched my heart. Nothing in the world seemed more important than the safety of my child. In an instant I knew I would sacrifice the Empire.

"No! Don't think dark thoughts," I coaxed myself. "It hasn't come to that!" Placing hands gently upon my abdomen, I apologized to he or she coming into a world filled with peril.

For hours I paced. Millions of thoughts swarmed my mind and I felt more terrified than ever. My heart told me to run away and protect my child. However, my mind committed to the role of Emperor.

"Summer!" Quan Bao's voice called, "The tunnels have been breached! We must leave!"

My training took over. Instinctively, I grabbed a sword, trembling at the knowledge my body harbored sacred life. Three more Ying Guardians appeared by my side. I didn't see Hanming. I wanted to ask about him, but feared bad news would cripple me. I needed to reach safety, for the sake of my child.

I ran close behind Quan Bao, making sharp turns. We stopped occasionally at locked doors. Each required a different code but Quan Bao knew them all.

When we exited, I gasped, stumbling as memories drowned me. My emotions affected the blue from my womb, causing it to spill into my mother's sitting room. Dust covered the furniture, but nothing else had changed.

Before I could take in the echoes left by my mother, a Ying Guardian pulled me to the courtyard. There, Hanming rushed to my side. I noticed a bandage around his leg. He was otherwise unharmed.

He saw me looking. "Just scratch," his arm moved protectively around me, easing tension. A spot of warmth entered my heart as I looked forward to telling him about our child.

Quan Bao hurried us along.

"Winter, STOP!" Silk Deer's voice reverberated through the air.

Searing pain dug into my shoulder. An arrow struck not far from my previous wound. A cry escaped, but my steps didn't slow.

Five Ying Guardians turned immediately to the origin of the shot. The rest continued to rush me along.

I peered over my shoulder. Through frayed feathers of the arrow, I watched my brother slide down shingles. He hopped into a tree and pulled another shaft from his quiver, fitting it into his bow. Even at my distance, I could tell his eyes burned as if nothing in the world could stop him.

From the far end of the courtyard, Silk Deer raced, shouting at the top of her lungs. My senses sharpened and the next events played slowly.

Silk Deer made good time skipping across rooftops. She leapt into the tree and lunged onto my brother. A second before, he had released the arrow.

Aimed for me.

I could've easily blocked or dodged. The path of the arrow was easy to anticipate.

What I didn't expect, was Hanming.

He stepped in front of me, back towards the oncoming object. His arms closed tightly in an embrace; his cheek to mine.

Something nudged above my heart and warmth spread down my chest. Blue drowned my vision as he exhaled in pain.

Hanming collapsed.

I held onto him, screaming his name. I prayed the wound wasn't mortal as his blood covered my front.

But when I saw the arrow protruding from Hanming's heart, an odd noise rose from my throat like a dying beast.

At my cries, a tired hand brushed hair from my eyes. The same gesture Hanming did many years ago. It calmed me enough to clutch his fingers. I stared into Hanming's eyes, "Please stay!" I quaked, every ounce of me resisting his life slipping. "I'm with your child. We must raise him together!"

His eyes flicked with delight and Hanming opened his lips to speak.

Only blood poured out.

Without warning, his hand dropped and his body gave a shudder.

The blue around him softened… fading to nothing.

I sat stunned, unable to accept his life flame no longer burned.

"Hanming?" I shook him, hoping to return breath. "Please,

don't go. You need to come home to me everyday" I sobbed. "One day, we'll no longer need worry about losing our lives."

His face remained still. I kissed his lips, hoping to rekindle his soul. "Please, Hanming," I begged. He'd left so abruptly I couldn't accept the loss. "Please don't be so cold to me. You know I don't like it," I groveled weakly.

Time ceased to move as I waited for any sign of hope. Yet no matter what I said or did, the man I pined over for years was gone.

Spots appeared in my peripheral as feverishness took control. In stuttered motion, I set my husband gently to the ground and rose. I glared to where the Ying Guardians surrounded my brother. Silk Deer stood in between them, explaining urgently.

Desire for revenge paid in blood consumed me, leaving me blind to all emotions except loss. I darted between the Ying Guardians and slashed wildly. Silk Deer jumped forward to block. I pushed her away and aimed for my brother's heart.

I wasn't going to miss.

Winter didn't move. He stood waiting. Eyes soulful.

At the last second, Spider's words surfaced in my mind. "The road of vengeance is not one of return."

The shroud of darkness lifted and I peeked into my brother's eyes. In a flash, I saw our father, mother, Yu Longjing, and Ting.

This is my brother…

I'd let my enemies win the battle over my soul. The desires in me became like them, willing to kill even my own blood.

My wrist flinched.

My blade sunk into Winter's shoulder.

He hardly cringed as his uninjured arm found its way around me. "My sister, my sister" he sobbed, "Youngest sister, you're safe…"

I heard relief, indicating his nerves had diminished to little more than strained hope. He must've searched endlessly, fearing me dead. With so much happening, I couldn't allocate more resources to find him.

Yet, if someone had told him his sister was the Emperor, would he have believed it?

"Winter, I'll never forgive you!" I wailed like a child, but my arms wrapped tightly in return. My heart bled as my fists pounded feebly.

I knew things would never be the same between us again.

Grief and mourning consumed me as elation made my head light. The mix became too much and I slipped from consciousness.

I awoke in the Emperor's bedchamber. Winter sat beside me, asleep with his head propped on an arm. Silk Deer curled against his shoulder, snoring softly. Sprawled on the ground nearby was Elk.

I pulled myself to a seated position, wincing from my shoulder. Memories of Hanming's last moments played in my mind and tears spilled. I bit my sleeve in frustration and a sluggish sensation depressed me all over.

We were here. Meaning the Yu Empire won. Yet, I felt defeated, and didn't wish to take another breath.

At the thought of never breathing again, fear and exasperation evaporated. Weightlessness visited and I wished never to part from the carefree sensation.

I peered around and spotted a pair of scissors. It sat beside thread, probably leftover from stitching my shoulder. I reached for the blades and positioned them above my wrists. A pleased sigh welcomed the idea of reuniting with my love.

As my fingers tightened to stab, a flood of the most magnificent blue billowed forth. It swathed me with the sensation of life, spreading from my womb. In this hue, I sensed the same love I shared with Hanming. It enticed spiritedly and my grip on the scissors weakened.

I dropped the blades and sobbed. My hands clutched my belly and a prick of joy began to form in my sorrow-drenched heart.

As I wept, the blue energy continued to dance. A small hand slipped around my shoulder and Silk Deer leaned her head to my temple. Her tears fell with mine.

~*~

In following moons, I couldn't speak to Winter. I refused to even look at him. Silk Deer told me I shouldn't be so hard. Winter couldn't have known Hanming would move into the path of the arrow.

I said nothing in response. She may be right, but it didn't

lessen my sorrow. Instead, I busied myself with state affairs.

For unknown reasons, the Lan Kingdom ceased their attack and withdrew. My loyal Generals caught in the Middle Courts returned to my side and subdued the High Court coup. Rebellion leaders were executed; their subordinates pardoned.

I addressed the issue of our defenses and ordered the Generals to fortify the outer walls, should another attack come. Fortunately, our troops from outlying territories arrived, tripling our militia.

My Lords wrote an inspirational speech and I recited it to the Empire.

Afterwards, I visited the mourning chambers where Hanming's body laid. He appeared content on the cold slab, burial vestments tied elegantly. Even in death, he'd never looked more handsome.

I reminisced about our time together, recalling his words by the waterfall. He'd been tormented, thinking I'd been sentenced to death for helping him escape the dungeon. Perhaps he stepped in front of the arrow because he couldn't live with the thought of my death a second time.

I didn't blame him. If our positions were switched, I would've done the same.

Or perhaps his generous heart did it for my brother. Winter would never forgive himself if I'd died by his hand.

I leaned forward and brushed my lips against his. The cold skin reminded me he was gone. "Goodbye, my love," I choked.

"I was fortunate to have found you."

I gave his face one last longing glance before I exited.

When he burned on the pyre, much of me left with him. I folded my hands in masculine fashion, but truthfully, as a protective gesture of our child in my womb. The blue following me day and night was the sole comfort in my life. I practiced the meditation technique the Empress had taught and felt my health weaken. It didn't matter. The child needed to enter this world, even at the cost of my life. I only needed to keep the Empire stable until an heir of three powerful bloodlines could take over.

Then, I would be free to join Hanming.

Chapter Forty:
Empire of Summer

When I took the mandate to rule, I had little experience in the world and even less with court affairs. I allowed the evil of others to infect me and found myself standing on the edge of a precipice, nearly plunging into an abyss of blood and tyranny.

I could've been one of those people too far gone to be saved, like the woman I'd met in the dungeon years ago.

The child in my womb pulled me back.

Losing Hanming reminded me I wasn't indestructible. I finally understood the words he'd spoken long ago. "Those who don't revere life will lose it in more ways than one."

The equation wasn't as simple as I'd thought.

I'd lost respect for lives because they belonged to my traitors. And the universe took from me: a life I could've lived with my beloved.

Instead of hardening, the lingering of Hanming's love and our child reminded me of kindness and nurture. My Empire wasn't my enemy, rather my ward. The proper way was not to control through fear, but prosper through guidance. A shaky balance persisted within the walls of the palace. Though many Lords didn't see eye to eye with me, at least they supported the Yu Empire.

"We're all broken. The world is broken," Spider said on a day I felt exceptionally low. "The ones who keep it going are those who never cease to strive for betterment."

It would be a while before the words fully soaked in.

As the end of autumn rolled around, a messenger from the Lan Kingdom approached our outer gates. Carrying a white flag and followed by a small band of a dozen men, a General expressed desire to call upon the Emperor.

Word reached me quickly. Along with it came the name of the messenger: General Wen.

My ears perked and I asked to have "him" brought forth.

Three days later, a blindfolded woman dressed in men's armor knelt before me.

When the blindfold lifted, shock crossed General Wen's face. She remembered me from the woods. A corner of her lips turned in the smallest of smiles. It quickly disappeared as she bowed, announcing her name and rank.

I commanded her to stand and asked her to speak her business.

"Your majesty," she spoke in a grand voice, "I bring news

from the Lan Kingdom. A revolution has taken place after the death of our late King. His brother, Prince Ku Rentu now rules."

Upon hearing the name of my friend, I grew hopeful. It made sense General Wen stood before me. Prince Ku Rentu trusted her.

She continued, "He wishes to send condolences. The Empress passed in our Kingdom due to poor health. It was always our intention to return her as an extension of peace. Unfortunately, that's not possible. Instead, King Ku Rentu wishes to extend the hand of his sister in marriage. If she can sit beside your majesty as Empress, it would show we wish for harmony and cooperation."

"Thank you, General Wen," I said politely. "I will discuss with my Lords. You're welcome here as a guest until you have my answer. Please respect my Empire and restrict your movements to your courtyard."

"Thank you, your majesty," she said with a bow.

That night, dressed as a High Court maid, I stole to General Wen's chambers. We were alone and she greeted me amicably. I asked her about King Ku Rentu and she informed me he was well. She filled me in on all that'd transpired.

Her troops were significantly weakened by my Generals' sabotage so she had retreated to the Lan Kingdom before the attack on my palace. There, she found Prince Ku Rentu amidst a power struggle. With the aid of Ku Cuixin, she helped him take the Kingdom.

"As King, Ku Rentu's first order was to cease attack on the

Zhenxun. When he and I sat down to talk in private, he told me about a strange Princess who facilitated his release from the Tanguts." We shared a giggle. "Once I told stories about the encounter with you in the woods, he sent me to extend a peace offering to the Yu Emperor. My second mission was to locate Princess Summer and see how she fared."

I stood and twirled dramatically. It was the most I'd been able to emote since the attempted coup.

"Imagine my shock when I discovered you're the Emperor!"

"You mustn't tell anyone," I said with utmost sincerity. "Princess Summer is dead."

General Wen frowned, "Has she officially been declared deceased?"

"Not officially…" I trailed. "I meant it figuratively."

"Good, because I have an idea," she said. "We should strengthen the bond further between our Empires. You should offer Princess Summer's hand in marriage to King Ku Rentu, and become his Queen," General Wen nodded.

The suggestion caught me off guard. With ruling the Yu Empire, I didn't think I could take on another identity. I told her as much. "Besides, I need to figure out how to keep my secret from Ku Rentu's sister if I'm to accept the marriage proposal as Emperor."

General Wen chuckled, "*I* am the sister, Ku Wenlian. Rest assured, your secret is safe."

I grinned. Things were looking brighter.

"Oh, I forgot," her face dropped. "This plan won't work. I heard you're already married."

Dark clouds appeared before my eyes, "I'm a widow."

General Wen sat silently for a moment. Neither of us could find words. Eventually, she squeezed my hand in sympathy.

The remaining Lords were mostly my father's supporters. The few dissidents weren't allied to the Yao house. They did all share wariness of the discord leading to the coup and were happy to accept an alliance with the Lan Kingdom.

As Emperor, I took Princess Ku Wenlian's hand in marriage. She became my spouse, and like my father, I valued my Empress' advice and friendship. In turn, I ordered Princess Summer to wed King Ku Rentu.

As I peered from my third red veil, this one of imperial silk, I gave Ku Rentu a smile. It wasn't a smile of love, rather a bond forged through secrets and shared turmoil.

Ku Cuixin stood at the ceremony. He embraced me and whispered, "I'm sorry for your loss, Princess, but know Hanming cherished you fervently and you'll always be my daughter."

I thanked him, but my words felt hollow with the longing of lost love.

After the wedding, I became "The Elusive Queen of the North." I used the excuse of ill health to keep from the public's eye, and returned to the Yu Empire. When my stomach showed,

I added layers to my robes as if I'd put on weight. Ku Wenlian made false whiskers for me to wear.

When it neared time for me to give birth, I traveled to the Lan Kingdom. Winter, who naturally grew whiskers, temporarily assumed my duties. Since most officials remained bowed before the Emperor, few saw our face long enough to question slight differences in resemblance.

The few who did wear puzzled expressions hesitated to speak.

Winter kept mostly out of sight, blaming his elusiveness and more aged appearance on poor rest.

In the Lan Kingdom, I dressed as Queen and made a show of my large belly. I did indeed carry a child of the Lan family. I paraded about the palace as maids cooed over my beauty and grace.

I felt more like a pumpkin.

I did find relief in being a woman again. It reminded me how demure I once felt, alone with Hanming.

I crossed paths with General Hong a few times, pleased to see he'd been promoted to personally serve King Ku Rentu. He didn't recognize me and I said nothing.

I committed to the story of ill health, which wasn't farfetched since the Lan qigong lowered my energy.

When time came to give birth, a dozen maids carried me to the highest floor of the pagoda. As I gazed from the windows, it felt as if I were flying in the clouds. I was told all Lan children were born in the heavens to receive the blessings of the Three Sovereigns.

I labored all day and when night came, I saw our Xin. I smiled, whispering, "Hanming, your child is entering this world. I hope you've met him before he's to arrive."

Birth felt excruciating, but I bore it proudly. When I heard the cries of a baby, my heart somersaulted. "It's a son!" the physician shouted with joy, "The Lan Kingdom has an heir!"

I beamed, reaching for my child.

Without warning, a sharp pain caused me to cringe. I let out a cry as my womb felt a kick like many I'd received during pregnancy.

The physician and the nurses quickly returned to their posts. Not long after, another child came into the world. "It's a daughter!" they exclaimed. The physician joked, "Do you have any more?"

With tears of joy, I cradled two beautiful children. In agreement with King Ku Rentu, I named the son Lan Ming, the daughter, Lan Tai. I remained with them for a moon, soaking in every second. I continued to practice the Lan meditation, nestling them in my aura.

Too soon came my time to leave. I held my children close and kissed both tenderly. I brought out my mother's gold coins. They had gone on incredible adventures, and a part of me believed they were charmed. I divided them amongst my children, so a small piece of me could stay with them. And perhaps the charm would protect them too, my precious heirs to three bloodlines.

Ku Cuixin promised he'd personally see to their proper upbringing. With that, I left them in the North Kingdom with their distant cousin, King Ku Rentu. He would raise them as their father.

After I left, news traveled through the Lan Kingdom their Queen passed away. My children would never know me as their mother. The heaviness of it forever lives in my heart.

When I returned to Zhenxun, Winter resumed his role as a Prince. He took Silk Deer as his bride and I'd never seen her happier. Elk returned to the tree bandits but was granted permission to return whenever he wished.

Despite increasing harmony, an issue needed to be addressed. The Empress Ku Wenlian needed to bear an heir. Since I couldn't, in secret it was decided the closet male would perform the task. My brother hesitantly agreed.

Silk Deer became discordant and left, and Winter fell into melancholy.

I felt for her. Silk Deer didn't bargain for the life we lived. Tree bandits were monogamous and kept their numbers low. It allowed them to be nomadic, traveling throughout the seasons.

With my people, men took multiple wives to birth children and build Empires.

When the heir was born, we named him Yu Shaokang. He will call me father. His true father he shall call uncle.

I reminded myself it was all for the Empire.

~*~

Years later, Silk Deer returned to Zhenxun to see me. She carried Hutu wrapped in linens and scented herb packets. "He passed peacefully," she informed.

We buried him in my mother's courtyard. It was the first I'd returned since Hanming's death.

As Silk Deer and I stood reminiscing about our time with Hutu in the cave, I sniffed, noticing orange flowers. The scent became synonymous with the most memorable moments of my life. It reminded of the simplicity of my childhood and the love of my mother. I remembered her falling ill too.

Lastly, staining across all memories was the day I lost Hanming.

The Empress' words came to me, breaking through lasting grief. "Always remember your innocence. It will lead you to make proper decisions." The orange blossoms took on a new meaning.

"I'll be leaving soon," Silk Deer informed me.

"Without speaking to Winter?" I thought of my brother, miserable in having driven Silk Deer away.

She frowned. "I believe it's best."

I read on her face that her mind was set. Yet, I believed minds changed when confronted by the heart.

I arranged to meet her the next day for tea. I then retreated to my study, and for the first time in years, wrote to Winter. I asked him to meet me for tea at the same time and location.

I didn't go for tea.

Afterwards, Silk Deer never left the palace.

My brother never looked happier, nor did he ever take another wife.

As time wore on, the pain of loss never faded. Instead, it grew to become a part of me. I lost count how many times I experienced a memorable moment and wished to share it with Hanming… only to remember he's gone. Never did the misery lessen, but overtime, I realized pain and love share the same root. It's through loss I learned to appreciate beauty not seen with eyes, but felt in our souls. It allowed me to cherish the fragile balance of the world.

I still look to the Xin in the sky. As long as it remains, I have faith the world will continue to fill with compassion.

During one of his visits, Elk brought the chest Winter and I had found in the decimated coastal Empire. In my spare time, I read the journals. The last Tai Emperor recorded words from his divination master. It foretold the demise of the Tai Empire by the ocean rising. It also predicted a rule so long it would receive a name in history.

"Dynasty of Summer" he called it, for the way it flourished. Its reach would be vast and deep like the ocean, absorbing surrounding Kingdoms.

Yet as all things, it will come to an end after five centuries. When oceans retreat, it takes everything, as it will the Tai Empire. All riches, inventions and wisdom of the Dynasty of Summer will be washed away in time too. Until nothing more than a name shall remain.

The words startled me. My mother stressed to me I was yang water. Powerful and omnipresent. Could I be the ocean the divinations spoke of?

But like summer, life will return, perhaps not in its original state. In future generations of the world, our influence will reappear, even if in different forms.

The citizens in Zhenxun already call us the "Empire of Summer."

The Ying Guardians investigated and reported it to stem from a misnomer. Tree bandits passing through asked for the ruler, Princess Summer. City folk found it amusing that foreigners could be so confused. They told the tree bandits no one by that name existed.

I didn't find it surprising, since no one remembers a consort's daughter.

However, the city folk liked the thought of our Empire being as prosperous as the season of summer and the name took root.

The Empire grows more stable each year as my father's supporters expand faith in me. King Ku Rentu often defers to the Yu Empire for advice. I knew he respected his sister and much of the reverence shifted to me. Over time, bridges were fixed and more built. Slowly, it seemed as if we were of one Empire.

Zhan Ji worked closely with old clans in the Nan Kingdom, restoring their honor. The territory was given some autonomy.

Old leaders were granted unlimited audience with me. To have a Lan Empress helped assuage bitterness.

I hope people don't flatter meaninglessly when they say I'm a just Emperor. Disgrace soils my heart from impetuous behavior during the coup. But once I discovered I carried Hanming's children, I strove to become an exemplary character they could admire, even from afar.

As years rolled by, my nephew Yu Shaokang grew bright. He reminds me much of Winter as a child. It felt strange to have him call me father, but the boy's adoration made me optimistic to think I would've been a great parent.

One thing I know for certain. If my daughter ever asked me, "What's a girl's role in the world?"

My answer would be, "Anything she could imagine, and some things she's yet to."

Even Emperor.

~*~

In later years, I left the palace often, claiming to go for hunts. Instead, I visited the tree bandits, or stayed as a guest in the Lan Kingdom to see my children. It injures me, but I've always kept my identity as their mother hidden. I've come to accept they will never know me. Or their father.

In an ideal world, I would've raised them with the tree bandits; jumping from branch to branch, with Hanming by my side. However, a different destiny called. I cannot interfere with what fate holds.

I still fantasize.

Perhaps I can fake my death.

I like the idea of drowning in a lake because few know I'm a strong swimmer. At least, strong enough to survive a merciless river.

I could leave a secret letter for Lan Ming and Lan Tai. For when they're older.

Or maybe, I'll leave this journal.

I could draw a map and lead them to me; living with tree bandits in their cave. I'd share the joys of fishing and sleeping amongst branches. If they wish to swim in the river, I'd give advice like Silk Deer once did for me. Perhaps then, I can reveal my identity as their mother and tell them about their father.

I could show them our Xin in the sky, and tell them how much I loved him.

... The End

Please leave a review on Goodreads.com!

For latest news, check out our blog:
space-tigers.com/blog

Follow @ticanazhu on instagram to see what she's up to!
And @spacetigers.publishing on instagram for updates!

About the Author:

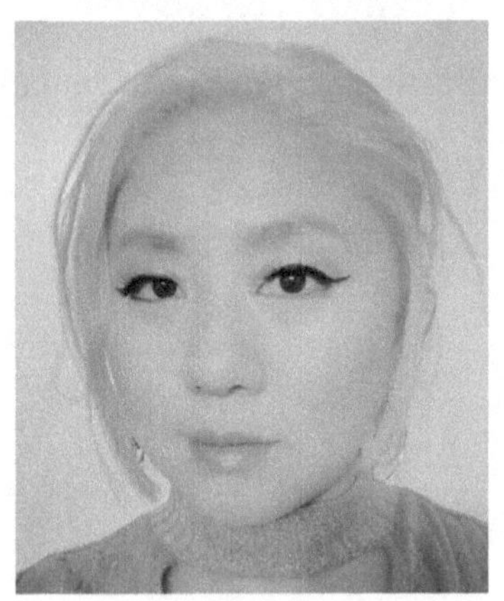

Ticana Zhu is a free spirit with a traditional heart. Her stories embody this essence, playing at the tension between what one wishes to do and what needs to be done. Her main characters are Asian; many channeling her experiences growing up on two sides of the world. She prefers to write memoir style, getting into the psyche of the protagonist. Ticana writes historical and science fiction, occasionally fantasy.

Ticana's back burner project is a science-fiction novel centered on the mythical creatures: Phoenix, Dragon, and Kirin. The main character, Rosi finds herself a part of an elite soldier division on Mars. Struggling to keep up, Rosi discovers she'll one day hold the power of Phoenix: to reshape the universe.

Author's Notes:

Thank you for following Princess Summer through her adventures! Here are some fun facts about the story. The tales she draws inspiration from—such as the one about the little fox who gets his tail wet and the sagging ridge pole—come from the I-ching or Zhou Yi (Book of Changes).

It's said FuXi (one of the Three Sovereigns) was the one who invented the I-ching. It was used for counting and tracking the change in seasons. Later, its use extended into divinations. However, the most notable record of it occured with King Wen at the end of the Shang Dynasty (the Dynasty after Xia).

There were a few inventions in Dynasty of Summer that weren't era-accurate. I thought they were too interesting to leave out (such as the earthquake sensor in Part One, clock incense, and saltpetre). They appeared in later dynasties. I hoped to explain it away in the last chapter where it's said the inventions were washed away in time… only to reappear later!

General Hou Yi comes from the myth about the lady on the moon with her jade rabbit. The tale of Chang'e has many different versions. What doesn't change is that Hou Yi was her spouse.

Yu Shaokang is named after Yu the Great's grandson—also a character in history.

Ying Guardians are "Shadow" (影) Guardians.

I hoped you've enjoyed reading! Please check out more of my works! *kisses*

Acknowledgments

Many thanks to all those who've purchased <u>Dynasty of Summer: Part One</u>! Even more so that you've bought Part Two! I hope you've enjoyed Princess Summer's journey.

I'd like to thank my husband for supporting my publishing endeavors, as crazy as they can get sometimes!

Special thanks to Sibley for always enthusiastically coming to my events and being the first to scoop up my books! Also to Debbie who's pointed me to helpful events. Last but not least, I'd like to thank Gloria—my aerial silks instructor. Because of her, I was able to put myself in Princess Summer's shoes when she escaped from the blood bandits! (Though I still can't climb silks the way Summer did, at least I understand the mechanics behind it!)

Discover Other Titles by Space Tigers Publishing:

Cycles of the Lights Series
(in chronology)
by: Ava Reiss

Fall of Ima   *full-length novel for Young Adults*

Vesper's Curse   *novella for Young Adults*

The Seed of Life   *full-length novel for New Adults*

Stillness in the Storm   *full-length novel for New Adults*
coming in 2022

The Cycles of the Lights series follows the primordial souls, En and Il as they immerse themselves into the cosmos of their creation. Battling karmic entanglements, they strive to find their way back to each other.

En and Il have no memory of their primordial identities. They incarnate like the multitude of other souls in the grand universe. The only thing they sense for certain is the inexplicable draw between them.

Each novel in the series follows the mortal lives led by En and Il. As they face exciting trials in their paths, they must remember who they are.

For Young Adults—prequel to The Seed of Life

Meliora lives on the Earth-like planet of Ima where days are idyllic and worries never last. Tension enters the north continent as her father, the King of a prominent sovereignty passes away. Her mother is left with the crown, but shows no interest in ruling. In desperation to find a cure for the hereditary disease that took her husband, Queen Vesper travels off-planet to study sorcery. Magic had long been banned on Ima, leaving desperate questions in her wake. To make matters worse, soon after her departure, Queen Vesper ceases communication.

The lone successor to the throne is teenage Meliora, who feels shy of the task. With her best friend, Jedrek by her side, she musters the strength to lead. Meliora's reign is short lived as the previous Queen returns after years of silence. Though once close, the woman now wielding magic isn't the mother she remembers. Includes pen and ink illustrations of scenes by Ava Reiss.

At age 23, Kameclara achieved her childhood dream: becoming an operative of the Intergalactic Military. They're deadly effective and highly revered; protecting their home planet, Teroma, is their main task.

Yet, Kameclara always felt it was the stars that called to her, not a sense of duty. Their frozen planet circled the edge of the la system, barely hospitable. She'd always felt there must be another place more like home. She longed to find it, and the Intergalactic Military afforded the chance.

Within the first week of becoming green-lit, Kameclara and her team are taken into the fold of the planet's deepest secrets. They learn their system contains nine planets, not the seven they were taught in school. Hidden deep in their sun's expansive corona are the planets, Jema, and Ima. As if the news didn't astound enough, Kameclara is handed her first mission. Instead of traveling outward into the stars, the operatives are headed to Jema, where they have a base.

Along the journey, Kameclara discovers there's no end to the Intergalactic Military's secrets. At first they're told they're to secure the Jeman base. Then, Kameclara learns of the Seed of Life, an item said to hold the fate of all her people… and the true purpose of their mission.

THE SEED OF LIFE

CHAPTER ONE

Kameclara stepped to the edge of a half-mile drop. An enormous cavern spread before her. Wall to wall of habbadite clay waited, capable of changing into myriads of dangers in an instant. She felt clacking beneath her mission boots. The clay remained solid… for the moment.

Her expression remained serene. She was never one to display much emotion. Yet beneath her skin, blood drummed, anticipating a rush of excitement. She flicked her wavy, black hair over her shoulder. This was her final evaluation to become a green-lit operative of the Intergalactic Military—one of the planet's elite. Since she was a child, Kameclara had looked forward to this day. Why?

Because operatives traversed stars.

Truthfully, it was no further than the Molta Belt—the asteroid ring outside their planet, Teroma's, orbit. The "Intergalactic" part of their military name was more hopes of reaching further in the future. Yet it was beyond where many on their planet ever hoped to go.

Kameclara celebrated her twenty-third birthday days ago. This final test was the perfect present. She adored a good challenge.

Her hand went to the weapon at her hip. She wouldn't need it. It remained a rite of passage for each team to finish their graduation run by the grace of their skill. She had completed five ans of intense training. Not to mention the two ans of vetting before that.

That's seven birthdays.

Once they aced this final test—and there was little doubt they would—the nation of Orareca's present operatives would retire with commendations, or become officers.

Kameclara already knew she'd never retire. Not if she could help it.

She lifted her arms, appreciating the material hugging her skin. Highly elastic, it allowed for a full-range of movement. Yet remained resilient enough for space travel. Lengthening her spine into a stretch, Kameclara's eyes caught a smooth rectangle in the ceiling—the only object not made of habbadite clay. Somewhere behind the one-way window, Teroman officers watched.

She knew there were more than usual to judge the graduation run. They were probably in the midst of cooking up a surprise or two, preparing to send electric signals to the habbadite clay. On command, the substance would take on various properties. The material was confiscated from enemies over a millennium ago. With Teroman engineering, it became a valuable training tool.

Beside Kameclara, her squad-mate let out a whistle. "What'll it be this time?" the white-haired young woman stared across the expanse. She kept her locks short and pulled to the side.

"Don't tell me you're nervous, Sy?" Kameclara teased. She knew none of them were.

Kameclara had two partners she lived and trained with, Syralise and Leera. They were on their nation's Alpha Team. Each team comprised of twelve squads of three. Those squads were ranked by ability. Kameclara and her partners made up Alpha-Je—the leading squad.

Syralise gave an easy laugh, "Nah. I think we've seen it all over the ans."

Leera shrugged, "Remember, real test's when we're alone in the field."

A shrill siren echoed across the expanse, a warning the exam was about to begin. Bumps formed on Kameclara's skin. Her composure kept steady. A characteristic she inherited from her father.

"Here we go!" someone cried.

The edge of the cliff lurched upwards and she braced with thirty-five teammates. She noticed the habbadite floor shifting. Large boulders peeled from now fluid surfaces. They lifted lazily into the air and hovered.

Pressure on her feet eased. Kameclara nodded to herself. Gravity was neutralized for this exam. It wouldn't be a first. She'd run thousands of similar scenarios. Scoffing, she thought the training cavern strangely felt like a second home.

"Yeah!" Syralise cried enthusiastically. She bounced energetically on her toes. The rapidly rising cliff didn't affect her footing.

Kameclara glanced to Leera to get a read. The lanky woman crouched low as she slapped on her helmet. Bits of auburn hair poked around her neck. By her posture, Kameclara knew the eyes behind the protective glass were keenly studying the unfolding landscape. It was Leera's turn to lead. The three rotated command every mission. Syralise led the last, and Kameclara would lead the next.

"Operatives prepare," an officer's voice came from inside her helmet. Kameclara had it balanced around her crown. She pushed it down. The sphere glided seamlessly over her glossy hair, keeping thick waves in check. Compression lining calibrated, hugging comfortably to her skull. Her coms were synced with her squad-mates.

"First squad to strike the buzzer wins," an officer announced, the voice piping directly into her ear.

No sooner were the words spoken, thirty-six operatives leapt from the cliff, keen on being first to complete the mission. The ledge they stood on a moment before smashed into the ceiling.

Air rushed past Kameclara as she landed on a floating boulder. She noted wind generators firing at random intervals from the walls. Objects chancing near them swirled mercilessly, pushed at frenzied speeds. There was enough force to cause permanent damage. Even their jumpsuits suits couldn't save them. Kameclara made a mental note to steer clear.

She kept her squad-mates in periphery while hopping around, avoiding careening blocks. Kameclara scanned the cavern, searching for anything that could be a buzzer. Nano-particles in the fabric of her gear compressed when needed, decreasing joint impact. Should the material be torn, the rest would constrict a small degree, mitigating blood loss.

"I need assistance," Syralise's voice came through.

Kameclara landed solidly, grabbing onto a nook. It was safer to adhere to large boulders. They offered some protection to debris compared to her free-floating. She craned her neck above. Syralise had landed too, but her boulder proved amorphous. Her legs were sunk into soft habbadite.

"On your left," Leera's voice came through as she dashed passed Kameclara. Syralise reached out an arm. Leera pushed from a rock and grabbed hold of Syralise, yanking her from the mire. They separated mid-air and landed on fresh boulders. Both proved solid.

Leera's helmet swooped in an arc, scoping a wide range. Kameclara knew her partner liked to take in as much information as possible before announcing a plan of attack.

As she stood by, Kameclara noticed other squads also discovering the erratic nature of their environment. Some had trouble getting unstuck.

She couldn't help but grin. Habbadite caverns had always been her favorite. Anything could happen. In previous weeks they'd finished exams in stealth, weapons, and labyrinths. All with strategy incorporated. She found those routine and a bit tiresome.

Kameclara recalled an evening a few weeks ago. She had gone to a lounge with her partners to enjoy music. Some people their age attempted to chat them up. "What do you do for fun?"

Kameclara smirked playfully, dodging a piece of habbadite. *If only we could show them this…*

Leera had curtly explained they were not out to make friends. "We're unwinding before our next Intergalactic Military exam."

The others took a step back, giggling nervously. Kameclara wished her partner hadn't given up their vocation, especially so coldly. Some citizens were afraid of them. Keeping a healthy image was important.

"Stay scattered," came Leera's first command, as she switched to another boulder.

It snapped Kameclara to the present. "Heading?"

"Most squads are checking boulders individually for the buzzer," Leera observed.

Kameclara's hand became stuck to a boulder she tried to push away. Grabbing hold of a smaller rock, she shoved it into the mire and wriggled loose.

"There," Leera pointed to the furthest wall. "There's a permanent wind stream firing from the base of the wall. All others are intermittent. Worth inspecting."

"Roger," Syralise chirped as she somersaulted from her perch. The three propelled from hovering habbadite as they navigated the gravity-free field.

Kameclara spotted two members of Alpha-I squad heading in

the same direction. "Interference on left," she radioed her squad.

"Sy," Leera commanded, "Inspect boulders in the wall blocked by the wind stream. Kame, assist me in interception."

"Got it, Boss!'" Syralise responded. As the most agile of the three, she wove her way through flying objects. She was careful to make contact with one appendage at a time. Should she be ensnared, her other limbs could grab onto neighboring chunks to pull herself loose.

Kameclara and Leera greeted members of Alpha-I with straight-on tackles. They were ranked just behind Alpha-Je.

Kameclara's target leaped and she missed. Following with a quick pivot, she pushed off the boulder and grabbed his foot. Catching sight of the emblem on his belt, Kameclara recognized Brock. She grinned. His right knee was still weak from a previous exam.

Brock pulled Kameclara into a wind stream. The rush of air slammed them both into an amorphous block. Kameclara's arms and shoulders were caught. Only Brock's hand was mired. Before he could clear himself, Kameclara quickly wrapped her legs around his right knee. She jerked mercilessly and he lost balance. His right side fell into the sticky boulder. Placing a hand on his back, Kameclara pulled herself loose.

"That's for the last run," she shouted playfully, kicking away. He'd stolen her ladder.

Kameclara noticed Leera in a grapple with Embledon. As she dashed to help, a shadow caught her eye. It was Verniv, the third member of Alpha-I.

A burst of air came from the wall. Kameclara pushed into its path, far enough to not be injured. It launched her into Verniv. The Alpha-I member detected her a split second before, and rolled out of reach.

Kameclara grabbed an outcropping to reposition herself. She caught a fist from Verniv as she recovered her balance. The two sparred amidst dancing boulders, neither able to best the other. Physically, all members of Alpha Team were equally matched.

Syralise's voice came through Kameclara's helmet. "Found a button," she breathed. "It was hidden behind a rock I smashed." She grunted in annoyance. "I've tried to strike it but the wind stream's too strong. It pushes away anything in its path."

"Kame, to the button," Leera commanded.

Kameclara abandoned the fight with Verniv and followed orders.

Syralise's discovery drew the attention of other operatives and all raced towards the same destination. One reached Syralise and they engaged in combat.

Leera was known for speed. Kameclara observed her squadmate grab a fist-sized rock as she dashed from one habbadite structure to the next. Soon, Leera was near Syralise. With a quick whip of the arm, the rock struck the opponent's helmet. It distracted him long enough for Syralise to land a well-placed kick. The opponent fell into a boulder.

Good! It's amorphous!

He was stuck.

"Sy, you're on defense. Keep all away from the button." Leera somersaulted to avoid a habbadite collision. She continued, "Kame, strike the button on the count of three."

Alpha-Je positioned themselves.

"One," Leera landed her feet into the mired block that had trapped Syralise's opponent.

He whipped his head to her in alarm, wondering why anyone would choose to be caught.

"Two," Leera twisted her torso, pulling the boulder with her. The large structure bowled towards the wall, mere yards beneath the button.

"Three!"

Kameclara launched from her perch as Leera's boulder cut off the wind stream. Her palm struck the button, but it wasn't enough force. She grabbed hold of a groove in the wall and threw her shoulder into the nub.

Kameclara felt a click.

A buzz filled the cavern as Leera's boulder rushed upwards. Kameclara flipped backwards, missing it by a hair.

Before Alpha-Je could cheer, gravity laid claim to the cavern. Habbadite boulders dropped suddenly. All members of Alpha Team scrambled to avoid being crushed. Kameclara propelled herself against one large rock to avoid another. Pushing off falling objects, she made her way to the top.

When she did land, shock absorbent boots protected her

ankles and knees. Nearby, her squad-mates peered about in anticipation, unharmed. Officers hadn't announced the end of the exam. Anything could still happen.

The habbadite clay crumbled into tiny pieces, enormous boulders melting. Kameclara jogged towards her squad-mates. Her eyes narrowed as the clay reshaped itself. "Are those arms and legs?"

No answer came. Hesitant postures alerted her to their uncertainty.

Kameclara crouched near Syralise and Leera as her eyes rose with the formation of the clay. They turned into creatures she knew all too well. Each stood four to five times taller than the average Teroman. These were Ressogurey forms. One of three alien races threatening Teroma. Their size, matched with intelligence, made them an exceptionally difficult opponent.

Without warning, a half-formed Ressogurey struck. An Alpha Team member was slammed into the ground. She cried in pain as her squad-mates rushed to her side.

A crackle came over the coms as Leera switched her channel to include the entire team. "Take-down formation Cephei!"

When no officers were present during a mission, command was determined by squad rank. Alpha-Je ranked first, and Leera was presently in charge. When not in competition with one another, the squads of Alpha Team trained in countless configurations. Cephei was one devised against Ressogurreys.

As the creatures thundered towards them, Alpha Team commenced their counter-attack. The weakness of the Ressogureys was their soft abdomen. The habbadite rendered these enemies with plated armor covering their undersides.

Kameclara raced towards a looming beast with Syralise by her side. Leera reached it first and pinned a leg as wide as her body. With a well-placed kick onto the other leg, the creature crashed to the ground.

Syralise evaded a swinging arm and launched herself into the air. Kameclara aimed attacks at the creature's head to keep it distracted. Syralise landed on its back and reached down, grabbing hold of its plated armor.

Kameclara ducked from a blow and slipped beneath the creature. She struck a crucial joint in its armor as she exited between its legs. Syralise yanked off the protective plate. Kameclara and Leera simultaneously landed devastating blows, felling their opponent. Around them, other squads of Alpha Team did the same.

Ressogureys were the reason they were grouped in threes. In direct combat, they could efficiently neutralize them.

Alpha Team continued until all beasts returned to inanimate lumps of material.

The cavern fell silent. Kameclara huffed, bending over her knees. From the corner of her eye, she noticed a rock twitch. It skittered until it met with a larger lump of habbadite.

"They're reforming," she observed. The hairs on her neck raised in excitement. She loved it when situations changed in an instant.

"The button's reset," Brock reported to Leera. Kameclara swung her eyes to the far wall and ascertained the large button had indeed popped out. In the back of her mind, she wondered what retaliation Brock had planned for their next skirmish.

"My guess is the Ressogurey structures will likely come at us repeatedly until we hit the buzzer a second time," Syralise reported.

"We've an opening," Leera observed as the first Ressogurey simulation reared its head. Its arms had yet to form. "Pyramid formation. Beneath original target. Now!" she commanded.

Immediately, members of Alpha Team raced to gather beneath the button. The wind stream had shut off, so none could ride it upwards.

Alpha-Je had been furthest from the button. By the time they reached the pyramid, they were near the top. Leera stood on Kameclara and Syralise's shoulders. Even then, she couldn't reach.

"We don't have time to restructure. We need to vault," Leera ordered, eying a charging horde. The operatives we vulnerable, stacked against the wall.

Kameclara laced her hands with Syralise. Leera placed a foot into the crook and they launched her into the air. The slender operative lifted her arm high as newly formed Ressogureys reached the pyramid. Kameclara could only imagine her teammates at the base bracing for assault. She tensed too, should she fall.

Leera struck the button with all her might.

Another buzz ripped through the space. Ressogureys crumbled into loose habbadite pebbles, cascading around the feet of operatives sighing in unison.

They caught Leera as she came down.

"Disband," the redhead ordered.

Alpha Team lowered themselves to solid ground. All operatives still on high alert.

"Exam complete," came over their coms.

Kameclara exhaled sharply, filled with relief and disappointment. She was just getting warmed up.

Habbadite pebbles at their feet skittered to form a staircase. Clay on a wall peeled aside, revealing double doors. The operatives stood in formation, awaiting permission to exit. Kameclara noticed lasers weapons on the ground, previously embedded in the habbadite. They had defeated the Ressogureys before the forms could utilize them.

"Proceed to briefing hall," an officer commanded.

The operatives trooped up the steps, giving one another supportive pats. They wanted to congratulate each other, but hadn't heard affirmation if they'd passed.

They entered a large space and took formation before a Captain. Not long after, a Major appeared. The name, "Uteni" emblazoned on her chest.

She marched to Leera. "Very clever. You've beaten the record. Congratulations on holding the shortest time in completing the final evaluation."

Leera saluted, "With respect, Sir, the victory belongs to all of Alpha Team."

A proud look shined on Major Uteni's face. "Absolutely. In training we pit you against each other because competition bears improvement. But the real test is how quickly you recognize the need to work together."

"Sir!"

Major Uteni's eyes shone with pride. "It's the one thing you can never forget when you're in the field: In unity we triumph."

Leera nodded sharply. "I'll remember, Sir."

Major Uteni faced the team, a wide grin across her face. "You're all green-lit for missions!"

Kameclara saluted with the rest of her team. No more chaperoning from experienced operatives. Next time they were in the field, they were on their own.

Her eyes gazed at the slate-gray ceiling, knowing a star-studded heaven spread beyond. She hoped to see it in person soon.